LION OF THE NORTH

Book 3 in the English Mercenary Series

By

Griff Hosker

Lion of the North

Published by Sword Books Limited 2025
Copyright ©Griff Hosker

The author has asserted their moral right under the Copyright, Designs and Patents Act, 1988, to be identified as the author of this work.
All Rights reserved. No part of this publication may be reproduced, copied, stored in a retrieval system, or transmitted, in any form or by any means, without the prior written consent of the copyright holder, nor be otherwise circulated in any form of binding or cover other than that in which it is published and without a similar condition being imposed on the subsequent purchaser. A CIP catalogue record for this title is available from the British Library.

No generative artificial intelligence (AI) was used in the writing of this work. The author expressly prohibits any entity from using this publication for purposes of training AI technologies to generate text, including without limitation technologies that are capable of generating works in the same style or genre as this publication. The author reserves all rights to license use of this work for generative AI training and development of machine learning language models.

About the Author

Griff Hosker was born in St Helens, Lancashire in 1950. A former teacher, an avid historian and a passionate writer, Griff has penned around 200 novels, which span over 2000 years of history and almost 20 million words, all meticulously researched. Walk with legendary kings, queens and generals across battlefields; picture kingdoms as they rise and fall and experience history as it comes alive. Welcome to an adventure through time with Griff.

For more information, please head over to Griff's website and sign up for his mailing list. Griff loves to engage with his readers and welcomes you to get in touch.

www.griffhosker.com

X: @HoskerGriff

Facebook: Griff Hosker at Sword Books

Thank you for reading, we hope you enjoy the journey.

Dedication

To all new friends I made on the trip to the Teutoburg Forest, especially the Born family.

Contents

Prologue 1
Chapter 1 8
Chapter 2 23
Chapter 3 35
Chapter 4 50
Chapter 5 63
Chapter 6 77
Chapter 7 91
Chapter 8 105
Chapter 9 120
Chapter 10 135
Chapter 11 148
Chapter 12 161
Chapter 13 175
Chapter 14 188
Chapter 15 201
Chapter 16 214
Epilogue 229
Glossary 235
Historical Background 236
Other books by Griff Hosker 239

Lion of the North

Real People in the Book

Protestant Leaders

King Frederick V of Bohemia
King James 1st of England and (King James VI) Scotland
King Christian IVth of Denmark - King James' brother-in-law
King Gustavus Adolphus of Sweden
Axel Gustafsson Oxenstierna - Chancellor of Sweden
John George of Saxony - Elector of Saxony
Samuel von Winterfield - German quartermaster
General Hohenlohe - Bohemian general
Georg Friedrich - Margrave of Baden-Durlach
Christian the Younger of Brunswick
William - Duke of Saxe-Weimar
Sir Horace Vere - King James' commander in the Palatinate
Ernst von Mansfield - Mercenary leader
George Villiers - Duke of Buckingham
Prince Francis Albert of Saxe-Lauenburg
Lennart Torstensson - commander of the Swedish artillery
Count Gustav Horn - Swedish general
Johan Banér - Swedish general and diplomat
Karl Gustav Wrangel - Swedish general
Bogislaw XIV, Duke of Pomerania
George, Duke of Brunswick-Lüneburg
Hans Georg von Arnim-Boitzenburg - Saxon field marshal
Wolf Heinrich von Baudissin - German cavalry commander under King Gustavus
George William - Elector of Brandenburg
Charles William - Leader of Magdeburg
John Leslie - Scottish general
John Hepburn - Scottish general
Robert Munro - Scottish general
Sir James Ramsay - 'Black Ramsay' Scottish general
Marquess James Hamilton, 1st Duke of Hamilton
Torsten Stålhandske - Commander of the Hakkapeliitta (Finnish light horsemen)
Sigismund III Vasa King of Poland
Bishop Arachy Grochowski - Polish bishop
Kasper Doenhoff - Polish courtier

Catholic leaders

Johannes Tserklaes, Count of Tilly - Commander of the Catholic League armies
Emperor Ferdinand II, King of Spain and Holy Roman Emperor
Albrecht von Wallenstein of Friedland and Mecklenburg - Imperial general
Charles Bonaventure de Longueval, 2nd Count of Bucquoy - Imperial general.
Colonel Dodo zu Innhausen und Knyphausen - German mercenary
Tommaso Caracciolo, Count of Roccarainola - Spanish mercenary
Graf zu Pappenheim - Imperial general
Heinrich Holk - Danish mercenary leader
Johann Philipp Kratz von Scharffenstein (defects to the Swedes after the battle of Rain)

Others

Cardinal Richelieu of France
Sir Richard Young - aide to King James
Sir Théodore de Mayerne - King James' Physician
Edward Zouch - Knight Marshal
John Felton - soldier
King Charles of England
Queen Henrietta Marie of England
John Sigismund, Elector of Brandenburg and Duke of Prussia

Bretherton's Horse

Colonel James Bretherton
Captain Alexander Stirling - Wolf Company
Lieutenant Dick Dickson - Wildcat Company
Lieutenant Peter Jennings - Hunting Dog Company
Sergeant Davy Campbell - Fox Company
Sergeant Alistair Wilson - Otter Company
Corporal David Seymour - Badger Company
Corporal Ralph Longstaff - Hawk Company
Corporal Alan Summerville - Stag Company
Dermot Murphy - Trumpeter
John Gilmour - Standard Bearer

Prologue

The house looked just like the others in the street that lay nestled beyond the main throughfare. This was the heart of Brandenburg and the houses were all grand. Formidable looking gates allowed even carriages through but both the gates and the main door were guarded and visitors had to be invited. This house was not one which blazoned its identity. The guards were discreet and wore no livery. They were not even visible until someone came to the door and then they would appear. They were not pretty guards chosen for their good looks, but for their skills. These guards were hired swords. In another life they would have been killers. They had the scarred faces and gnarled knuckles that bespoke men who knew how to use their fists as well as their weapons. Those tools of their trade hung from their belts. They had good swords but not the kind that had to be used two handed. These were razor sharp swords that could be used along with a parrying dagger. That they had two daggers, one in their belts and one in the top of their boots also bespoke a military background. The two pistols that were in their holsters were always loaded but they were a last resort, for firearms were noisy. These guards preferred bladed weapons or their fists.

The noble who approached the door was alone. He had been told to do so by the messenger who had contacted him. His men waited but they were out of sight, just around the corner in the next street where they guarded the horses. He did not fear assassination. If he shouted then they could reach him in moments. The reason for his visit was simple. He had been approached by a priest who had promised him land if he went to the house. As surety for his safety that priest was now held by his men. He was, however, intrigued. This was winter. There were no battles fought in winter, even in this religious war that had torn the heart from the heartland of the empire. Why had he been summoned? The priest had said that it would be in his personal interest and there might be land and more for him. That had ensured that he would attend. He fought for the Protestant side but that was for pragmatic reasons, he hoped that they would return to him the lands he felt were his. He had one cause, his own.

As he raised his hand to knock he hesitated. He was not a brave man. He had fought at Breitenfeld but his pistols had not been fired and his sword had remained sheathed until there was no risk to him. He had made sure that others were around him to do both the fighting and risk the shot and shell that could end a man's life. He had been seen close to the fighting and, if men spoke of it, then they might say that he was in the thick of it. The reality was that he was not. He had shouted commands and warnings but his aides had been the ones who had unsheathed their swords. Of course, when it was clear that they were going to win and the Imperial tercios were being slaughtered he waved his sword, spurred on his horse and played the part of a gallant cavalier. He took a deep breath. He decided that this was worth the risk and he rapped on the door.

The two men who opened it made him start and take a step back. He felt terrified by their faces. That was their purpose and they were there as a deterrent to casual callers. The crosses hanging from their necks marked them as Catholics but there was nothing Christian about the two men. The noble was so stunned that he was silent. However, it was clear that he was expected for the inner door was opened and the two men stood apart to allow him to enter. He did so trepidatiously. One of the guards scanned the street to look for watchers while the other led him silently down the corridor, lit by brands in sconces. He wondered if they were mutes. Another guard stood at the door and he was left there, almost like a parcel waiting to be delivered. The man who stood outside the door was another like the two weapon laden men who had admitted him but there was something different about him. The noble had seen enough battles to recognise nationalities. He had a full beard as well as a sharp nose and he looked at the noble with piercing hawklike eyes. This one had the look of a Polish Cossack. They were men who served the Polish king. Their ancestors had come from the steppes and were now a regiment loyal to the king. They were fierce soldiers who made the Croats seem like nuns. The man said nothing but opened the door and slipped inside. It gave the young noble the opportunity to study the house. There was nothing about the interior which suggested a woman's hand. Everything was functional. There were neither drapes nor paintings on the walls. The brands that burned gave light but were not pretty. This was the home of a man who did not care for decoration. The door opened and the silent guard gestured for him to enter. As he passed the man his sword and dagger were deftly taken. He was about to object but the guard glared at him. He entered the room, the door closed and he looked around. There was a table on which lay a jug and two goblets. A fire burned in the hearth and there were two chairs, their backs to him. Was he alone?

He moved towards the table to pour himself a goblet and almost jumped from his skin when a voice came from one of the chairs, "You can drink later."

He moved closer to the voice and saw two men seated in the chairs. The one who had spoken was an older man. From his dress he was a priest of some kind. He guessed he had some senior post because he wore expensive rings upon his fingers. He also saw, in the corner and hidden in the shadows, another man.

The second seated man who addressed him was younger and had the sharp eyes of a zealot. They burned. He spoke, "We need to find out, before we proceed, your views on this war."

He found his voice, "I am sorry, who are you?"

The older man said, "I am Bishop Arachy Grochowski and I serve King Sigismund of Poland."

He knew that King Sigismund was ill. It had been common knowledge in the camp of King Gustavus Adolphus. The Swedish king had fought a long and successful campaign against King Sigismund who had claimed the Swedish throne. This began to make sense because King Sigismund hated King Gustavus. Having spoken once and feeling on more secure ground the noble went on, "And what does the King of Poland want with me? My disputed lands are not in Poland."

The younger man, the zealot who had not revealed his identity, nodded, "We know that. Do not get ahead of yourself. Answer our questions and then all will be revealed."

"And if I choose to leave?"

"There is the door and it will not be barred to you. Leave." There was something in the man's look that suggested his health might be harmed if he did leave.

"No, I shall stay and hear your words. Who are you?"

The man smiled but there was no warmth in the smile. It was a cold one and made the visitor shiver. "The man who will replace the land you lost with something of equal value and will not cause you to lose any men to gain it." He was hooked. His disputed lands meant nothing to him except as an income. He was used to a rich life and he did not like the life of a campaigning warrior. He served King Gustavus in the hope of having his land returned. He could not help but give half a smile. The man continued, "I can see that I have piqued your interest. Now, how do you feel about King Gustavus Adolphus?"

He frowned. Was this some sort of elaborate trap? Were these men masquerading as Catholics? "I do not understand the question. You know I serve King Gustavus and I am one of his aides."

The man smiled again. This time it was a silkier smile, "Yes, but we also know that your heart is not in this fight, is it? In the last battle for instance, we know that neither your sword nor your pistol was used."

How did they know that? Was there a spy amongst his own men? He said nothing.

"The king does not reward you. Others have been given commands but you merely follow his banner. To be honest you are little more than a titled servant. I ask again how do you feel about him? If he were no longer the leader or if he came to an untimely end would you grieve?"

He looked at the bishop who was watching him impassively. "Bishop, what is Poland's interest in this matter?"

"King Sigismund is coming to the end of his life. He is ready to face God but the loss of his lands to King Gustavus rankles. He would like to know that when he died King Gustavus was gone from this world."

"You wish King Gustavus dead?" He asked the question of the courtier. He wanted no misunderstandings.

"Do you wish him dead?"

The noble shook his head, "He has promised me the return of my lands when this war is over."

"And do you believe him?" He did not answer. "Your silence is eloquent. You are a practical and pragmatic man. Religion means nothing to you for you are self-serving." The courtier held up his hand to silence the anticipated objection. "I applaud such sentiments. If you are willing to end the life of King Gustavus then there is a reward for you in Poland, close to the border with Brandenburg. Świdnica is a prosperous place and has a greater income than your disputed lands which, by the time this war is over, will consist of corpses, weed filled fields covered in animal bones and burnt-out buildings. Świdnica is safe and is beyond the war's ravages."

He thought about what he was being asked. He had men who worked for him who could do the deed but, equally, he knew that the bodyguards of the Swedish king might have something to say about that. "If I am dead then the reward means nothing. The king is protected."

The courtier leaned forward, "You have been in battle with the King of Sweden. Does he stay where it is safe?"

The noble shook his head, "No, he is reckless and has great courage,"

"And since his wounding he can no longer wear a cuirass and fights in a buff jacket." They had clearly thought this through. "When, in the heat of battle, you find yourself close to him what could be simpler than to slay him in the smoke and the din of death?"

"But that would mean that I was in danger too."

"Yes, you must pin your courage to the banner and stay close. Think of the reward."

"We are in winter camps at Mainz."

"But we know that in the Spring he will war in Bavaria. There will be battles."

"And you will give me the land now?"

The bishop shook his head, "The land comes when King Gustavus Adolphus is dead and not before."

The courtier smiled, "Men fight in this war for many reasons." He glanced at the shadowed figure in the corner, "Some fight for the domination of the empire. Some, like you, fight for other reasons and that is not a cause for us to disagree." The courtier stood and went to the table. The noble's eyes followed him and saw that as well as the wine and goblets there was a purse. The courtier picked it up, "We know that you have needs and one of them is gold." He picked up the purse. "This is, shall we say, the seal for the arrangement. The land will come when he is dead but this ensures that you will do what we ask." The noble could not keep the pleasure from his face. He could keep the gold and not bother to do the deed. The courtier moved the purse away from the noble. "Of course, if the deed is not done by the end of next year then this gold, all of this gold, will be returned to us." He nodded towards the door, "You have met my debt collectors, have you not?"

The smile of joy was replaced by a look of horror. The last thing he needed was to have those men hunting him. "Let me be clear, so long as I find some way to end the king's life by the end of the next campaigning season then I get to keep the gold and I will be given Świdnica?"

"That is right." The courtier put the purse down and poured three goblets of wine. He did so carefully, spilling not a drop and ensuring that all three had exactly the same amount. He was a calculating and meticulous man. The bishop stood to join them.

The noble thought of the battles that they had fought over the last year or so. King Gustavus had been lucky. A man only had so much luck. It might run out and if he took the gold then he could buy a better cuirass and be on hand to seize any opportunity that came his way. He did not particularly like the Swedish king. The king had not rewarded him as he saw fit. Others had been praised and given gifts. He had been ignored and overlooked. He was not enamoured of their cause. It did not matter to him if the empire slaughtered every Protestant in their lands so long as he had his own lands returned to him. He smiled and said, "I will do it."

The two Poles looked at each other and raised their goblets. The courtier said, "The fate of King Gustavus Adolphus is in your hands, my friend. Take your money and may God be with you."

As he stood the courtier said, "We have many spies in the court of King Gustavus. You need not know who they are but we have plans afoot which will starve the Swedes of powder and ball. We have men placed in his armies who command and will, at the apposite moment, pretend not to hear an order. They play their parts and you will play yours." He nodded. The young man said, "One more thing. You met Jan did you not?"

The noble frowned, "Who?"

The zealot said, "The one who allowed you to enter and took your weapons." He nodded. "It will not be for some time but he and others like him will come to seek employment. Take him on. He will ensure that the deed is done."

They had him. He was trapped. The Polish Cossack would ensure that he had to try. He had gold and the promise of land but he did not like that there were spies. He did not like to be watched. He was a careful man and he never made enemies of a superior. The inferiors were a different matter. The men had implied that it was amongst the leaders where the spies lay. He would keep his eyes and ears open.

It was as he passed through the doorway that he heard the courtier say, in Spanish, "That should ruffle some feathers, eh, Don Alvarado?" He now knew the identity of the shadowy third man. He would keep his ears open for his name in the future.

Chapter 1

The North Sea October 1631
The ship in which I sailed back from the Baltic was not a large one but it was fast. That had helped me decide to take it. I had been relieved to board the ship with my chests of gold and silver intact. I had travelled through land controlled by King Gustavus but the chests were clearly intended for bullion. I had not enjoyed a good night of sleep since leaving my regiment in Germany. I had just a couple of months to spend back in England and I had not seen my family for a long time. I needed to see my wife, Charlotte, and William, my son, as soon as I could. My son would now be walking and talking. I had missed the stages that led to that and I wanted to make the most of every moment I had been allowed to spend away from the war.

Captain Stewart was a dour Scotsman and thanks to the mercenary companies of Scottish soldiers who fought for King Gustavus and the Protestant alliance there were many such sailors who profited from the war. England and Scotland were ruled as one now and while, since Buckingham's disasters, they no longer fought the Spanish, they provided weapons, powder and, most importantly, mercenaries who fought for the Protestant cause.

The grizzled sea captain waved me over to the helm, "Another day, Colonel Bretherton, and we will reach Hartlepool. I am just sorry that I could not sail up the Tees for you."

I shook my head, "There is an agent in the port and I can reach home in a day. It would take you three days to negotiate the bends in the river. I thank you for such a quick voyage."

He nodded and took the clay pipe from his mouth. He tapped it against his palm and said to the helmsman, "Bring her up a point, Robbie."

"Aye, Captain."

"This will be my last voyage before February. It is time to take the old girl from the water and clean the hull. The last thing we need is to have the worms eating at her. I get to spend time with my family and then it will be back to the duty of ferrying supplies for the Swedes."

I knew how parlous and dangerous an existence sailors led.

"We had a great victory at Breitenfeld and we now have more of Germany returned to Protestant rule. Soon you may have to find another employer."

"There is always war, Colonel, and if there were not then we would just haul coal to feed the fires of the rich men in London."

I laughed, "Aye, they have hewn all the trees that there were."

He nodded his agreement, "If you like, Colonel, I can give you a passage back to Peenemunde, when you return to the war."

"Thank you, that would be helpful." I nodded, "I will speak with the agent, George Smith."

He nodded, "There will be gunpowder as well as cannon balls for that voyage. The crew do not like it for it means three days of cleaning when we reach the Baltic but it brings, with the weapons we shall carry, the greatest profit." He smiled, "It also means no lights and cold food so I fear that the voyage back may not be as pleasant for you."

He was right. King James supported the Protestant cause but the only soldiers that were supplied were mercenaries. Those who owned mines and made weapons and gunpowder had the greatest profit. England and Scotland had been spared the ruinous nature of religious war. The land had not been riven with indiscriminate death and destruction, not to mention disease and famine, as Germany and parts of the Netherlands had. I was glad that my wife and son had not been in danger. However, I still cursed the predatory Catholic Empire that sought to impose its will on the world. The war was also necessary to me for it had brought me a good living and an income. The two chests of coins that I carried with me were testament to that. I had saved my pay and made money from the weapons my company had captured and sold. I knew that I could retire because I had enough gold to buy more land and become a farmer. It would not happen. I was not a farmer and I had an association with Bretherton's Horse. The regiment I had been given had been a wild bunch of men when I had taken them over but thanks to hard work and discipline they were now the finest regiment of Light Horse in Gustavus Adolphus' army. I knew that men like Torsten Stålhandske who led the king's Finns might dispute that but I knew differently. They obeyed my orders and their wildness was controlled by good officers. I felt a bond with them. They were like brothers in arms and I knew that I would have to explain that to Charlotte. When she saw the gold then she would ask me to give up my sword.

It was not long after dawn when I saw the arms of the port of Hartlepool welcoming me as well as the ship. I knew then that I was close to home. I would have a day of hard riding and then I would be in the bosom of my family. We negotiated the narrow entrance and, even as we tied up at the place vacated by the collier, heading no doubt for London, another ship followed us in. It was a busy port. The captain had two of his men carry my belongings ashore. I had the chests, my armour, my war bag and my clothes. My weapons were festooned about my body. It was a habit I could not shake. It was as natural as making water in the morning and then donning my clothes. I was a soldier and it was what we did. Once I reached home I would put them in a chest and forget them until January.

George Smith, the Swedish agent, strode over. He was a mountain of a man and despite his name he was not English. When he saw me he beamed, "Colonel Bretherton, I did not expect to see you again. I thought you would be fighting the good fight for King Gustavus."

He looked at the pile of my belongings, "And I am guessing that you will need a riding horse and a sumpter?"

I nodded, "And as I will be sailing from here in February with Captain Stewart I would be obliged if you would let me stable them until my return."

He nodded, "That suits me. This is the last of the ships to arrive before winter. It would help me if you were to feed and stable them. My wife and I can now hunker down and enjoy warm fires and just listen to that icy east wind as it beats on St Hilda's walls."

I had been close to the east for the last couple of years and it did not feel as cold here. I knew that when I returned to Germany, in the spring, I would find it far colder. We went to his stable where I chose my own saddle. There was a time when I would not have been choosy. I now knew what I wanted. I saddled the hackney myself and as I did so I saw that the horses were good ones. By that I mean they were schooled and obedient. George helped me to load the chests, bags and war gear. I saw him raise his eyebrows when he loaded the two heavy chests but he said nothing. The chests were not large but their weight told him what they contained. As a precaution I loaded my pistols and put them in the holsters on the saddles. I mounted.

"Take care, Colonel." George pointed to the clouds to the northeast. "I am thinking that you shall have rain before you reach your home."

I nodded, "Aye, we endured a squall on the voyage here. I have a good hat and an oiled cloak. I shall return in time to take ship."

"And if the ship is delayed I have a room for you, Colonel." I knew then that he was paid well as the Swedish agent in Hartlepool.

When we reached his home he had my horses prepared while his wife gave me a freshly baked loaf for the journey. I was keen to get home and I mounted as soon as the horses were ready.

It took longer than I wished to negotiate the busy port and leave by the Middleton Gate. I left the town and headed down the road that headed to the Tees. Here there was nothing to stop the wind and I urged the horses on to cover the open ground. I had twenty-eight miles to travel and I only intended to stop to water the horses. I would not need food. I had an ale skin provided by George and the loaf given to me by his wife. I was a soldier and they would do. As I headed down the road that wound down the dunes to the Tees I could smell the smoke from the fires of the salt makers at Seaton. As the wind was blowing from the northeast, once I had passed it the smell lingered until I turned slightly more westerly to head for Norton and cross the marshland that lay before it. The best road passed through Stockton and then ran along the north bank of the Tees. Stockton would be the last large place that I passed. After that I knew that I would see nothing but small manors and farms: Sadberge, Great Burdon, Haughton le Skerne and Low Coniscliffe. Once I reached Low Coniscliffe then I would be almost home. I would be recognised and known by the people that I passed. Many of the men who toiled on the farms would have been trained by me when I had commanded the militia.

Lion of the North

I watered the horses in Stockton. The castle was largely empty for there was no lord of the manor. It was used, sometimes, as a gaol or, if there was local trouble then a garrison might occupy it. Since King James had united England and Scotland that was rare. I was not sure about his son, the new king. I had learned that he was less enthusiastic about the war against the Imperialists. That might be something to do with his French wife who was a strong Catholic.

The rain came when I was between Sadberge and Great Burdon. It had threatened all the way from Hartlepool and I had hoped to reach home before it arrived. Luckily it came from the northeast and I endured it on my cloaked back. I was glad that I had eaten the bread by Stockton. I was not a fan of soggy bread. The ale was also finished and I carried an empty skin. Like the ale skin the road was empty. There were few travellers and I suspect that they were enjoying meals at the inns like the Fighting Cocks and waiting to continue after the downpour. It was after Haughton that the land dropped a little as I headed for the crossing of the River Skerne. It hardly needed a bridge and was a river I would normally have forded but I did not want to risk becoming even wetter and so I headed for the bridge.

My cloak covered most of me and hung down to protect my legs and my sword. The two men who rose from the other side of the bridge must have been soaked to the skin. The fact that they were brigands was clear both from their dress and their weapons. They had worn, leather jacks that had seen better days, and a cudgel hung from each of their belts, while in their hands they held short swords. I guessed they were ex-soldiers. Certainly, the older one had that look while the younger one looked to be an apprentice. From their point of view all that they saw was a traveller who was alone and led a laden horse. The bridge was exactly halfway between the two villages and I could see why they had chosen it. I was on the top of the bridge and to turn was almost impossible.

The elder one, who had a few grey hairs in his lank hair, spoke. His voice told me that he was local, "Hold there, Master, and keep your hands where I can see them. I can see that you are a wealthy man while Tom here and me are poor. That does not seem right to us. Now, if you will share with us what you carry, equally mind, then we shall let you keep your horses and carry on your way. That seems reasonable, does it not?"

I threw back the hood on my cloak and let go of the reins of the sumpter. He could now see my face. I wanted him to know who I was. "You speak reasonably as you threaten me and I will respond in kind. Here is my proposal. Sheathe your weapons and flee as fast as you can and hope that I never see you again. I am Colonel James Bretherton of Piercebridge and I do not take kindly to threats."

They looked at each other. The one called Tom, the younger one, looked less confident but the older one decided to bluster it out, "Fine words for a man alone and there are two of us. For the threat you have made we shall take all your goods and your animals. However, I desire to be away from this rain and I will let you keep your life." I saw the look in his eye which told me what he would do. I was doomed to die and then there would be no witnesses. My body would be stripped and by the time it was found would be almost unrecognisable. "At him Tom!" They both ran at me coming from two sides.

I threw back my cloak and drew my sword. As I did, I spurred the hackney. It was not Marcus, the horse I rode to war. This was a horse bred to be hired and she was slow but the heels dug into her flanks made her move. The dangerous one was the older man and he came at my left. I kicked my feet from my stirrups and I swung my sword over my horse's head to strike at his upper body. He was not expecting the blow and barely raised his sword in time to block it. It was a weak block and my sword drove his own blade towards his unprotected skull. His own shoddy sword saved him. Had he had a well sharpened weapon it would have driven into his skull but, as it was, the flat of his blade cracked into his head and he overbalanced and tumbled over the side of the bridge into the Skerne. Tom had not seen his friend's end and he lunged up at me. I swung my right leg and before the sword reached me the tip of my boot cracked into his face. I saw the light leave his eyes as he fell over the other side of the bridge and like his friend ended up in the water.

I rode from the bridge and, after sheathing my sword, dismounted. I went to the youth called Tom. He was almost face down in the Skerne and in danger of drowning. I turned him over and dragged him to the bank. I did not want him to drown. Then I took the sword. It was a poor one. I jammed the end into a crack in the bridge and bent it double. It was now useless as a weapon. The other man was not in the river when I went to the other side. I saw him disappearing south. He had abandoned his friend. I saw that his sword was in the water and I rendered that useless too.

I had wasted enough time. I would tell the local judge of the incident when time allowed. I recovered the sumpter and mounted my horse. I rode on, suddenly aware that the rain had stopped. Low Coniscliffe had no constable but I reined in at the large farmhouse that stood close to the village green. The farmer walked over. He touched his cap, recognising me, "Captain Bretherton, you are back." To the farmer, like most of the other militia, I was and would always be Captain Bretherton, the man who trained them.

"I am, Bob." I gestured behind me, "At the crossing of the Skerne two footpads tried to relieve me of my belongings. One was called Tom."

He shook his head, "Tom is not so bad. He is a strong lad but he just goes along with his uncle. John Taylor was a soldier but no one would have him serve with them. They say he was an archer but then gunpowder came in and fewer people used men with war bows. He is a strong man and could fell a chap with one blow. He is a thief, a brawler and a bully."

"Why are they not in gaol? Had I been a merchant and not a soldier then I would have lost everything."

"It is finding them, Captain. They have hideouts all over the valley and they move. John is a nasty piece of work but he is as cunning as a fox. Come the end of the month, when we have our weapon training, I will tell Captain Jackson and we will seek them out."

I nodded my thanks and headed along the road. I was not confident. Captain Jackson was over sixty years of age. He had the rank because his family had influence. He did not know one end of a pike from the other. I shook my head in anger at myself. If I lived at home such men as the two thieves would not be tolerated. I put the two men from my mind as I neared the end of the village. I could hear the Tees. The rain had raised its level and it was noisy. I smiled as I spied my village. The horses were weary but I wanted to gallop and get into the warmth of my home and family as soon as I could. The hooves of the horses clattering down the road that led to the bridge announced my arrival.

John Cunningham had the house next to the bridge and he called out, as I neared my gate, "Colonel, Sir, you are home." Others, hearing his cry, shouted their welcomes and I waved.

It was dusk because the days were short and few visitors passed over the bridge once it was dark. The result was that doors opened and heads peered out at the noise which grew as I neared my home. I saw lights at my home as the noise reached within. It was Margaret who acted as a housekeeper for us who came to my door as I turned into the yard.

"It is the colonel! He has returned!" She turned within and shouted, "Ted, come and take the colonel's horses to the stable."

I dismounted as a young man I did not recognise raced out of the house and, whilst knuckling his forehead, took the reins of the horses. Taking off my hat I hurried to the beckoning light of the door and saw Charlotte standing, protected by the lintel, waiting for me. Her hand held the tinier one of William, my son who had been a babe when I had left. He was shyly standing behind his mother. I put my arms out and enveloped my wife. She kissed my cheek. I was aware that I had not shaved since leaving Germany and I stank of both horse and the sea.

I heard a whimper and, as I pulled away and looked down, saw that William looked afraid. I smiled, "Do not fret, William, I am your father, returned for Christmas."

Charlotte reached down and picked him up, "I have told you of your father, the brave soldier who fights for God. He is here." I saw that my wife had been weeping silently. I smiled and was relieved when my son also smiled and then put his hand out to touch my face. He pulled it back and said, "Rough!"

I laughed, "He can speak!"

I heard Margaret say behind me as she closed the door, "He can that, Colonel, trouble is sometimes he doesn't want to shut up and his questions would test the patience of a saint!"

I saw the kitchen door open and Elizabeth the cook stood there. She beamed, "God be praised you are home, Colonel, and whole. Mistress, I can add an extra bunny to the pot for dinner or …"

I waved my hand, "Whatever you will be eating is fine, Elizabeth."

Charlotte sniffed, "And while it is cooking you can have a bath. Margaret, fill a bath for the colonel." She shook her head, "We have nothing in. We have yet to begin to fill the larder for Christmas."

"This will do."

I took off my cloak and saw William's eyes widen when he saw the sword and pistols. "I will go and put these in the bed chamber where they are safe."

Charlotte handed me a lit candle, "We do not waste money, husband, by lighting rooms we do not use." I smiled as I took it. Our home had two floors and I tramped up the stairs, ducking to avoid cracking my head.

The house smelled familiar now. When I had walked in I had sniffed the air and been aware of the difference. I was back in England and England did not smell like Germany and my home smelled of Charlotte and dried herbs. When I entered our bed chamber I saw the small bed next to our bigger one. I had wondered, as I travelled home, if William would have his own room. There was one for him but he still slept in his mother's room. I went to the chest in the corner. It was not completely empty because there were some old weapons within but it had not been opened since I had left. I put my sword, sword belt, daggers, pistols and holsters inside. I closed it and hoped I would not need to open it again until I returned to the war. I took off my jacket and then sat on the bed to pull my boots from my feet. The boots I would wear at home were not the ones I used as Colonel Bretherton who led Bretherton's Light Horse to war. For the next weeks I was shedding that skin and adopting another. I went to the wardrobe and took out clothes that had not been worn since I had left for Germany. I hoped that they still fitted. I took them and headed downstairs. At the bottom of the stairs, the youth called Ted waited with my clothes bag. I saw the two chests and the war gear by the door.

"Ted is it?" He nodded, "Put my war gear in the chest in the corner of the bed chamber and find my razor. Bring it to the bathhouse. You can assist."

"Yes, Colonel." His voice had the twang of Northumbria.

At the door to the dining room, I was aware that William was peering at me, I paused and smiled, "I will be as quick as I can, William, and then we can talk."

The bathhouse was simply a room that was attached to the back of the house. Warmed by the fire from the kitchen, it was a functional room. The wooden bath had a linen cloth liner to prevent splinters and while it had to be filled and emptied by hand there was a channel that led to a pipe under the door and it fed the hog bog. The pigs and the chickens did not seem to mind the wastewater. Margaret had lit a couple of candles and there were herbs in the water. She and Elizabeth brought two more pails of hot water and they were hurled in.

Margaret pointed to the hook on the wall that backed on to the kitchen, "There is your towel, Colonel. We will give you privacy now."

As I hung the clothes I would wear on the other hooks, I said, "Ted will bring my shaving gear. He can help me." As I began to unfasten the shirt I said, "Who is Ted and what happened to Alan?"

Elizabeth had been about to leave but she stopped and turned, "Ted is my sister's son, Colonel. They lived up Birtley way. His father died of a wasting disease and poor Polly followed six months later. He had no one and walked all the way here, God bless him. He was half dead when he arrived." She looked nervously at me, "The mistress took him on. He is a good worker, Colonel."

I smiled and said, "I was not criticising, Elizabeth, I was curious and did not want to offend by a careless comment. Your words have helped me."

I saw the relief on her face, "You are a good man, Colonel, and we are glad to have you home again. The mistress has missed you."

"And Alan?"

She looked sad again, "In the autumn we had heavy rain. He fell into the river, took a chill and died within a week. We buried him in the graveyard but we were the only mourners. It is sad when people die and no one comes." She smiled as if to dispel the memory of death, "We have all missed you, Colonel, and it is good to have you home again."

The door closed and I undressed. She would miss me again for my visit was a brief one. I reflected that I had barely known Alan but she was right, it was sad when the dead were not mourned. We had not lost many men from the regiment but those that had died were mourned. I piled my dirty clothes on the floor. They had been washed whilst on campaign but they had been given a soldier's wash. I knew that the women of the house would make them look and smell better. I stepped into the water. It was deliciously hot and I sank into it carefully. I did not want the water to spill. The ladies had put in just enough and only my head was above the water. I sank my head beneath it. I could not remember the last time I had washed my hair. I did not think there was wildlife within but Ted would tell me better, I did not want to bring anything to our bed that would offend Charlotte.

I raised my head and heard a rap on the door, "Enter, Ted." He came in nervously, his eyes fixed on the ground. I was a soldier and having emptied my bowels before now in full sight of my horsemen I was not precious about my naked form. "Come Ted, you can act as my body servant."

"Yes, my lord."

I laughed, "I am not a lord, Ted, I am just a colonel."

He frowned, "But the mistress said that you were a captain."

"I was but things change. I have much to tell you all when we eat. Tell me, Ted, do you shave?"

"Yes," he hesitated, "Colonel."

"Good." He nodded, "Then you can shave me but first check my hair will you? I have campaigned in the field for so long I am surprised that birds do not nest in my hair."

He laughed and after putting down my razor he stood behind me and I felt his fingers as he ran them through my long hair. "No, Colonel, it is all clean."

"Good. I shall have my wife cut it when time allows. Now, while you shave me you can tell me your tale. Anyone who can walk from Birtley to Piercebridge has a story to tell."

His story, sadly, was typical. His father had been a tenant farmer and when he had died Ted and his mother had been expected to continue to pay the rent on the farm. As Ted's mother was ill so the farm was neglected and as soon as Ted's mother died, the young man was evicted immediately. There were plenty of men willing to pay the lord of the manor the rent. It allowed the noble to live well, far from the northeast. There were more landowners of land in the north living in London than on their own land. On campaign I had met many such nobles. None were English but the life they led was the same.

"And are you happy here?"

He paused in his shaving and beamed, "Colonel, this is like heaven. I have my own room and I enjoy the work." His face clouded, "You are not thinking of letting me go are you?"

"Good heavens, no. I am a soldier and my work is not in this land but abroad. I am pleased that my wife has such a rock as you."

I saw that my words had pleased him and he continued to shave me with a smile upon his face. "There." He stood back.

I ran my fingers over my face. It was smooth. I stood, "Good, you have done well. Fetch me my towel and you can help me to dress."

"I can get a couple of coals from the fire to heat up the water again, if you wish, Colonel."

"No, I am clean and ready to dress."

The clothes still fitted. That was not a surprise really for we did not eat well enough for my girth to have grown. Ted picked up my clothes, "I will take these to the laundry, Colonel. Shall I return your razor to your bed chamber?"

"You can indeed."

I headed for the dining room and as I entered I could smell the aroma of rabbit stew with herbs and wild mushrooms. Charlotte and William were already seated and Margaret hovered next to my wife. Charlotte clapped her hands together, "Much better, husband, although I think we need to tame those flowing locks."

"Just so." I sat next to William. "And now I am home and the world is well once more."

I looked hungrily at the stew and went to take the serving spoon. Charlotte shook her head, "First we say Grace."

I nodded. I was now in a different world. The world of soldiers lay, thankfully, on the other side of the German Sea. There we ate as soon as we had food. We said Grace when we remembered. We were grateful for the food but too hungry not to eat immediately it was laid before us.

Grace said, the plates were loaded with food. There was fresh bread and it was good bread. In Germany we often ate what they called black bread. It was filling but not to my taste. Here the bread was delicious in its own right, but when used to mop up the gravy from the stew it was as fine a feast as I could remember. Once the edge had been taken from my appetite I told them of the war. It was, of course, a cleaned-up version. I told them of victories and not the slaughter. I regaled my son and wife with stories of the Lion of the North, Gustavus Adolphus. I could see that my wife was proud of me. I saw the smile on my wife's face; however, as she took it all in I saw the smile turn to a frown.

"Does that mean you are not done with war? You will be returning to serve the Swedish king?"

I nodded and dabbed my mouth. I took a swig of wine and said, "The war is almost done. King Gustavus has the beating of Tilly and soon the Protestants of Germany will have their freedom. Then I promise, I will return home."

She looked sad, "I thought you were home for good. Are those chests you brought not filled with coins?"

"They are."

"Then why do you need to return?" I said nothing. "When you took on this task it was for money. You have that money."

I sighed, "You are right but I cannot leave the job half finished. My love, I am good at what I do. They need me not to lead just my company but a brigade. If I am not there then I fear that the war will last longer."

"James, that sounds like the sin of vanity."

"You are right." I put my hand across William to take Charlotte's. "I promised that I would return and I am a man of my word but I will give the king notice that I intend to leave. He has the service of my sword for one year. How is that? I will return to the king in early spring and I will be back here one year from now. I will be home before November of next year."

"You promise?"

"I promise." Sometimes a man makes a promise but fate or the world conspire to make him break that promise.

Margaret took William to bed and that allowed Charlotte and I to talk more openly. She did not harp on about my decision to return but she spoke of the farm and how we might use my coins to improve it. "Ted has ideas, James, and with the money you have brought then they can be implemented. He spoke of cows and sheep."

"Has not the trade for wool diminished?"

She shook her head, "The war in Germany has driven up prices. Those who farm sheep cannot keep up with the demand."

"Cows?"

"Cheese can be made from their milk and calves can be sold for profit. The peace has made many people more prosperous and they like to emulate the great and the good. Beef is a good way to make more money."

I looked at her and held her hand, "Make money?"

"If money will keep you at home then, aye. I have missed you, James. Cuddling our son for the last couple of years has given me comfort but I need the strength of my husband's arms."

I stood and took her hand, "Then let us talk no more of my leaving. That will come when that comes. Let us retire."

When we reached our chamber I saw that Margaret, Elizabeth and Ted had moved William's bed into the small room adjoining ours. We would be alone. That night we were like wantons. When William awoke in the middle of the night and cried for his mother the joy was temporarily suspended but it had been enough. I was home.

Lion of the North

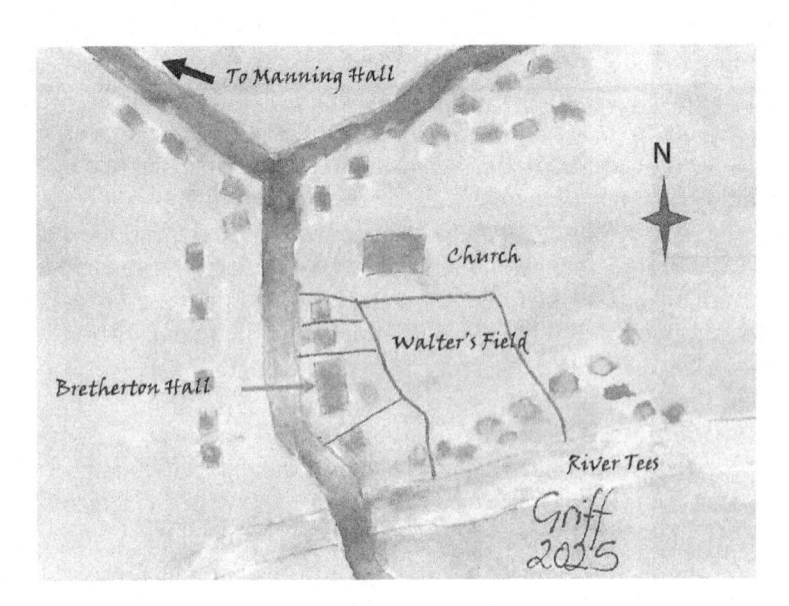

Piercebridge 1631

Chapter 2

I discovered that little boys are like soldiers on campaign, they wake early. The sun had yet to crack across the horizon when he climbed up on to our bed. I could see that he would demand much of my time. Charlotte realised my dilemma. "William, let us dress you and then you and Ted can show your father what we have done with the land since he was away." She looked at me, "It will give us the opportunity to wash your clothes."

That suited me and with William's hand in mine I walked my land to see what Ted had planned. My home fronted the road but the land to the back was a large piece of fallow land. We had a small plot to grow vegetables and some fruit trees and bushes but that was all. "Colonel," he pointed to a piece of land beyond the drystone wall that marked our boundary, "that piece of fallow land is for sale. Old Walter of Gainford died and he had no children. It adjoins yours and would be perfect for grazing animals. There are stones beneath the soil that make ploughing hard. Also, the slope is too steep for ploughing. As you can see there are also trees with roots that make the turning of the soil hard. The animals can drink from the river." I looked at the land and saw that there was a hedgerow and a gate at the far end. John Cunningham had, like me, a large plot but his adjoined the river. Walter's land lay beyond it and bordered not only the river and John Cunningham's land but my neighbour's too. It would give me a much larger piece of land. Was it too much?

I tried to remember what Walter had done with the land but could not think. "What was it that Walter did when he farmed here?"

"He tried to grow beans, my lord, and the crop from the Americas, potatoes. He failed."

I knew that this crop of tubers discovered by Raleigh was a new thing. "Could we grow them here?"

He frowned, "I think so, Colonel. Master Miles over at Langton grows them."

I nodded. I knew Miles. He had been a pikeman I had trained in the militia. "Then you and I will ride there some time in the next week. I would pick his brains." I also knew that Miles Langton would be able to give me news about the area. The attack so close to my home had made me fear for my family. When I returned to Germany would they be in danger from lawlessness? I had not mentioned the attack to Charlotte. I felt there was no need.

When that was done, we wandered the village. I was greeted by smiles and respect by all that we met for without a lord of the manor I was the closest they had to one to whom they could turn with their troubles and complaints. My father's friend, Roger, had a huge hall but it lay beyond the village in large grounds and I was closer. It had helped that I had trained the militia and the men all called me captain. As I walked the village I was not going to correct those who used the wrong title but Ted put them straight. It seemed to enhance my position. I listened to all their complaints; I could do little about them and, having realised that the people of Germany had far more to complain about felt that their carpings were just the sounding of air. England and Scotland were enjoying that rarity, peace. Their complaints about the lords who ruled, in absentia, the lands that they farmed were justified. I paid for the land I farmed. I had enough gold and silver not to worry about an income but farmers who relied on the weather and nature often found that they did not make as much profit at the end of the year. The absentee landlords did not care. They expected a regular income to keep them in the lifestyle that they enjoyed. I decided that when I had the opportunity I would speak to any lords of the manor that I met. My father's friend, Roger, whilst not a lord moved in those circles and he might be able to offer advice.

I had not asked my wife if William had been trained to make water but his shuffling gait on the way home made me wonder. As soon as Margaret saw him she took his hand, "Come Master William, you have done well for you have been out a long time but let us ensure that we have no accidents." She flashed me a look which might have been one of criticism. "And then we shall have you fed. You must be starving after such a long walk." I had not thought about the little boy keeping up with his father.

I turned to Ted, "Thank you for this morning, Ted. I can see that you are a valuable asset for my home."

Lion of the North

He seemed to grow an inch or two and he beamed, "A pleasure, Colonel. From the Mistress' words I expected you to be a fine man and you have not disappointed. I shall go and attend to my chores. As the stable now has four horses, it will need mucking out more regularly."

"Have my horses been ridden?"

"Master Roger and his son come over once a month and let them stretch their legs, Colonel. I do not ride."

"Then we shall remedy that. Tomorrow is your first lesson." Ted was a useful addition to the household but I would help to give him even more skills.

We arrived back in time for lunch and I could not help but smile. On campaign regular meals were rare and to sit at a table with a roaring fire and being waited on was something to be enjoyed. The last of the rabbit stew had been augmented with root vegetables and we enjoyed a delicious pie. The chutney that came with it was also delicious and the beer that Elizabeth and Margaret had brewed was the best I had drunk in a long time. I was pleased to see that my son also had a healthy appetite. When the meal was finished Charlotte smiled, "It is rarer these days, husband, but I think our son will need a nap this afternoon. You tired him out."

"But we only walked a few miles."

"A few miles to you are a great adventure to him."

She was right and when he began to doze Margaret took him up to bed. Left alone, for Elizabeth cleared the table, Charlotte said, "I think we should invite Roger and his son for Christmas. It is time we repaid them for their kindness when I first arrived not to mention when you were in Germany and I know he will wish to have a long talk with you."

"Why wait for Christmas? Let us invite him to dine with us this Sunday. I planned on riding to see him tomorrow in any case." I nodded toward the kitchen, "I thought to teach Ted how to ride. He needs that skill."

She frowned, "Why?"

"When I come home from the wars I do not intend to simply vegetate here in Piercebridge. I want to make a difference to this land." I was thinking about the bandits but did not elaborate.

She smiled, "I wondered if your words last night were to fob me off. It is good that you intend to carry them out."

"I have seen what war can do to a land. King Gustavus is the only man who can bring this divisive and destructive war to an end."

She sipped her beer and was thoughtful. "You will be paid for your service?"

"Of course."

"I have not examined the chests you brought. Are they full?"

"They are." I knew that when the first chest was opened she would be astounded at the gold and silver that lay within.

"And your future pay?"

"I am now a colonel and King Gustavus wants me, in the fullness of time, to be a brigadier general. There will be more in the future."

"Then you need someone to watch over you."

I laughed, "If you have met my regiment then you would know that is unnecessary. Besides, I had a servant, Trooper Ashcroft." That part was true but I knew that Alexander Stirling, the man I had promoted to captain, would now be using him as a servant.

"I was thinking of the time my father and I were attacked on the road. You were lucky to travel from Frankfurt to home and not risk danger. You cannot guarantee such luck."

Her words were a little close to home for me. I had decided not to tell her of the attack. It would only worry her. I nodded, "If I can find someone who is suitable then I will take them."

As I finished my ale I reflected that it was not a bad idea. A servant who could watch my horses and double as a bodyguard was no bad thing. What I had learned from my time serving the Protestant cause was that there were assassins and killers. Men changed sides so frequently that it was often hard to truly discriminate between friend and foe.

The next morning, I rose a little earlier and slipped out of the bed chamber, leaving my son and my wife happily asleep. William had complained about sleeping alone and he was in the bed in our room. I had clearly tired out William for he had not stirred all night. Elizabeth was in the kitchen preparing breakfast,

"You are up early, Colonel." There was criticism in her voice for I was upsetting the natural rhythm and routine of the house.

"You need not worry about me. I was just going to see the horses. I will ride today."

She shook her head, "There will be rain, Colonel."

"Then I shall wrap up."

She gave me a look to suggest that I might apply for the post of village idiot. She shook her head.

I donned my cloak, which hung from the hooks in the hall and, after taking a couple of apples from the fruit bowl, went out, passing the clucking chickens in the hogbog, to the stable where I could hear the four horses. Jack was my main horse. Bluebell was a sumpter. She could be ridden but I normally used her to carry my armour and spare weapons. She would be a good horse for Ted to ride. I might exercise George Smith's horses but my priority was my animals. Jack recognised me and neighed and nodded his head at my arrival. I gave him one of the apples, "The master is home, Jack, and I shall try to ride you each and every day." He munched on the apple and nodded his head as I stroked his ears.

I heard Ted's voice from behind me, "By, but you can see he likes you. Won't give me the time of day."

I tossed the other apple to him, "Here, feed this to Bluebell. You are riding her today and this makes her your friend. If you want Jack to be your friend then bring him occasional treats too. Horses are like dogs, they can be bought, up to a point."

He fed Bluebell and looked nervously at Jack. "I am happy to try to ride Bluebell, Colonel, but Jack terrifies me."

"And horses can sense that fear, Ted. You must overcome it. We have a couple of months while I am home and I hope to make you a rider before I return to the war." I gave Jack one last pat and then said, "Let us breakfast and then come back to saddle the horses. Have you a cloak?" He shook his head, "I have an old one. A rider needs a cloak. If you cannot ride in all weathers then, in the Tees Valley, you do not ride at all."

Charlotte and William, along with Margaret, were in the kitchen when we returned. I could see from Elizabeth's face that she was unhappy to have so many people in her kitchen. I whisked William up into my arms and said, "Let us to the dining room, eh, and let Elizabeth get herself sorted."

I noticed that Ted went to help Elizabeth. He was a good worker. William had a chair at the table but one which kept him safe. I placed him in it and Charlotte gave him a spoon to hold. As Margaret brought in the food I said, "I thought to ride and see Roger today." I asked it somewhat trepidatiously as I was aware that she had only had one day with me and I was riding off.

She nodded her approval, "He has been so kind to us, and his son, Peter, they came to visit once a month and not only rode the horses but helped Ted to see what jobs needed to be done. Peter will make a good father. He entertained William well."

I laughed, "He is yet to be married."

"Oh, I forgot to tell you, there is a marriage planned for March. He is to marry one of the younger daughters of Sir George Armstrong. The Armstrongs are an old family and not carpet barons."

I did not know the knight but knew that Peter had done well for himself if he was to marry into a noble family. "Good. Thank you for forewarning me."

It was a hearty breakfast and if Elizabeth was right about the weather then I would need it. The ride was not a long one. Roger Manning lived in the largest house in the village although it was a mile beyond the last house. As mine was amongst the first we would have a ride of almost two miles. It was when I bade farewell and headed to the kitchen that I heard the rain begin to pound on the cobbles in my yard.

Charlotte took William's hand and said, "Delay your visit. Wait until the rain has stopped."

I shook my head, "I need to show Ted how to ride. We can spend some time in the barn and then leave when this rain abates a little." I sighed, "Typical, I arrive home and this cursed rain stops me from riding."

It was a good plan but like all such plans was far from perfect. Had we not had oiled cloaks then we would have been soaked before we even reached the stables. "Take off your cloak."

I led my horse from the stall and when Ted had taken off his cloak, showed him how to fit the blanket, the saddle and then tighten the girth. "Some horses are clever and trick you into thinking that the girth is tight when it is not. Always check. I am lucky, Jack is not like that. Now fetch Bluebell." When the sumpter was out of the stall, I watched as Ted did what I had done. He was clearly nervous but he managed it well. "Now let us don our cloaks and head for the barn." The rain still pelted but we did not have far to hurry. Once inside Ted made to take off his cloak. I dropped Jack's reins and shook my head, "You need to be able to mount while encumbered. Now, hold on to the saddle and the reins. Put your left foot in the stirrup." When he had done that I went to hold Bluebell's bridle, "Now swing your leg up and over the back." It was lucky that Bluebell was a sumpter, he would not have managed to swing his leg over Jack.

He looked pleased with himself, "That was easier than I expected."

I smiled, "Because I was holding her head. If she had moved…aye, you did well now put your right foot in the stirrup." He did not find that so easy. "While the rain is heavy we will ride here in the barn. It means you will just be walking and that may help." I told him that he was in command. I taught him to use his heels along with his knees and hands to augment his voice. I was patient because the rain still pounded. I could see that this would have to be a daily exercise. When I was satisfied I went to the doors and, peering up in the sky, saw that it was growing lighter. I donned my cloak and led Jack from the barn, "Come, Ted, tell your horse to walk on."

He gave the command and Bluebell obeyed. She had heard my command but Ted was not to know that. The rain was no longer hard. It was petering out into a drizzle that would still be unpleasant but would be bearable. I closed the barn doors and then mounted. We would be trotting through the village and I knew that Ted would find that motion disconcerting. I said, "Bluebell will follow Jack but remember, Ted, you are still in command." I realised, as we trotted through my gates that one day I would be teaching William to ride. It made me smile in anticipation. Despite the weather, people were still out and about. Work needed to be done no matter what the weather and soon winter would be upon us and might prevent any work being done. It was a relatively short ride to Roger Manning's home but it was far enough for Ted. We left the houses of the village and rode for another mile before we saw the imposing gates of the Manning mansion, as the villagers called it. I knew that his buttocks would be burning as his thighs and calf muscles were red raw already from gripping the horse.

The Manning mansion had been the home of a lord but that had been more than a century ago. The lord had fallen foul of Queen Mary, Bloody Mary as she was known. He had been a staunch Protestant and that Catholic monarch had taken his head and then his land. Roger's grandfather had been a successful wool merchant and had snapped up a bargain. The family had lived there ever since. It had been enlarged and improved thanks to the wool market. Roger now kept his own flocks of sheep. This was not a knight's land with pretty gardens and all the affectations of nobility, it was a working estate. When I had lived with Roger, after my father's death, I had begun to see what a good businessman he was but it was only since I had served alongside lords and nobles that I had seen the difference between men like Roger and nobles. He had a bailiff, shepherds and workers who ensured that his lands were well maintained. He was a rich man and by managing the land and his people he became even richer. The nobles I had met just seemed to spend money rather than making it. I knew that he would happily have supported me when my father perished in the river but I had wanted to be my own man.

The hall had many chimneys and I saw the smoke spiralling into the cloudy sky. The rain had ceased by the time we clattered into his yard. I had dropped my hood and was just wearing the woollen cap that kept my ears warm. Two of Roger's men raced from the side door as we reined in. They recognised me. The elder said, "Welcome home, Colonel Bretherton. Are you home for good?"

I shook my head as I dismounted, "No, Ralph, but long enough. This is Ted. He is a new rider. Can you look after him while I speak with Master Roger?"

"Of course. Paul, help Colonel Bretherton's man to dismount."

I handed my reins to Ralph and the door opened. My father's dearest friend appeared in the doorway. He had aged slightly. His thinning hair was flecked with grey and there was a slight paunch but the eyes and the smile were still the same.

He held his arms out to embrace me, "James. You look well." We hugged because he was the nearest thing I had to a family and other conventions went by the board. I felt safe with Roger. In his presence I was no longer a colonel but a young man who had been lost and needed the guidance and friendship of a good man.

He stood back, "Welcome, Ted. I see your master is teaching you to ride."

Ted had managed to dismount but he was standing with his legs wide apart, "Yes, Sir, but I am not sure that is a good thing."

Ralph said, "Come with me, we have some salve that will help."

I entered the grand house. The warmth from the many fires hit me as I walked in. That was a sign of wealth. Despite the fact that Roger and his son lived alone with just servants, fires were lit in every room. He liked his comfort and could afford the wood. We went to a small sitting room where a merry fire blazed. Roger paused at the door and shouted, "Catherine, buttered ale in the sitting room."

A disembodied voice called back, "Yes, Master Roger."

As we sat I said, "No Peter?"

He smiled, "You have heard that he is to be wed?" I nodded. "He is visiting with his young lady. Her father has a manor, Durham way."

"He has made a good marriage. Her father is a knight."

Roger shook his head, "An impecunious one. Sir George likes to live as though he is the Earl of Northumberland rather than a knight who does not attend to his land enough."

"Are you happy about the marriage?"

"Peter is enamoured of her for she is pretty and while I would be happy for him to marry any woman so long as she was a good one, he set his heart on one who is as pretty as Charlotte."

"I was lucky."

"In my experience a man makes his own luck." The ale came in and when it was poured Roger toasted me, "To you. I pray you are home for some time." Those words initiated a conversation about my time in Germany. He listened patiently for he was a clever man. He knew that the war in Germany could affect his profits. Roger was not a knight. He was a man who knew how to make money. When I had finished he said, "You have done well, and from what you imply more promotion in the offing?"

"Perhaps but I have promised Charlotte I will give but one more year to the life of a mercenary."

"You do not do yourself justice. You are fighting a holy war."

Shaking my head I said, "There is nothing holy about this war, Roger."

We then chatted about Charlotte and my son. I mentioned the land I intended to buy and Roger confirmed Ted's view. "Old Walter was unlucky. It happens. He did not have enough coins set aside to cover the shortfall in income and he needed to sell. He died before he could so. I think the loss of income led to his death. I know the lawyer dealing with the estate and I will speak with him. I am not sure there are heirs but there are debts that need to be cleared. If you buy it then his debt will be cleared." Roger acted as a sort of unofficial lawmaker in the area. I invited him to lunch on Sunday, which he accepted and then mentioned Christmas. He shook his head, "I fear that I will be with Peter. We have been invited by Sir George. I think he is trying to impress me."

I was slightly disappointed but I knew that it would be a cosy Christmas with just my family. I was about to leave when I remembered the attack on the bridge. I told him and he became immediately serious. "You should have told me as soon as you arrived. We cannot have such lawlessness."

"From what I was told, Roger, such events are not uncommon."

"Then on Saturday I will mount some men and see to this pair of villains. Would you come? You can identify them."

"Of course."

He shook his head, "This is the problem we have here in the borders. London thinks that now we are one land there is no trouble, but there is. Men here were used to the freedom to rob on both sides of the borders. The old days of knights who were vigilant are long gone. The likes of Sir George have grown complacent. They live the life of nobles but have forgotten that nobility brings with it obligations."

As I rode home I knew that I would have to speak to Charlotte about the attack. When we reached the stables I let Ted unsaddle the horses, "Are you happier about the riding now, Ted?"

He nodded, "Ralph gave me some tips and the salve helped. I shall persevere, Colonel, for I would be the best servant that you could wish for."

I smiled, "You should know, Ted, that I am unused to servants, just be yourself and I shall be content."

I waited until after the meal when Margaret had taken William to play to speak to Charlotte. The wet ground outside meant that the only game he could play was jumping in muddy puddles and, whilst it might be agreeable to him, it would not be to my wife or my housekeeper. When we sat alone warming ourselves by the fire Charlotte shook her head, "Curse this weather. We have all the washing to dry and no dry air."

In the grand scheme of things that was a minor problem but I knew that it would have upset their plans. Washing day was always followed by drying day and then ironing day. "Roger will come for lunch on Sunday but Peter is in Durham. They will also both be there for Christmas."

"Then it will just be us. We do not need to slaughter a pig. The old goose will do. I will have Ted fatten her up. She stopped laying some months ago and is living on borrowed time."

There was no sentiment on a working farm.

"Oh, and I will be riding with him on Saturday."

She looked up, her perceptive eyes boring into me, "Why?"

I could have lied or come up with a story that would explain it but I knew that such lies would come back to haunt me. I told the truth. "When I was on my way home a couple of footpads waylaid me at the bridge over the Skerne. Roger wishes to apprehend them."

She nodded and then said, quietly, "You did not tell me."

I tried a smile, "I did not want to worry you, my love. It was nothing."

Her voice was heavy with sarcasm, "Oh, so they had no weapons?"

"They had weapons but they were not a threat."

"James Bretherton, I want no more deceptions from you. I fear for your life when you are not here but I expect you to tell me all. I am not a weak woman. You have provided well for us but I need to know that there are no secrets hidden from me. Do you understand?"

I nodded, "You are right and I am sorry."

I saw her composing herself. She was angry with me. "And what will happen to these men when they are taken?"

"I honestly do not know. I suppose they will be tried."

"They could be hanged?"

"That is a possibility." I thought back to Bob Chester's words. He had said that Tom was easily led. Would it be right to hang a youth who had made one mistake? From Bob's comments I had no doubt that Tom's uncle, John, deserved to hang but Tom, I saw him, in light of Bob's words, to be different. If this was my regiment I would apportion the punishment using my common sense. Would English law display such reasonable judgements? I told her what Bob had said.

She composed herself and said, "You were not hurt in the attack?" I shook my head. "Then it seems to me that this John, the younger man's uncle, deserves to be punished. He has led the boy astray and from your words would have done you mortal harm. I am not sure that the taking of his life is justified although the Old Testament teaches us that there should be an eye for an eye. The younger one, though, might be redeemed. When you hunt them, husband, be mindful that this is not war."

I had been away from my wife for so long that I had forgotten her father had been a preacher. Such upbringings gave values that ran deep.

Chapter 3

When I told Ted, on Friday, that I would be riding with Master Manning on Saturday, he asked me why. When I told him the reason, he wanted to come. I shook my head, "One day, Ted, when I have another hackney for you to ride and you are skilled with reins in your hands then you can come with me and welcome but, for now, you are a liability. You do not have enough skills and I cannot hunt two bandits and watch out for you."

He nodded, "I understand, Colonel, but it just makes me even more determined to acquire those skills."

I rose early and dressed for the hunt. I had my clothes already laid out. As I was dressing I heard the rush of water as the rains further upstream made the river deeper, white tipped and filled with debris. Unless we were very unlucky the bridge would not be damaged. This was not the hunt that nobles enjoyed, chasing animals until they were weary and then setting a pack of hounds upon them. When Roger and I hunted it was for food. This hunt would also be different for we would be hunting that most dangerous of prey, man. After dressing in a leather jack, I strapped on my sword and I took four pistols. I had spent some time on Friday with Ted showing him how to clean and maintain the pistols. They were ready to fire. I wore, not the hat with the plumed blue feather and wide brim that marked me as an officer, but a simple beaver skin hat that would protect my ears and keep me warm. I also wore my leather gauntlets.

Roger and his half dozen men arrived not long after dawn. I saw that Ralph rode with him and his men all sported a short sword and a pistol. Like me Roger had four pistols. I knew that if we had to use our pistols then we would have failed for we wanted prisoners so that justice could be seen to be administered.

Charlotte, wrapped against the cold and with William in a woollen shawl came to the door. "Would you like refreshments?"

"Gracious, Mistress Charlotte, but we will defer that until our return."

When I was mounted we headed up, through the village and past the church to head east to the next village. We did not have far to ride to reach Bob Chester's farm. He knuckled his forehead, "I wondered when you would return, Colonel. I spread the word and the rumour is that the two of them, along with another four fellow brigands are holed up in Coatham Woods." He pointed to the Skerne Bridge and beyond. I knew where that was. It lay just a mile and a half from the hamlet of Great Burdon. It teemed with wildlife and the poached animals and timber would keep bandits fed and protected. There were trails in the woods but a man on foot could easily evade hunters.

Roger, nodding, said, "This is a good time of year to hunt. The leaves are shedding and they will need to use fires to cook and for warmth."

Ralph shook his head, "Master, we thought it was just four men. Have we enough to take on six or more?"

Roger smiled, "Colonel Bretherton has taken on the might of Spain and Austria, I feel confident that with his right arm and clever wit we can overcome half a dozen bandits."

I rode with Roger. There was no rain but the wind was an icy one and I was glad I had my good cloak about my shoulders. It also protected Jack's back. While Roger also had a long riding cloak I saw that his men just had capes. Some were oiled leather ones and a couple were sealskin ones. Seals basked at the Tees Estuary and there were hunters and fishermen there who profited from the bounty. I wondered what the bandits would do in the rains. The dwellings they used would be hovels. We used them on campaign. They were made from using branches to make a frame, like the letter A and then covering them with leaf covered branches. In Germany the pines that grew there made good hovels. Coatham Wood had deciduous trees.

There were few farms on the track we took. The river valley was the best place to farm. When we clattered over the Skerne bridge I saw that the rains had made the little river break its banks. We were dry crossing the bridge but then the horses found the going harder for there was more mud than we normally experienced and climbing to the higher ground towards Haughton was hard. The land dried a little as it rose towards the distant woods. That it was their hideout made sense now for that was the direction the bandit called John had taken when he had abandoned his nephew. Once we were close to the woods we halted.

Roger turned to me, "You are the military man, James, what do you suggest?"

"Even with this damp ground they will hear us coming for we ride horses and make noise. That means they will run, unless, of course, they think to attack us."

Roger said, "There are six of us, surely that is unlikely."

"If it was just you and I they might risk it." He raised his eyebrows in surprise. "They have no pistols and I damaged two of their swords. I do not fear even six of them. If we prime our pistols then that should cow them." I nodded to Ralph, "If you and the others take a long sweep around the woods, I am guessing that there will be another trail into it, we will take the main one. We will bait them with two men on good horses and when you hear voices then you close the trap."

Ralph looked at Roger who nodded, "We will wait here for the count of five hundred, Ralph. If you hear a pistol then head to the sound."

Ralph cast a stern look at me and then said, "You watch out for yourself, Master Manning. These bandits are not worth you to suffer an injury." It was clear he did not like the plan.

When they had gone I said, "Ralph seems to disapprove of me."

"He is protective of me, that is all. I confess that it seems risky to me not to say reckless. I am a little fearful of this venture yet you ooze confidence."

I had not thought about it but he was right. I nodded, "I suppose I am confident. I have found that being bold, at the right time, often brings the victory."

"And that marks you as a soldier and me as a farmer. You have changed, James. I barely recognise the young man who lived with me all those years ago."

I knew that I had changed. War had done that. I think I was a better man for I had faced adversity but it was always for others to judge the calibre of a man. All else was vanity.

We loaded our pistols. I had two holsters in my saddles. I had made sure that they were well greased before I left home. I knew that I could pull them and prepare them for firing quickly. I had learned the secret was to pull one, and fire and then do the second and, if it was needed the third. The worst thing to do was panic and try to do things quickly. Just the drawing of the pistols might be enough to cow the bandits. It would not work for Spanish or Austrian horsemen. They would be wearing a cuirass and be, in any case, fearless. I knew that my wheellocks had a priming cover so that they could be primed and there was no danger of the powder falling out. It would be my wheellocks that would bring us a result.

When it was done I said, "Shall we?"

I made sure that Jack was ahead of Roger's horse. The trees were not too thick at the edge of the wood. They had been copsed or taken for building work in the local villages and farms. After a few hundred paces they became thicker and the trail twisted and turned. It was clear that horses did not use it over much. I was listening and smelling. When I had dragged the bandit's unconscious form from the river I had noticed that he had stunk. Roger and I smelled like roses by comparison. We might be able to smell them even if they had no fire. I observed the absence of bird noise. That might have been us but I could not hear any noise from further ahead. Were we being tracked? The wind did not help us but, when the path turned sharply to the right, I caught a whiff first of unwashed bodies and then of woodsmoke. I drew a pistol and readied it. Jack was a good horse and allowed me to ride with just my knees. I could draw a second and still ride if I chose. I said nothing but I knew that Roger, riding just behind me, would have emulated me and drawn his pistol. I noticed that we were heading slightly downhill and Jack was eager. That meant there was water ahead. It all began to make sense. They would have made a camp close to water. I also discerned that the wood was becoming lighter ahead and that, too, suggested a good place to camp. It had been cleared in the past, perhaps by charcoal burners. I slowed the keen Jack and peered ahead. I thought I caught a glimpse, not of a man's form but clothing. I reined in at the edge of the clearing. I took in that there was a fire burning which appeared to be dying and that there were blankets laid around it beneath hovels. There were half-hewn trees which suggested seats. Half of a young deer hung from the limbs of a tree. If nothing else it showed me that they were poachers. I felt Roger's horse move next to my leg. I dug my heels in and Jack moved into the camp. Three men rose from behind the half-hewn trees. The one in the centre was the bandit called John. I did not recognise the other two and I did not see Tom. John had a bow with a nocked arrow. Bob had told me he had been an archer. The other two were armed, one with a sword and the other a wood axe. I did not look for the rest of the bandits but I knew that they would be close, probably behind us. Smelling the fire and the men had given me an advantage. I had a primed pistol and the three men were less than thirty paces from me. I did not fear the bow.

I said calmly, for I wanted to take John and his nephew without violence, "We are here to apprehend the men who tried to rob me at Skerne Bridge. I see that one is before me. Lay down your weapons and I swear that there will be a fair trial."

Roger said, "Poaching is a crime."

It was the man next to John who spoke. I saw that he was the better dressed of the three of them. He had a sword and, as I studied it I realised that it was a good sword. His boots were also better than those of a brigand. He addressed me by name and rank, "Colonel Bretherton, there are six of us and just two of you. This man," I noticed he did not say his name, "is one of us and we would not have him taken. Give up your weapons and we will sell you back to your families." He smiled, "We will let you live."

I felt shivers run up my spine. The man had used not only my name but my rank. How did he know me? I did not want to turn my attention from the three men but I was desperate to see the two who were with Tom and probably behind us.

Roger became angry and he urged his horse next to mine. As he distracted the three men I drew my second pistol surreptitiously. Roger pointed the forefinger on his right hand at them, "Enough of this. I hold the assizes in this valley and I will try the six of you. The butchered deer is clear evidence of poaching. Lay down your weapons."

The man with the sword suddenly shouted, "Now!" He and the axeman moved to the side as John pulled back on the bow. I reacted. My hand came up in a blur and I fired. There was the heartbeat of a delay and then the pistol cracked and smoke plumed. I heard the twang of a bow and I kicked Jack in the flanks. He lurched to my left as I holstered one pistol and levelled the second.

Roger cursed, "Treachery!" He was not a soldier and they were wasted words. I aimed the pistol at the shadow in the smoke and, urging Jack forward, rode through the smoke I had created towards the man with the sword. It was then I saw that he had rammed his sword into the soft soil and had drawn a pistol. This man was no bandit. He was priming it for it was a matchlock and he blew on the lighted fuse. He was a soldier and that became clear to me now. As the smoke cleared I raised the second pistol and even though I was moving quickly I aimed at his middle. His pistol rose and I squeezed my trigger. He was ten paces from me when the ball struck his face and even as he fell backwards he discharged his own pistol into the air. The axeman ran at me and I barely had time to holster my pistol and draw my sword. Jack's speed and natural reactions saved me. He swerved away from the swinging blade. I managed to flail and swash my sword at the axe. I caught the haft and prevented it from touching either me or my brave horse. I heard the pistol in Roger's hand bark and then the sound of hooves as Ralph brought the others in a belated attempt at rescue. The axeman raised his axe to hack at Jack and I slashed at him with my long sword. Any thoughts of wounding him and making him a prisoner disappeared at the thought of an injured horse. My blade sliced across his neck and, as the blood spurted and his knees collapsed, he died.

I whirled my horse around and saw Tom lying prostrate on the ground, his arms and legs spread out, shouting, "I surrender." I saw that he was the only one who was left alive. Roger's pistol had slain one of the bandits and the last had been hacked by Ralph and Harry as he had tried to flee. If he wanted to save his life then Tom had done the right thing.

I saw that Roger's arm had been hurt. I rode to him and dismounted. I let Jack's reins drop. "You are wounded."

"Aye, it was the arrow. Damned thing hurts."

I saw that it had nicked his upper arm. I took the cloth from my neck and fastened it around the upper arm to stop the bleeding. I shouted, "Ralph, have someone watch your master."

"Aye, Colonel. What do we do with this cowardly one who did not dare to fight us? String him up now?"

I shook my head and walked over to the last of the bandits, "No, he gets a trial as we promised him. Are the others dead?"

As I went to pull Tom to his feet I saw Roger's men turning over the corpses to check for signs of life. I realised, when Tom faced me, that I must have broken his nose when I had kicked him. His face was blackened, bruised and turning yellow around his eyes. He looked terrified. I saw that he was only slightly older than Ted. He looked thin and the dirt and scruffy beard had made him look older. He was shaking. "Don't let them hang me, Colonel. I never hurt anyone. I did not fight you. I know I have sinned and committed a crime. I will take my punishment."

"You tried to attack me." My voice was calm and measured. There was no anger in it.

He looked down, shamefacedly, "I am sorry, Colonel. My uncle said that if we showed determination then our victims would surrender their goods. I thought, on the bridge, you would surrender. We never struck anyone we didn't have to. At least I never did."

I pointed at his uncle, "But he did."

He nodded, "Yes, Colonel, he could be cruel."

"Then why did you stay with him?"

"Where else could I go? I still do not know who my father was and my mother died when I was but twelve. John came and took me. I know it was not mercy. He needed someone who would work with him for no one else would."

"What about these other four?"

He shook his head, "Two of them came last week, not long before you did and the other two, the soldier and his friend arrived the day after you. Even my uncle was afeard of them. I think three of them were foreigners." To someone from Northumberland that could be almost anyone. The man who had known my name had been from this island.

I heard the mutterings of Ralph and the others. They wanted to hurt Tom and I knew why. They had been tardy. Their master had been hurt and the plan had almost failed. They wanted to blame someone. I said, quietly, "Stay by me, Tom." His story was the same as many of the men who served with me in

Bretherton's Horse. I knew that there would be others in this land who were just like Tom. Life was not fair. I walked over to the soldier. Ralph and Harry had turned him over. His skin was the same colour as mine. German winters were cold but the summer sun burnt the skin. He still had the slightly darker skin of one who had lived beyond England. I took his purse and opened it. As I poured the coins in my hand I understood more. The coins were from Germany, Spain and France. There were more silver coins than copper. I picked up his sword and pistol. They were both good ones. What was a soldier doing here hiding in Coatham Woods? "Which was the other one who came with this man?"

He walked me over to the man slain by Roger. It was clear that he was a soldier too. His weapons, whilst not as good as the ones on the leader I had killed, were good ones. His purse also showed that he had served abroad. I suddenly said, "These four men, did they walk here?"

He shook his head, "No, Colonel. They had horses. This man and the other who came not long ago had better ones."

"Where are they?"

He pointed to the north, "Hidden there."

"Take me to them. Ralph and Harry, come with me."

I saw Ralph look at Roger. The wounded man now had his arm in a sling and sat on the log drinking from his coistrel. He waved and said irritably, "Go with the Colonel, he is in command."

Ralph and Harry came reluctantly. For some reason they seemed to blame me for the wound to their master. Tom led and Ralph grabbed his arm, "No running, mind! I will cut you down like a dog if you try."

I snapped, my voice commanding, "And you, Ralph, will obey my commands."

"He is a bandit, Colonel, why treat him well?"

"Because he surrendered and I say so. If you cannot obey orders then rejoin the others." He glared at me but nodded. I said, "This man says that there are four horses. That is the only reason that I need you."

The horses were tethered in a hidden glade and a rough natural looking pen had been built. Two were hackneys while two were sumpters. There was one good saddle with a pair of holsters and a second saddle that looked military. The other two were worn and old. "Saddle them, Ralph, and bring them to the camp. They can bring the bodies back. The men need to be buried."

Harry snorted, "Just leave them here to rot."

I sighed, "And would you have men fear to come where their spirits wander? Do you wish Coatham Woods to be haunted?"

I saw the fear on Harry's face, "No, Colonel."

"Then we take the bodies back."

By the time Tom and I returned, the bodies had been laid out. I sat on the log next to Roger. "Tom, tell me all. The truth will save you."

"You want everything?"

"I want to know what happened after these four joined you."

"Jurgen and Klaus, as I said, came a day before… before the day of the bridge over the Skerne. They were foreigners but they had sumpters. I think my uncle was trying to work out how to get the horses from them. He let them stay because they shared food with us. When we ate they wanted to know about the area. They left the day we…that day. We went to the bridge because my uncle wanted to impress them when they returned. They came back, late the next day, with these other two. Lieutenant Robert," he nodded towards the soldier I had killed, "he took charge. He said they were here to get you, Colonel. He promised my uncle and me money if we helped. When he found out about how you had escaped our attack he said he was not surprised."

I looked again at the man I had slain. My ball had made a mess of his face but there was something about him that was now familiar. I moved his jack and saw the red sash around his waist. He was one of the English mercenaries who had followed Heinrich Holk. I had helped to thwart him and his men. Was this some act of revenge or were the king's enemies trying to eliminate his leaders?

"What was your plan?"

"Lieutenant Robert planned on going to your house. When the man told us your name my uncle said he knew it and said that you had no real protection and he could get us in. The rain the other day made the lieutenant wait, for the Skerne burst its banks. We planned on coming tomorrow, Sunday night. When we heard your horses the lieutenant told us what to do. He said for the three of us to hide in the trees and when you entered surround you."

The rain I had cursed had helped us. I shuddered at the thought of these men coming to my home. I had thought I had left the war behind but it had followed me. The silver in the purse was now explained.

Roger said, "It seems a little extreme to send four men to England to kill you, James. Perhaps this man is lying to save his skin."

I shook my head, "I believe Tom, for this makes sense. This lieutenant served a cruel Danish mercenary. They ravaged and raped their way across Germany. I helped to stop them. Perhaps I am a marked man and more of a threat than I know. Assassination is not an English thing but I know that our enemies are happy to engage such killers."

I saw Roger nodding as Ralph and Harry led the four horses into the camp, "What now?"

"We take the bodies back. They need to be buried. As I said to Ralph and Harry, we do not need their spirits walking this land."

"And this one?" He used his good hand to point to Tom.

"Let me deal with him."

He cocked an eye in surprise, "You would hang him yourself?"

"Tom told me that he never hurt anyone and I believe him. He does not deserve to hang."

Roger shook his head, "It was you who they attempted to rob and, by his own admission, you and your family that were threatened; I suppose you have the right but I wonder at your decision." He stood, "Put the bodies on the horses and tether this man." He looked at me, "You can decide what to do with him but I will not risk him running. That is my command." He had taken charge now that the fighting was over. I nodded.

We headed back to Piercebridge. When we passed Low Coniscliffe the villagers came out. Bob Chester smiled, "I see you have them." The smile left his face when he saw the tethered Tom. "What will happen to poor Tom?"

I said, "I have yet to decide, Bob."

I heard the sympathy in his voice, "He made a mistake. A man should not die for one mistake."

"I will make a decision on this matter, Bob. You will have to trust me to make the right decision when I have thought on it."

We rode on and as we clattered down the road to the village, people came out from their houses. Roger said, "Ralph, take the bodies to the church. I will come with you and speak to the minister." He looked at me, "You are determined?"

"I will speak with Charlotte and we will watch this youth."

He nodded and looked at the horses, "I do not need these animals. Do you wish them?"

I realised that I could use them. Ted needed a better horse. I nodded, "If you do not want to use them then aye."

"I will send them back and I will return to dine with you on the morrow." He rubbed his arm, "First, I shall need to see a doctor."

Charlotte and Ted had come to the door. Seeing the tether around Tom's neck I saw Charlotte start. I dismounted and took the rope from his neck. I said, quietly, "Swear that you will not run."

His eyes were wide with fear, "I do not wish to die, Colonel, and I believe that you are a fair man. I have done wrong and I swear that I will accept any punishment that you decide to impose and I will not run."

"Very well." I waved Ted over. "Ted, take Jack to the stable and take Tom here with you. Watch him. He has promised that he will not run."

Ted gave Tom the same look that Ralph and Harry had but he nodded, "Yes, Colonel."

The two men headed to the stable. Charlotte said, "There is a tale here." Before we had even entered she stopped and said, "Is he one of those who attacked you?"

"He is."

"And the other?"

"Dead."

"Margaret, take William and bathe him. I need to talk to the colonel before we dine." I shed my cloak and gauntlets and went to the small sitting room recently vacated by my wife. Her needlework was still there. "What do you intend? Have you decided?"

I nodded and, mindful of our conversation the previous day told her the truth. I told her the story that Tom had told me. She tried to hide her feelings but her face betrayed her when I spoke of their plan to raid the house. I had time to think about this on the way home. "I confess, Charlotte, that the chests of coins I brought may have been a lure. This Lieutenant Robert could have planned to kill me but also profit by my death. The sooner we spend as much of the money as we can the better." I knew that once I returned to the war I would double what we had.

She sat and picked up the needlework. I knew that it helped her to think. "The youth, Tom, I think he is a victim here." She looked at me, "The broken nose you gave him seems, to me, punishment enough for a botched robbery."

I smiled, "You are right but people like Ralph and Harry think the way most of those around here will think. People will expect retribution of some kind."

"Then they are not Christian. When he is able, a Christian forgives and I cannot see the benefit in this matter of punishment."

I could see that whatever I said my wife had already made up my mind. I was a soldier and I knew when a frontal charge was the right move and when a retreat was the wiser choice. I retreated. "And what is it you have in mind?"

"First we clean him up. He stinks." It was not a cruel comment although it sounded like one. "We feed him and clothe him."

I nodded. All of that was understandable but I knew that Charlotte had more in mind. "And?"

"And then you hire him and make him into the man he should have been. We redeem the sinner." Charlotte's father had been a preacher and his influence clearly ran deep.

"Are you sure? Think of William."

"William needs to see this. The world is not a land of milk and honey. There is cruelty and injustice. He has to see that there is good in all men. Sometimes God needs a helping hand to draw out that goodness and hide the dark." She reached out to touch my hand, "You are a good man. The stories you told me of your company and how you melded them into one make that clear. While you are home, save Tom."

"And when I am gone?"

"Then he will work with Ted." She saw the doubt on my face. "I looked into his eyes and I saw a young, frightened boy in a youth's body. From what you say it was his uncle who was the devil. Tom was not swayed by the temptations offered. I am content."

She laid down her needlework and took my arm. We went to the kitchen. We both knew that was where Ted would have taken Tom. Elizabeth was cooking but watching Tom. He sat on a stool in the corner looking very sorry for himself. Ted was drinking a mug of ale. Charlotte said, "Have you offered ale to our guest, Ted?"

Ted almost choked on the ale. He spluttered, "Our guest?"

My wife's voice was firm, "All visitors to our home are guests. Ale, if you please." I saw Elizabeth's smile. She and Margaret knew my wife even better than I did. When Tom had the ale in his dirty hand she continued, "Now, Tom, the colonel has told me your story. You do not wish to die." He nodded. I think he was too scared to speak for my wife's tone was firm and stern. The redemption of a soul was a serious business. "We wish to offer you a place in this house." I smiled for Elizabeth, Ted and Tom all had the same expression on their face. It was one of absolute shock. "Now there are rules and before you are offered this sanctuary I want you to hear them." He nodded but this time his mouth remained closed. "First, you will be stripped, bathed and your head shaved. We will burn these rags and you will be reborn in new clothes. You will live here in this house." She looked at Ted. "You will share a room with Ted and in that way you will better learn our ways." She stared at Ted until he nodded his acceptance of the dictate. "This is a Christian house and you will behave in a Christian manner. There will be no blasphemy and you will, while you live here, pray each day. Can you read?" He shook his head. "Then you can join Ted for his lessons. You need to be able to read for in that way enlightenment will come."

There was something almost evangelical in the way my wife spoke. It seemed that all of her father's teachings had resurfaced or, perhaps, they had always been there and I had just failed to see them.

She looked at me. It was clearly my turn to say something. I would not dream of trying to speak in the same manner. It was not my way. "Tom, I agree with all that my wife has said but if you are to live under my roof then you will need to work. You have heard our words. First, do you agree to my wife's terms?"

He nodded, "With all my heart. I am a Christian and I am sorry for my actions."

It was the right thing to say. "Good, and what work can you do?"

He frowned and looked nervous again. He shook his head, "I do not know, Colonel. When I lived with my mother I tended the vegetables…" he tailed off.

"That is a start and I am guessing that you have the skills of one who lived in the woods. You can trap, hunt, chop wood, build hurdles, fish…?"

He beamed, "Of course, but I did not think of those as skills, Colonel. I was just trying to survive."

"And in my experience just surviving in this world is a skill."

My wife said, "Enough talk, it is all settled and we have much to do. Ted, fill the bath. James, go and find the old clothes you wore as a youth. They should fit him. I will fetch my shears and when I have taken the worst away Ted can shave his head." She suddenly stopped and her voice softened as she said, "Elizabeth, Tom will eat in here with Ted, is that acceptable?"

She smiled, "Of course, Mistress Charlotte. I think I have the measure of this soul that needs to be salvaged."

"Then be about your business. William will be ready for his food soon and I want him to see a clean Tom and not the wild beast that lurks in the corner." There was a smile on her face to take the insult from her words.

By the time I had found clothes that I thought would fit, Tom had been shorn and was in the bath. Ted was shaving his head and I saw the dead wildlife floating in the water. Ted had used the rough soap that rid a body of dirt and now I saw the marks of an outdoor life. His hands and neck apart his body was as white as snow. I also saw his ribs. He had not eaten well. I hung the clothes on the hooks. He looked embarrassed.

I said, "You will feel cold when you are dressed and when you leave the hall you shall need a hat." He nodded. "Ted will give you an eating spoon and," I paused, "an eating knife. I pray you do not abuse it."

"Colonel, I am grateful to you. This is the second time you saved my life."

"The second time?"

"My uncle told me that he escaped because you took the time to pull me from the Skerne. Had you not done so I would have drowned. I owe you two lives and my oath was easily given for I had already sworn one to myself that I owed it to you to protect you."

I almost smiled to think that this half-grown emaciated youth would ever be able to save me but I did not for he meant it and I knew that stranger things had happened. "Then let us start your new life here, Tom…of the Woods." He smiled and nodded. As I later came to learn the name Taylor did not fit. His mother had been forced to retain the name for she was abandoned and its association with the bandit John was painful. To Charlotte he was always simply, Tom, but I kept the name, Tom of the Woods. I knew other Toms who served in the regiment. This gave my new servant an identity.

Ralph and Harry had returned the animals while Tom was being bathed. I spoke to them and saw them peering beyond me to spy out the man they wanted to hang. I just smiled and thanked them. After they had eaten Ted and Tom had their first job and that was to see to the new horses. It gave Charlotte and I the opportunity to speak.

She seemed at peace as she spoke, "I think that God has sent us Tom. We have been blessed with William but Tom is a challenge. He is formed already and not a piece of clay to be moulded. Let us see what we can achieve, eh, husband?"

She was right but it was not what I had expected when I had returned from the wars.

Chapter 4

Charlotte wanted everything to be just right for the meal. We had spoken of the disapproval Roger had shown when I had dealt clemency to Tom rather than retribution. She saw the meal as a way of mending bridges. She and Margaret spent most of the morning in the kitchen and that left me with William. I did not mind for I could get to know him and my wife would not be there to see my mistakes. The hardest part was fielding the barrage of questions with which he bombarded me. They were all about Tom. Even when I answered them they seemed to prompt even more questions or sometimes he repeated the question. It was clear that I did not know children. When Margaret returned to take him to make water, I was exhausted and relieved. I went to the dining room and saw Tom and Ted, under the supervision of my wife, laying the table.

She looked up at me and saw the questions on my face. She smiled, "I have been remiss with Ted and the arrival of Tom has prompted me to remedy that omission. The two of them can learn the skills of house servants too. If they should choose to leave our service then they have many more skills with which to find employment."

I just nodded. I doubted that either of them would wish to leave us but, if they did, the reasons in both cases would be different ones. "And what are we serving our guest?"

"Ted has found two hens that no longer lay. They are cooking now in a pot with root vegetables and some wine. I believe the French call it coq au vin. It is fancy enough for Roger but easy enough for Elizabeth to manage. We have a bramble and apple pie for pudding although I believe the great and the good call such things desserts. Does that suit?"

"So long as there is a mature cheese to go with the port I brought home then I am a happy man." Port was one of my indulgences and I had bought some in the port before leaving with Captain Stewart.

We had not given Roger a time to dine and he arrived at noon. We had all seen him at church that morning but Roger had his own pew and we had just nodded to him. After the services it was others who accosted him to ask about his arm. I think it was only he who noticed Tom and I am not sure he even recognised the shaven headed and smartly dressed young man who looked nothing like the wretch who had abased himself before us. Certainly, when he arrived and Ted and Tom waited to take both his horse and his cloak, it took him a moment to see that it was a reborn Tom. He waited until they had gone before he said, "So, you are not punishing him?" There was definitely criticism in his tone.

I smiled, "Some might say that the loss of freedom and becoming a servant were punishments enough."

We entered the hall and he shook his head, "You know what I mean. If you take a wild animal into your house then you take a risk."

I stopped and faced Roger, "You are my father's oldest friend and the man who saved me but if you cannot tell the difference between a wild animal and a man then I despair."

He studied me and then nodded, "Perhaps if Caroline was still alive I might agree but I live in a world of men who demand that Tom be hanged."

"Then it is a good thing that the decision lies with us and we are intelligent men who can act rationally and not as barbaric beasts."

I had always looked up to Roger. He had been my saviour when my father had died and I knew that but for him I might have ended up like Tom. That single moment changed how I viewed him. We were no longer as close. Perhaps it was the influence of Charlotte but it seemed to me that where I could see no difference in Tom and me he did, and that disparity was down to our birth and upbringing. I was born to parents who were close to being noble while Tom was illegitimate.

Despite the abrasive conversation the meal went extremely well. The food was excellent for Elizabeth was a good cook and my wife knew how to concoct a menu. The slow cooking in the wine had rendered the older birds succulent. The wine I had to accompany the birds was excellent and who could fail to enjoy our own brambles and apples with Elizabeth's delicate pastry? The cream from the cow's milk went perfectly with it. The cheese and port served with freshly baked bread, for me, was a perfect end to the meal.

Roger sat with Charlotte and I in the cosy sitting room. Ted and Tom were enjoying their own lunch of the leftovers. Tom's face, as he carried the platters out, told me that it was, for him, a feast. Margaret was amusing William and the three of us were able to talk. I thought it best to keep clear of Tom and his position. As we had spoken of William during the meal I turned my attention to politics. I did so because Roger seemed keen to speak.

"The king, it seems, is trying to make changes to the way the Scots worship."

Charlotte shook her head, "The church does not need interference from a king. Why does he do this?"

Roger gave an irritated snort, "It is the queen. She is a Catholic and French. She still has her own confessor. It rankles with her that she was never crowned and refuses to acknowledge the title of Queen Mary. She titles herself as Queen Henrietta Maria."

I nodded, "I know that many who serve King Gustavus wonder at the lack of military aid from England. King Charles' father supported the cause."

Roger sighed and sipped a little more of the port, "And for that you can blame the Duke of Buckingham. He made disastrous military decisions and his campaigns cost money, lost men and gained us nothing. The king tired of failure. The king now taxes ships and Impropriations. The taxes from those are used by the king and they hurt the Puritans. They are less than happy about his ways. There is unrest." He smiled, "He is even managing to make taxes out of nothing. He allows monopolies, such as soap, which he taxes. He encourages deforestation and gains taxes from the timber. He has reintroduced the Distraint of Knighthood."

Charlotte frowned, "And what is that?"

"An old law not used since Tudor times. Men who earn more than £40 a year can present themselves in London where they are knighted. Once they are they become liable for taxes. The king has also claimed back the ancient hunting forests that were allowed to be common land. He is a throwback to monarchs who believed in a divine right to rule. I fear for this land."

I realised that the land was becoming divided. Already there were secret Catholics and the Puritans were a sect that were extreme Protestants. King Charles was in danger of dividing it even more. I smiled and poured more port, "It is better than what I have seen in Europe, Roger. Here we have parliament and we have laws which men obey."

He shook his head, "We do at the moment but that may change." He knew more about British politics than I did but his words were a warning. The mood was soured.

Charlotte tried to lighten it, "And when will the wedding be?"

"In June. You are both invited…"

Charlotte shook her head, "James will be away and I would not attend alone. Besides, there is William. We shall send a gift, of course."

I knew from his tone that he was disappointed, "And you, James, you do not tire of war? You intend to return to Germany?"

"Of course I do for the task is not yet finished. The Papists want to strangle Protestantism. You would not believe the things I have seen done. So long as King Gustavus fights on I will be at his side. He is an enlightened monarch and one of the fairest men I have ever met."

"Then you will be there for longer than one year."

I shook my head, "The king is a great general and he has the beating of our enemies. His leaders, in the main, are good ones and his tactics have them confounded. I may be back within the year if all goes well. Northern Germany is already rescued and it is Bavaria and Austria that demand his attention. When those Catholic countries are defeated then they will sue for peace and I shall return home and give up the sword."

That he did not stay long after the meal had ended told me that he disapproved of my decision about Tom's future. I would still be his friend and still respect him, how could I do anything else after what he had done for me and living in the same village, but I knew it would never be the same between us in the future.

After we had put William to bed I sat with Charlotte and we talked. The putting to bed took a little longer these days as I now had to tell him a story. I knew that I would soon run out of the ones I knew, the ones my mother had told me and I would have to find ones I did not know.

I said, "Roger thinks we have made a mistake with Tom."

"You know, James, that I thought that when my father died his teachings would be forgotten and, for a time, they lay hidden somewhere here." She patted her head, "I was distracted first, by marriage and this house, and then William. I thought that I did not need my father's teachings. William and your absence have made me think otherwise. I think we have to do right by one another. It is not because the church tells us to but because it is the right thing to do. I want William to know how to behave and treat other people when he grows and not simply go along with what everyone else thinks. I believe that you and I are right and Roger and his men are wrong. He is still our friend but I will not change the way we live to fit in with another." She smiled, "You and I will make a better man of Tom. What is it you called him, Tom of the Woods?"

I was content. "Aye, that is how I named him." Of course, over the years the name changed to simply Tom Wood. That was the way with some names. They changed over time. He knew who he was and answered to all the names even when someone he knew from his past called him Tom Taylor.

With the visit out of the way we could prepare for Christmas. Part of that would necessitate a visit to Durham. It had a market and there we could buy all that we could not find locally. Christmas was a time for whatever luxuries one could afford and thanks to the war I had coins to spare. This would also be an opportunity for Tom and Ted to ride. On the Monday after the meal we went to the stable to examine the four horses we had taken. They were not the best of horses. All were mares. The two hackneys were little better than the horse George Smith had loaned me. I deduced that the four men had come from abroad and bought the animals as cheaply as they could. We had no names for them. Tom could not remember the riders addressing them and he said that they had not bothered much about the animals. The way a man treated an animal, horse or dog, it mattered not, told me much about a man. The two horses I had brought from Hartlepool were not the best of animals but I had fed them and had them groomed each day. They had responded well and George would be getting back better animals. The day was cold but bright and, wrapped against the cold, we took all the horses into the yard. I knew that this would be intimidating for Tom. He had little experience of horses and all that Ted had done, in my absence, was groom the horses. It had been Peter and Roger who had exercised Jack.

Tom had only been with us for two days but already he looked like a different man. I had seen a scowling and potentially dangerous man at Skerne Bridge but now he could not keep the smile from his face. His blackened nose and face were both becoming their normal colour. Had we found him the day after my kick had disfigured him then his nose might have been straightened. Tom did not seem to harbour a grudge. He was well wrapped against the cold. The old clothes I had outgrown were well made and warm. He seemed happy.

"Well, we have four animals to name. What do you think?"

Ted rubbed his chin, "It seems to me, Colonel, for the two sumpters, that as Bluebell is named after a flower why not do the same for the other two?"

I nodded, "That seems like a sensible idea." I pointed to the one nearest to Ted, "Name that one then."

He went to the horse and stroked it. Smiling he said, "Rose." He nodded to the back door where Charlotte had planted a climbing rose. "It will please the mistress for she likes roses."

"Good. Tom, the other."

He emulated Ted but also put his head next to the horse. He smiled, but it was a sad smile, "Lily, Colonel."

"Lily?"

"Yes, Colonel, when my mother died the reverend placed a single lily on the grave. It was a pauper's grave and that was the only flower. It will remind me of my mother."

"What was your mother's name?"

He hesitated and then sighed, "It was Rose."

Ted looked aghast and shook his head, "Then we will rename the other... I did not know."

Tom said, "No, we have named her, and besides, I am reminded of my mother twice over. This is all good, Ted."

That briefest of conversations told me much. The two young men got on and, as I would be leaving them to look after my family, then that was a good thing. It also determined that I would name the other two animals and avoid any such problems. I walked over to the two hackneys and took their halters in my hands. I looked into their eyes. Horses have such wonderfully deep eyes. I never regard them as dumb animals for I had seen, in battle, horses show more courage than any warrior. They were brave and, if treated right, loyal unto death. I chose names that were female but classical in nature. That way they would not be confused with any women that we knew. "Dido and Cleopatra were great queens in antiquity. Let us see if noble names help these two to aspire to greatness." The name, Cleopatra, inevitably became shortened to Cleo. All four animals soon responded to their new names. Perhaps they had not even been addressed before. They looked to have endured miserable lives.

"Now we need to make them into better horses. Once we have groomed them we will take them into the paddock. When we have legally acquired Walter's land we can let them graze there before we plant crops." Roger had set the sale in motion. We had given the gold to the lawyer handling the sale and by January I would have doubled the land I owned. I helped the two to groom the horses. For Tom it was all new but he seemed to have a natural affinity to horses. Bob Chester's words came back to me, *'a good heart'*, he appeared to be right. That done I let the two men lead them to the small paddock to join Jack and Bluebell. They would soon make the paddock a muddy morass and then we would have to feed them hay and cereal. That was something else we would need from Durham. We would need to visit the chandlers.

That done I returned to the warmth of the house. I went to the small room I called a study. I think that in a previous life it had been a guard room for a porter but Charlotte had repurposed it so I could be alone. I now used it properly for the first time. I had placed my chests of coins there for it was a safe place and I had sheets of paper, ink and quills. I used the paper to account for all the coins. I had, of course, counted them once before but that had been in Germany. I had spent some already. Once I had the coins counted and returned to their chests I wrote down how much I had. It was still not the fortune my father had lost when his ship and hopes had foundered, but it was getting there. As I looked at the columns of figures I had to work out how I could continue to make money once I was no longer a soldier. I was no farmer. Ted could farm but I could not expect him to earn money for me while I did nothing. I was a soldier and those skills would not aid me here in England.

I had also thought about the attack since I had returned home. This Lieutenant Robert would not just have come to take my life. It was an expense to come to England and buy two horses. The profit would come from the taking of my gold. Our enemies were also paid and they would know that the victorious army always had more money. The money that I had could be a curse.

There was a knock on the door and Ted stood there. I saw Tom just behind him, "The horses are in the paddock, Colonel, what else would you have us do?"

"The saddles and horse furniture we took, I am guessing that it is not the best. Repair what you can and make a list of what needs to be replaced."

"Yes, Colonel." They left.

Horses, horse furniture and weapons I knew but farming...It was then that the idea came to me. The land we were buying from Walter's estate was huge but only half of it was suitable for crops. The other was too close to the river, there were trees that prevented ploughing and it was steep. Jack was a stallion and if I bought mares that were suitable for breeding then I could breed horses. I had two mares whom whilst not the best, with care and close attention might produce reasonable horses. The more I thought about it the more sense it made. I liked horses and the breeding of such animals could be learned. I put the quill down and felt quite self-satisfied. It would be the unknown but it was a challenge. It was also something I felt more confident about doing. Ted and Tom would need more skills but we had a year for them to gain such skills. It was as I put the chests under the desk that I suddenly thought of my regiment. There were men there who looked after our horses. When I left the war and returned home there might be others, men like Stephen of Alnmouth who had served and then returned to England. There might be men who would wish for a life after the killing. I was planning for a future after war.

Charlotte came to find me, "It is time for lunch." She looked at my inky fingers, "And what have you been writing?"

I smiled, "I have been planning for our future. When we have Walter's land and I have left the service of King Gustavus, I fancy a life as a horse breeder."

I saw her pause. My wife was quick witted and had the ability to sift through ideas and to evaluate them. She nodded, "Men always need horses. Riding horses?"

It was good that she asked me questions for those questions prompted more ideas, "I had thought so but we have sumpters and with the right stallion we could breed draughthorses."

"And there are enough coins?"

"There will be when I return, but, my love, I am planning for the future. Remember when last I had no work… then I was able to train the militia. Now that income would not provide enough money for a wife, son and servants. I have more to think of these days."

"Then I will do all that I can to help you." I saw, in her eyes, her mind working, "It will mean more building."

"When we have the new land we can turn the paddock into the new stables and make the old stables into…" I shrugged, "I am not sure."

"And I will have a year to come up with a plan. All of this is not on your shoulders alone, James, we share the burden."

I went out, after lunch, to speak to my two men. I walked them through the gate to the new field. "Ted, I have thought of your ideas and changed them a little. This land will be ours in January. However, I thought to use it, first, for our horses." He nodded. "The upper part, that which is flattest, can be used for the crops you wish to plant. I leave that decision to you for you are a farmer and I am not. The lower part, closer to the river will be for animals."

"Cattle and sheep, Colonel."

I smiled, "Part of it but I also intend to breed horses. That will not be until I leave the army but I wanted the two of you to be prepared."

Ted frowned, "Breeding horses? That is a mighty step, Colonel."

"It is and, at the moment there are things I lack to ensure we make a success of it. There is no point in starting something that is doomed to failure. We have a year to solve the problems but I want you two to think about those problems while I am away."

While Ted nodded Tom asked, "You will be leaving, Colonel?"

I suddenly realised that Tom was not privy to that information. "Aye, Tom, I am a colonel of a regiment which serves King Gustavus of Sweden. When Spring comes I will return to Germany until, well, this time next year and then I shall be home for good." I saw that this disturbed him, "What is amiss? Does that not suit you?"

"Colonel, you have saved my life twice. War is a dangerous business, so I hear, and I would be on hand to save you, if I can." He was sincere, almost passionate. He had been reborn.

I smiled and saw Ted doing the same, "I am a good soldier, Tom, you are a callow youth and the one who would be in danger on the battlefield is you and not me."

"Colonel, do you have a servant? I mean one who comes with you to battle and watches your horse, cleans your weapons and the like?"

"I did but he now serves another officer, Tom."

"Do other officers have such servants?"

"They do."

"Then take me, Colonel. You are right I am callow and I have no experience but neither have I any farming skills. I know that I was bandit but living with my uncle taught me how to fight. Let me learn to be a servant and a soldier."

"Ted will need help."

Ted said, "Colonel, until a couple of days ago I expected to do all this on my own. I am unused to having help. If Tom wishes this as his path then who am I to stand in his way? Besides, you said yourself that we cannot do anything for a while. I will buy the sheep and the cows in spring when the young are born. Tom and I have January and until you leave in February to make the pens for the animals. It will be this time next year, when the animals have fertilised the fields and you have draught animals to plough, that the real work will begin. By your own admission, Colonel, then you will be back and Tom can help me."

He was right and I had not even thought about draught animals. The sumpters could pull the plough but bullocks or heavy horses would be better. "Let me think about this, Tom. We have time. For now the two of you need to work with the horses and make them stronger and you, Tom, need the same riding lessons as Ted. We begin in the morning."

That night, as I lay in bed with Charlotte in my arms, we spoke. We had finally managed to get William to sleep in his own room. He had woken on Saturday night and come into our bed but Sunday had seen him stay there. We hoped that Monday would be the same for we needed some privacy. After cuddling I told her what Tom had said. To my surprise it delighted her, "Now we see that we have done God's work. Already the soul we have saved comes to help us. You need someone to watch out for you."

I chuckled quietly, "I have a whole regiment to do that."

"You know what I mean. You are a senior officer and while I do not know how armies work I know that the senior officer is someone who is at the top of his tree. You need a servant and if Tom thinks that he owes you a life then what better man to watch your back?"

I did not go to sleep immediately for my wife and the former bandit had set my mind to working. Would I be putting the young man in danger? As parlous as the life he had led as a bandit had been, he would be entering a much more dangerous world. I also knew that I would have to train him not only to ride but to use weapons. I would defer the decision until after Christmas.

When I woke I put my mind to the trip to Durham. I wanted to make it in the first week of December. One advantage of the new horses was that Charlotte now had a horse that was better than a sumpter to ride. She could ride and was able to control horses well. Both Cleopatra and Dido appeared to be docile animals. I knew that we would need to take a sumpter and, as I would have William on my lap that meant taking either Tom or Ted. Before the seed of a soldier's servant had been planted in my mind I had planned on taking Ted. Now I saw that it would be Tom who would come. If nothing else it would give him the chance to run. I did not think he would but by taking him I was placing temptation before him.

We spent the next couple of weeks improving the riding skills of both men. I let them choose their own mounts. Ted chose Dido and Tom, Cleopatra. They had repaired the reins, bridles and girths as well as waxing the saddles. We spent an hour each morning and an hour each evening riding the lands along the river. By the start of the second week I was confident enough to let them canter and then gallop. They no longer clung for dear life to the saddle. Each day saw an improvement. At the end of the second week, after a particularly heavy rainstorm upstream we found ourselves, in late afternoon, at the ford we normally used to cross the river but it was in flood. We could have ridden back to the bridge but that would have added a mile to our journey. I took a chance for this was a skill I had used before and could teach them.

"We will swim the horses across." They both looked terrified. I said, "The level of the water is higher but it is not a dangerous current. Your horses can swim. Every horse can. I doubt that these have ever had to and so this is as much about schooling your horses as you. When the water reaches your boots then take your feet from the stirrups and lie flat on your hackney's back and hold the mane. I will lead and your mounts will follow. If you are in trouble then shout. I will come for you."

They both nodded but I knew that neither wished to risk the river. I doubted that they could swim. Later I realised it showed the trust they had in me. Perhaps it was the same with the men in my regiment. They followed me because they trusted me. I entered the river and headed Jack upstream. The river was not wide and it was ten paces before I felt him start to swim. I took my feet from my stirrups and looked behind. The two hackneys were following me. We had to swim for a mere ten paces and then Jack found the bottom and I put my feet back in the stirrups. I slowed and turned to watch the other two. Terror was written all over their faces but their horses were swimming well. As soon as their hooves touched bottom I saw the fear replaced by broad smiles. Once we reached the other bank the horses shook themselves and my two men grinned. Their confidence grew immeasurably in that moment. They had swum a river.

I also taught them to use the wheellock pistol. I had six of them and while they were expensive they were much better than the matchlocks which required a lighted fuse to be applied to the pan. There was still a slight delay when the wheellock was fired but it was far briefer than the matchlock. "Now the advantage of this weapon is that you can prime it and with the cover slid over then you can fire quickly." I pointed to the spring-loaded arm and said, "This is the dog. In this position," I demonstrated, "it is safe and in this, it is armed. You need to maintain the weapon for it has many parts and if one fails then the gun may not fire. I have six of these. When I have shown you how to use them then, while I am home, you can maintain one each." That was the start of the lessons in the use of pistols.

By the time November ended the weather was much colder. We had endured frosts. There was no snow yet but it had threatened. We had seen sleety rain that promised snow in a month or so. We restricted our rides to once a day and the three of us went to collect firewood from the river. We took the driftwood that had been brought from upstream in the floods first. We managed to secure most of our firewood that way. It was put to dry close by the bread oven and covered with an old, oiled cloak that was no longer serviceable. That done we copsed the trees that overhung the river. They would not be usable for some months but who knew how long winter might last?

Those tasks done, the leaves gathered to be used as compost and all the berries collected along with the autumn fruit, we prepared for what would be for William, a grand adventure.

Chapter 5

We wrapped well against the cold wind for the ride to Durham. It was a good twenty-five miles and whilst that was easy for me it might be too much for the others. I decided we would stay at an inn, in Durham, with which I was vaguely familiar. I had been there with my father and knew that the inn which lay close to the marketplace was one with stables. The inn, the Three Feathers, had comfortable rooms, as I recalled, and as we had gold as well as silver with us I knew that we could be accommodated. We left after breakfast. Margaret had wanted to come but Charlotte knew that our servant was no rider and she left Margaret to prepare the house for Christmas. With no William to watch over, she along with Elizabeth and Ted would have three days to clean the house and repair anything that needed to be repaired. We would take small roads until we reached the palace of the bishop at Auckland. From there it was a busy thoroughfare. I did not fear bandits but Tom and I went armed. He had a short sword and dagger and I had four pistols. Once Christmas was passed I would continue my lessons with Tom and Ted to show them how to use firearms. We had made a start but that was all.

William was cosily wrapped. He had a coat made of rabbit skins and a hat to match. My cloak covered both of us and Jack. He would be as warm within the tentlike cloak as he would at home. Everything he saw was of interest. This was the first time he had left the village and my ears were assaulted by his constant barrage of questions. It did not help that, as he did not know everything he saw, he often did not have the words and it was a lesson in learning new words as much as anything. Having said that it helped to pass the time. Charlotte spent the time getting to know Tom. He quickly learned how to lead the sumpter and once we had passed Bildershaw he was confident enough to answer my wife's questions whilst leading a sumpter and riding Cleopatra.

Once we were on the busier road we saw more travellers heading to and from the most important town in the Palatinate, some would say north of York and south of Edinburgh. When

King Henry had dissolved the monasteries he had been astute enough to know that a Prince Bishop in Durham was an ally he could use to his advantage. Although castles were no longer seen as powerful as they had once been, the river that encircled the rock that was Durham was still a place that could be defended and was a refuge. On the sumpter we had one chest of coins. That was not for spending but banking. Outside the city walls I knew, from the Swedish agent in Hartlepool, that there was a Jew who could be trusted. The port belonged to the Palatinate and most of the trade from Durham passed through the port. I intended to bank some of my money with him. Jews had been persecuted back in the time of the first King Edward, most notably by Simon de Montfort, but since then men had come to realise their value. A blind eye was turned to them. Officially they did not exist but there was a brotherhood of them in all the major towns and cities. Through their network it was possible to buy goods in far off lands without money moving. The Jews did it through bonds and parchment. I did not understand it but King Gustavus used them and that was good enough for me. Until I had spoken to the Jew then Tom would have to guard the chest in our room.

    We rode across the River Wear and passed through the gatehouse. The bishop kept guards there but our clothes, not to mention my sword, marked us as people of quality and we were allowed to pass through into the walled city. Tom looked fearful as we did so and that was understandable. He and his uncle would not only have been stopped from entering, but they might also have been incarcerated too. Once through the gate we turned right to head to the marketplace. I spied the Three Feathers immediately. I had not been there since before my father died but it had made a deep impression on me. I remembered the smell of ale and pipe smoke and large men with rough hands. I had never seen such people. I could not describe the furniture, the food or anything else but the smells and the men's hands had lingered. We headed for the gate to the courtyard. It was large enough to take a carriage or a wagon and I knew that, once upon a time, plays had been performed in the yard.

    I dismounted and an ostler called out for help. Tom took William from me and I went to help my wife. The men who came from the inn and the ostler went to unpack the sumpter. I went with Tom and we unstrapped the baggage. We would carry them. "We will be here for two nights. Treat our horses well and you shall be suitably rewarded."

"We shall give them our best attention, Sir." The ostler nodded to the servants, "Jamie, take their bags and we shall look after the animals."

Jamie slung two of our bags over his shoulders and the other man took the others. "Follow me, Sir, Madam, this is not a place to stand and we have a fine fire within."

I had to duck beneath the doorway. The wall of heat that greeted us as we entered confirmed the servant's opinion. He led us to an opening where a large florid man with a belly that bespoke good ale, waited for us, "Yes, Sir, how can we be of service?"

"We need rooms. I have a servant and there is my wife and son. We shall be here for two nights."

"I have just the thing, Sir. I have three rooms with connecting doors. We often use them for lords who visit the cathedral. There is a master bedroom and two smaller rooms. It has its own open fire and it is cosy." He hesitated and said, "If the price is too expensive…"

I smiled, "I am sure it will be fair."

He beamed, "Good, Jamie, take the bags up to the Lord's Suite. Your name, Sir, in case you have visitors?"

I doubted that I would but I nodded, "Colonel James Bretherton of Piercebridge."

He suddenly said, "Excuse my impertinence, Colonel, but you wouldn't be the commanding officer of Bretherton's Horse would you?"

"I am one and the same. How have you heard of me?"

"My nephew is Stephen of Alnmouth and he speaks well of you." The smile grew broader. "Welcome, Colonel. If you need anything, and I mean anything at all, then do not hesitate to ask. I am honoured to have under my roof such an esteemed warrior and one who fights the Papists." The landlord took us to the rooms and was at pains to point out all the features which, he assured me, were unique to not only his inn but the whole of Durham.

Once in the rooms, which were all that was promised and more, Charlotte shook her head, "I did not know I had married such a famous man and one who would be accorded such service."

"I am not, my love, and had Stephen of Alnmouth not been related then such a fuss would not have been made."

I am guessing that Harry Richardson, the innkeeper, must have been fond of Stephen for we were waited on like royalty during our stay. The servants in the tavern were most attentive and made a great fuss of William who revelled in it. For Tom it was an even more momentous occasion. He had never stayed in an inn and Charlotte insisted that he dine with us rather than with the servants. That first night he was so nervous that he found it hard to speak. He did not want to take advantage of us and, eventually, Charlotte ordered food for him. When the food came he was worried about the way he ate but Charlotte, once again, showed her kind nature. Over the next days he seemed to grow hour by hour as he gained confidence and stopped being quite so nervous.

We were tired and retired early. William, in a strange bed, woke early. We were amongst the first to breakfast. As we ate Charlotte said, "And what are your plans today, James?"

"I have to see about banking some of our money."

She nodded, "Then I will buy what we need and meet you at lunchtime. Shall we meet here at Sext?" I nodded, "Will you need Tom?"

I shook my head, "I will not be taking any money with me but I go to ensure that I can do what I need. If I need him it will be on the morrow."

"Good, then he can watch William." My son had taken to Tom. I think it was because Tom did whatever was asked of him. The previous night as we had prepared William for bed my son had Tom entertain him with funny songs and pulling faces. Tom did not seem to mind and it made life much easier for us.

I wrapped up and in lieu of my hat wore a cowled cloak. I had an address, obtained from George Smith, the Swedish agent in Hartlepool. It was outside the walls in a commercial area. I had my sword with me and a pair of pistols. I did not think that I would need them. They were a deterrent. I asked, at the gate, for directions. The sergeant at arms nodded and gave them to me but before he did he said, "You will be seeing the Jew then?"

"Why do you say that?"

He smiled, "No one, especially one dressed as well as you, Sir, asks for directions to that street unless they are visiting old Isaac." He pointed, "Easy to find. Knock on the door and wait. The man has more bolts on his door than enough."

King Edward had banned and then expelled all Jews in England more than three hundred years ago. They had not all left but gone into hiding. Many were men whose families had lived in England for many hundreds of years. They were English. There were also conversos. These were Jews who had, in Portugal and Spain, converted to Christianity. As the branch of Christianity they had converted to was Catholicism it was a moot point but most of the authorities turned a blind eye to the practice. So long as the Jews did not abuse their power, and that meant usury, they were tolerated.

I found the house and saw that unlike many of the others adjacent to it the door was solid looking and well made while the house itself was properly maintained. I knocked on the door and waited. The sergeant had said it was to allow the locks to be opened but I guessed there was some spy hole. I heard the locks being opened but they alone did not explain the delay. A huge man stood there. He was not a Jew. He was a bodyguard.

"Yes?"

He was, like my sword, a deterrent. He was there to put off those the Jew did not want to see or those who were not there on business.

"I am here to see Isaac." It was good that the sergeant had said his name. George had just called him *'The Jew'*.

"And who are you?"

"I am Colonel James Bretherton." For some reason I was loath to give him my address.

"And the purpose of your visit?"

My tone changed and I used my officer's voice. "Is between me and your master."

His eyes narrowed but I did not flinch. I had dealt with tougher men than him before now. "Wait here."

Lion of the North

The door closed and I heard a single bolt pulled across. I took it as slight acceptance that I was not a threat. I felt as though I was being scrutinised again. I continued to wait. This time when the bolt slid back and the door opened the giant gave me a smile that reminded me of an ill maintained graveyard. More teeth were missing than remained in his mouth and the ones that were there were uneven. "The master will see you." When I entered he pointed to the table that stood in the narrow passage, "Weapons there, Colonel." I obliged. At least he had used my title although his tone brooked no refusal.

The room we entered was well lit and that reflected the man who was seated at the table. He was dressed in plain but expensive clothes. The oil lamps illuminated everything and I saw that he needed the light for there were ledgers piled on a desk just behind him. He was an old man. His skin was wrinkled but his hawklike eyes were sharp and I felt myself being examined as I waited.

He smiled and his voice was without a trace of accent, "Sit, Colonel." He smiled, "Do not be intimidated by Alfred. He is very protective about me."

I nodded but said nothing. Alfred was clearly there to intimidate visitors.

"So, Colonel, you wish to borrow money."

I shook my head, "No, just the opposite."

I saw the look on his face change. He had made assumptions about me and already decided upon a course of action. My words had upset his ideas and I could see that he was unused to such events. "You wish to loan me money?"

I smiled and shook my head, "I serve King Gustavus and it was one of his officers who explained the system operated by people such as yourself. You loan money and collect the interest. However, you also store money and protect it. That is what I wish from you. I have made money from the war and I do not wish it to be a temptation to bandits and robbers. I believe it will be safer with you." I gestured at Alfred, "I can see that you know how to protect yourself and, I am guessing, coins."

He leaned back and played with the quill he held in his hands, "Interesting. You are, of course, right. My people do store money and guard it. As you probably realise for I can see that you are a clever man, Alfred is not my only protector." He reached over and picked up his wax tablet. He put the quill in the ink pot and then picked up his scribe. "Now, how long would you like us to guard your money?"

"At least a year and, in the event of my death," I smiled, "my profession means I must think of such things, then the money would be accessed by my wife, Charlotte Bretherton."

He paused in his scribing and looked at me, "You are prepared for such an eventuality?"

"A soldier who goes to war and expects to come back whole, or simply just return deludes himself. I do not wish to die and I will do all in my power to remain alive but I know that I must make such arrangements."

He smiled, "A wise man." He resumed his scribing. "And how much will I be guarding?"

"The gold is a mixture of Reichstaler and livres. There are three hundred of the former and two hundred of the latter. There is also a quantity of silver in various currencies."

He looked at me again and I saw surprise in his eyes, "This is truly a fortune. Perhaps I should take up the sword."

I laughed, "My friend, the man you employ, Alfred, would last moments only in battle. War is a profession and the men who fight it know their business."

"And you are clearly a master of it." He scribed and then wrote a figure down. He said, "I can offer you five per cent interest on your investment."

I would have settled for much less but I did not want him to know that. "You charge more than that for loans."

He smiled, "Indeed, but that is because such loans involve risks and there is always the expense of recovering such debts." I nodded. "You do not have the coins with you."

I shook my head, "If we are agreed then I will bring them tomorrow before I return to my home."

"I will have to count and weigh the coins."

"Of course."

He put down the tablet and put his fingers together, almost as though he was at prayer. "You are my most interesting customer to date and your visit has enlivened my day. Tell me, Colonel, how do you know you can trust me?"

"That is simple. You have taken the name Isaac Smith because you do not want to attract attention to yourself. I know that a blind eye is turned to your activities but if I chose to make a fuss I could. However, there is a simpler reason. I have men in my regiment who are loyal. If I thought for one moment that I was being robbed then I would bring a couple of them and recover my treasure. Trust me, Alfred and whoever else you have to guard you would not stand a chance against the men I would bring."

He smiled, "I believe you and you can trust me. When I have accounted for the gold and silver I will furnish you with my written surety of both its income and its guarantee of return. You are satisfied?"

I stood, "I am satisfied."

He looked at me and then Alfred, "Wait, without." His bodyguard obeyed instantly. "Colonel, I thank you for your business and, as it looks as though I may profit in the future from our association, I have some information for you." I waited. I could see him weighing up his words and choosing them carefully, "I have letters from my fellows in Germany, France…" he waved an airy hand, "all over Europe. My people may not have their own country but we are in every land. We are businessmen and regardless of what kings and emperors do we try to turn a profit. To that end we watch and listen. In a recent letter," he smiled, "written in code of course, I learned something that might interest you. Until you came through my door I had disregarded it but now that I have met you I feel obliged to tell you. Your King Gustavus, the Lion of the North, is now seen as a threat by his enemies."

I shook my head, "That is not news. He has defeated them at every turn."

"But now they see that if they rid the Protestant alliance of the king then they might achieve their end and destroy the rebellion."

"What are you saying?"

"That they will try to kill the king." He spread his arms, "For our business it matters little. Men will always need to use our services. Catholic or Protestant it matters not but I thought you should know."

"And for that I am grateful and I am happy that we have met and spoken. My treasure is safe, I think, with you." I held out my hand and he stood and took it. We shook hands. "And with this the bargain is made, Isaac Smith."

"It is, indeed, Colonel Bretherton."

It was when William had gone to bed and Tom was checking on the horses that I had the opportunity to speak to Charlotte. I told her all. "And you trust him?"

"I do. This is necessary. The money will grow with Isaac. There are men who will borrow from him and now he has even more funds to do so. We do not need this chest. I have a second one at home which, while containing less gold, will keep you for two or three years. I expect to come back with more profit and then I will give up the life of a mercenary."

We rose early and while Charlotte and William enjoyed a leisurely breakfast Tom and I headed for the Jew's house. This time I was admitted quicker and I did not have to yield my weapons. Tom stood protectively behind me as Isaac Smith counted the coins. He wrote down a figure and showed it to me. I nodded. He then inserted the numbers into a document he had already written. He signed and sealed it and handed it to me.

"Thank you." I made to rise.

He said, "One more thing." He took a small box from the desk. He handed it to me. "This is for your wife. If anything should happen to you then this is evidence of her identity." I opened the box and inside was a ring. It was a blue sapphire. He said, "The ring is a gift."

"Why?"

He shrugged, "I need some way to identify your wife and I do not think that you would bring your lady into this seedy world. I also like you. There are few men who would trust such a large amount of gold to a stranger and to do so for a family heartens me. I live in a world where men are greedy and seek only to enrich themselves. You settled for the first number I offered and that was surety for your family." He nodded to Tom, "And I can see that you engender great loyalty. I see in the eyes of the boy there that he would fight Alfred if he thought your life was in danger. I look forward to your return, Colonel, and I pray that you do. As much as I would like to meet your lady, I would prefer that she were not a widow, albeit a rich one."

With the ring and the document secured, we left.

We loaded the sumpter and it was laden. We were not carrying back the cereal and the seeds I had bought, the chandler promised delivery before Christmas. Charlotte had bought gifts as well as food, spices and wines that would make our celebration a memorable one. I had to show Tom how to load the sumpter so that she would not be injured and would complete the journey home without trouble. It meant we were later leaving than I had hoped. The last part of our journey would be in the dark. That could not be helped. I saved the ring as a surprise for our return.

William had his usual barrage of questions. Charlotte told him to be silent at one point but I said, "Let him ask. He needs to use the time we have together to ask as many questions as he can."

It was then I realised that my son had no concept of time. He asked, "You are not staying forever?"

"No, William, I have to return to the soldiers I lead and the king that I serve. Tom and I will have just a couple more months at home and then we will head across the sea."

"A month?"

I sighed, "How many sleeps is it until Christmas?"

He knew that and said, "Twenty-four." I knew that the number meant little to him. He could count to ten but after that numbers were meaningless. My wife and Margaret had done their best to teach him and I knew that he was better educated than any other child in the village but he was still a child.

"Then three times that number and I will leave. I will return when we light the next bone fire and prepare for the next Christmas."

The next questions were the hardest for me to answer. He asked me what I did. I have never chosen my words more carefully than I did on the ride back to Piercebridge.

The days until Christmas flew by. Part of that was that I knew I had to make Tom into a soldier. He would be my servant when I returned to Germany but in my world there were no bystanders. Tom would need to be able to defend himself and, if necessary, me. As Ted would be the one to stay at home and guard my wife, son and home, then he had to be trained too. Charlotte grew weary of the popping of pistols as we blank fired our weapons. Powder was relatively cheap but I did not want to waste ball until the two men were able to discharge their weapons without closing their eyes. It was almost Christmas when I let them fire balls for the first time. The deed for the new land was in my possession and we used the most distant part of the field where there were willows draped over the river. I placed a floured piece of wood on one of them and that was our target. It took four shots before Tom managed to hit the target. Ted had to move closer than the thirty paces where Tom had enjoyed success.

"I am sorry, Colonel, I am a failure."

I shook my head, "Ted, you are trying to be like me. I use the pistol one handed because I can. Tom here seems to be able to do the same. He has a strong right arm. When you aim use two hands to hold the pistol and take a wide stance." This time he hit the target and it was in the middle. "Now move back to your original place and try again." This time he hit the target. "This is the fault of a bad teacher, Ted, I should have asked you to use two hands from the start. Now we can stop. We have disturbed the peace enough and the poor willow has more than enough lead in him."

"Shall we try to recover the balls, Colonel?"

"If you wish, Tom, but it will mean we have to melt them down for they will be misshapen." I smiled, "Perhaps this is a good thing. I can show you how to make balls. It is something you can do, Ted, while I am away and you, Tom, will have to keep me well supplied when we are at war."

I also taught them to use swords. We practised with the ones taken in Coatham Wood. I had a good sword for Ted and a second for Tom. As they were blunt weapons we used a small buckler to learn the strokes of a swordsman. I wanted no accidents to upset my wife.

It was two days before Christmas and we were returning from the field after another practice when Tom asked me his question. It was bitterly cold but we were sweating. Tom said, "And have I learned all that I need, Colonel? Am I ready for this war in Germany?"

I shook my head, "I have given you a few skills but, as I discovered when I was but a little older than you, war and the life of a campaigner are the best teachers. You may well come to regret your decision, Tom."

He shook his head, "No, Colonel. The mistress has been teaching me to read and write. I had seen in the scriptures that I was a sinner. I was not evil, I know now that Uncle John was, but I was not a good man. I need to redeem myself." He smiled, "I like the story of the Prodigal Son for that seems like me. You forgave me despite the ills I tried to do to you. I am content and if I should fall in some foreign field then I know I will have done enough to, hopefully, secure my place in heaven."

I put my hand on his shoulder, "I would be happier if you kept yourself safe and returned with me so that you could protect William."

"Then let us do that, Colonel."

Christmas was especially wonderful. This was the first real Christmas that Tom had enjoyed and the first one where my son would remember having his father at the table. For Charlotte it was perfect. There was peace and harmony around the table and all seven of us dined in the dining hall. Elizabeth and Ted were not sure about it but Charlotte insisted and it was the right thing to do. The goose had been fattened up well and Elizabeth had cooked it to perfection. With stuffing and the expensive delicacy of potatoes we dined as well as any lord in his castle. I doubt that the Puritans would have approved for we had good wine and the pudding was flamed in a bottle of brandy we had bought in Durham. By the time the meal was ended no one felt able to move. We sat before a blazing fire and Tom and Ted enjoyed their first ever taste of Madeira. I ensured that they only had one for it was a heady drink. William played with the wooden sword and pistol I had bought for him in Durham and my wife smiled. When the meal was digested then the entertainment began. Margaret and Elizabeth began the merriment and they sang folk songs. They were both good singers.

Charlotte had a good voice too and when I pressed her she sang some Christmas hymns. When she had sung two she said, "And now it is time for you all to sing." She saw the fear on Ted and Tom's faces. "This is Christmas and we celebrate the birth of

Christ." They joined in and once they heard my slightly flatter tones they became encouraged and soon the house was filled with Christmas joy. It was perfection.

The preparations for our departure were different this time. I would be taking Tom with me and he had to pack for every eventuality. My wife had raided my old clothes but it had not been enough. When we had been in Durham she had found material and she and her women had sewn more shirts for both of us. They had knitted socks for the two of us as well as ensuring that we had adequate underwear. My wife was of the opinion that cleanliness was next to godliness. I packed everything I would need in my saddlebags. I had ball moulds, tools to repair pistols, flints and, as I always did, I packed the prayer book given to me by my mother. It was a comfort. We had spare blankets for they could be the difference between a warm night of rest and a frozen one without comfort. The sumpter would be laden although we could always wear our blankets around our chests, en banderole.

The night before we left was almost painful. Tom and I would be leaving early and goodbyes would be perfunctory at best. My wife and I cuddled and it was as we cuddled that Charlotte gave me the news that she thought we had made a brother or sister for William. "How do you know?"

Charlotte could be prim and proper when she chose. "James Bretherton, there are mysteries known only to women. Let me just say that there are ways I know these things. I think that we will have another child in July or early August. I have yet to see a midwife but Margaret and Elizabeth concur."

"The servants know?"

She laughed, "They are more than servants, James. They are a comfort to me."

Suddenly, I did not want to go. I knew that I had nothing to offer at the birthing but…

"So, James, you have even more reason to take care of yourself. If you have a choice of a reckless charge or watching the men you command do so then think of your son and your unborn child."

I sighed, "If it was only as simple as that, Charlotte. The king does not sit and watch. He is at the forefront. I promise that I will protect myself as much as I can. I have been lucky thus far and perhaps I will keep that luck."

"I will pray for you and I will trust to God rather than to fickle luck."

She buried her head on my shoulder and I felt the tears as she wept, silently. I just held her until she slept. She had given me more to think about as I returned to war. I would have more distractions when the balls flew, the cannons crashed and the swords sparked.

Chapter 6

Hartlepool February 1632

It had been a raw and cold journey to the port that was used by the Bishop of Durham. Ted had come with us so that he could take back the three riding horses and the sumpter. As soon as we had unpacked the sumpters we bade him farewell and he headed back to Piercebridge. His rump would be raw when he reached home and it would be after dark. He and Tom had bantered all the way north showing that they were now good friends. The training both on horseback and with weapons had done that. When they clasped arms it was the sign of genuine friendship.

When they had gone and we had taken George's sumpter and hackney into the stable the agent said, "Captain Stewart's ship is overdue. She should have docked last night or this morning. I fear that you will have to stay with me." He waved a hand at the warehouse, "We have balls and powder for the king."

I did not like that. I knew that we needed powder to fight the war but a wooden ship filled with powder made an already hard voyage that much more dangerous. I had forgotten that the captain had told me that would be his cargo. His wife fussed over us. She knew that I often met the king and she was keen to impress. George and his wife had one spare room and in it was just one bed. Tom was happy to use the straw filled paillasse George provided and lie, like a chamberlain, behind the door. Since Christmas Tom had changed, almost beyond recognition. The shaven head was now covered in brown hair and he would not feel the cold so much. He had also filled out. That was not only due to the good meals we enjoyed but the titbits and treats given to him by Elizabeth. Ted was the same. I think Elizabeth viewed them as the children she would never have. Tom now wore better boots. They had been mine and were more than serviceable but I preferred the cavalry boots which suited me on the battlefield. Tom would not be riding to war. His leather jack had been made especially for him. Not quite as good as the buff coat worn by the king, it would prevent cuts to his body should he get too close to danger. That was always possible. The jack would not stop a ball but I had no intention of letting Tom anywhere near the fighting. He would watch my horse and my belongings. His cambric shirts were good ones and he had three. Charlotte believed in cleanliness and Tom had been given lessons in washing clothes. I would no longer have to ask one of the troopers to wash my clothes for me. Ashcroft had done his best but Tom had been trained by Charlotte….The hat he wore on his head was not the broad brimmed one I wore. They were largely for officers. He had a montero or English fog hat. They were comfortable and warm with a brim that could be pulled down to protect a warrior's ears and neck. He was happy with it.

We ate a homely meal in the agent's home. George had an enormous plate of food. He was clearly a man who enjoyed eating. The dish had plenty of pickled vegetables. I said to Tom, as he ate, "This is the sort of fare you will enjoy in the next year."

George nodded, "My wife knows what I like."

I asked, "Will you know as soon as the ship docks?"

"Before. I pay a man to watch for the ships and as soon as he sights one out to the east he will tell me. If it is not the right ship then no matter. I will have had to endure a few moments of cold, that is all."

"Are you worried about the delay?"

He nodded, "The weather can cause a problem but for the last few days it has been quite benign." He frowned, "That is the right word?"

"It is."

"That means either a problem with the ship, and that I doubt, for Captain Stewart has had the whole winter to maintain his ship, or interference from man."

"He was just sailing from Scotland though. Surely that is safe from danger."

"You would think so with the Norse, Swedes and Danes all on the side of the Protestants but do not forget Ireland. There are Gaelic Irish and the Old English, both are Catholic. There are men who might like to cause mischief while pretending to serve the church."

"Pirates."

"Just so."

"But Captain Stewart would be empty."

George had cleared his plate and after wiping his mouth he pushed it away. His wife took it and scurried away to bring his pudding. "True, and a pirate would know that." He shrugged, "I am clutching at any answer which might explain his tardiness, Colonel. The last message we had was that King Gustavus was desperate for this powder and ball."

I knew why. The last battle had almost brought us victory. We had taken many artillery pieces but without ball and powder they were wasted. The king wanted a quick victory and then the war would be ended.

When Tom and I retired George did not. He took his pipe and said, "I will walk to the quay. My watcher will need relief."

"Wake me as soon as the ship arrives."

"I will."

Tom was a little relieved for it deferred the voyage and he was not looking forward to the sea. "Do not unpack your belongings, Tom."

"Yes, Colonel."

The bed I had been given was comfortable enough but my mind was a maelstrom. I was worried about the captain and the voyage not to mention the fact that my wife was with child. I did not sleep and when there was a tap on the bedroom door I was alert before Tom had even stirred.

George stood there, "Captain Stewart has arrived." He paused, "He is loading the ship. I am sorry, Colonel, but he says if you want a passage you must leave now. He intends on leaving on the next tide."

"Of course. Tom, we are leaving."

I suppose this was all new to Tom and he did not see anything untoward at rising not long after midnight to hurry through the dark to board the ship. We had nothing to pack and we donned our jackets and cloaks quickly. It was cold for this was February on the east coast of England and we wrapped our cloaks tightly about us as we hurried to the ship. We were all laden. We had Tom's clothes, my clothes and, of course, my armour and my weapons. George carried as much as we did.

I heard Captain Stewart long before we reached the ship. He did not care that it was late and people were abed. He roared

"Move yourselves, you lubbers. I want to be at sea before the tide has turned."

A voice said, "Captain, it is dark. Can we not have a light?"

"Damn and blast you! This is powder we load! There will be no flames." He saw us coming and nodded, "Thank you for being so prompt, Colonel. You know your own way to your cabin. We have no time to waste. Thank you, Mr Smith, I am much obliged."

We hurried up the gangplank. I say we but Tom edged his way nervously up the plank. It was lucky that they were using a crane to hoist the barrels of powder and crates of ball directly into the hold and the crew were not using the gangplanks. George led the way to the forecastle. I knew that the cabin was small, I had used it before but poor Tom was appalled. "Where do I sleep, Colonel?" He looked around and not seeing a bed said, "Where do you sleep?"

I smiled, "This night we do not sleep but when we do then all will be revealed." I placed the bag I was carrying on the floor.

George said, "I had best get ashore, too, Colonel. The last thing I wish to do is to upset the captain."

"Thank you for your hospitality."

He shrugged, "It was nothing. Fare ye well."

He strode down the gangplank. Such was his weight that I feared it might break.

I went with Tom to stand where we were out of the way but could still see the ship being loaded. I saw that the musket and cannon balls had been loaded first. The powder would be last. While balls would not be unduly affected by sea water, dampness in powder could prove fatal. The men were like ants as they swarmed over the cargo and hoisted it aboard. Tom and I were the only idlers on the ship. I knew why the captain was hastening. He had come in almost at low tide. He had been helped by having ballast only and no cargo. If he loaded quickly then he could leave on the high tide and if not then he would have to wait until the next high tide. The ship was already late and I knew that the captain prided himself on his punctuality. I was intrigued by the delay. Captain Stewart would tell me in his own time.

When the last barrel of powder was tied down Captain Stewart shouted, "Make secure. All hands to station."

I knew that having an agent expedited matters for the captain. The agent would deal with the fees and the customs. Nothing had been landed and that made life easier. The crew were well trained by the Scotsman and we were soon free from the land and edging towards the narrow entrance of the harbour. The two fires that burned at the arms were all that helped the captain as he navigated his way out to sea. Once he had set the sails and the two lights at the harbour entrance faded, he shouted, "First Mate, the crew did well. Open the new ale barrel."

There was a cheer from the crew. As well as powder and ball the ship had taken on more ale. It was always safer to drink ale than water and freshly brewed beer was eagerly anticipated. The second mate had come to the helm and Captain Stewart said, "Keep her on this course, Mr McKay. I shall talk with the colonel." He waved me over to the larboard quarter.

"Trouble, Captain?"

He nodded and went to take out his pipe. It was as though he suddenly remembered the powder and put it away. He grumbled, "I shall have to forgo tobacco until we dock. Aye, Colonel, I was not late because of any fault of my crew or the ship. The Spanish had two ships watching the passage south and they followed us."

"Spanish ships?"

"Privateers. Pirates by any other name. They sought to follow us. I managed to lose them by the Farne Islands. St Cuthbert saved us. I risked the causeway. I knew the tides and I knew my clearance. I made it and they, fearing the rocks, had to beat out to sea. I kept to the coast and I ducked into Warkworth Harbour. It is a fishing port and they would not expect me to use it. We hid there and watched them sail by. We had to wait until the next tide to continue south and each time we saw their sails we reefed ours." He pointed north, "They are still waiting for us but I know not where. They want my cargo." I waited for I knew that there was more. "They know we will be sailing to the Baltic and they are faster than we are. They will wait."

"But you have a plan."

He nodded, "Better that I deliver the cargo to the wrong place rather than lose it. We will sail to Rotterdam. It is a Protestant port and there is a Swedish agent there. If, when we have landed, you would ride to Mainz and tell the king, I will wait in port until an escort comes for the powder." His eyes burned bright in the dark, "Damn my eyes if I let the Papists take Protestant powder."

I did not answer immediately. I was calculating. The voyage to Rotterdam would be quicker and the journey from Rotterdam the same as it would have been from the Baltic. I would need at least two horses. I said, "I can do this, Captain Stewart, but I shall need horses."

"The agent in Rotterdam can oblige." For the first time I heard a little doubt in his voice as he said, "Will you be able to manage the journey? Can you speak Dutch?"

I nodded, "I spent the early years as a soldier fighting the Prince of Nassau. I can manage in both Dutch and German." He smiled. "What happens if the privateers catch us?"

"They will try to take us but they will know we carry powder and will not use their guns. They will try to board us. If they manage that then we are doomed. We have to stop them boarding. And now, Colonel, I need to get as much speed out of **'Maryanne'** as I can. The darkness is our friend. Once daylight dawns then with the clear skies that are promised they will see us and it will be a stern chase to reach our destination."

I waved Tom over, "Come Tom, I will show you how we sleep."

We went to the cabin. I left the door open to make the interior lighter but most of what I did was by feel. I found the hammocks and I slung one. I handed the other to Tom, "You will find two hooks. Sling your hammock between them."

"Hammocks, Colonel?"

"A nautical bed. That which you hold in your hand."

That done I helped him to climb into it. "I am not sure I like this, Colonel."

"Do not worry, the motion of the ship will send you to sleep."

"If you say so."

"And speaking of saying, your lessons begin in the morning."

"Lessons, Colonel?"

"Aye, Tom, you need to understand some Dutch and German. In the fullness of time you may even have a smattering of French and Spanish, but German is vital."

"What about Swedish, Sir? I mean, isn't the man we serve Swedish?"

"He is but as we are going to be campaigning in Germany it is that language which is the priority and as you and I will be travelling through the Netherlands then some Dutch would be useful."

I think my words had taken his mind off the hammock and I soon heard his snores.

The captain had been right. We woke to clear blue skies but a wind that pushed us south and east at a good rate. I slipped out of the hammock. I looked at Tom. He was awake but looked terrified, "How do I get out of this contraption, Colonel?"

"Easy. Hold on to the sides and then roll. I will stand here to make sure you come to no harm. I do not need my servant injured before we have even landed."

When he managed it he beamed. "Well that was easy enough and you are right, Colonel, that was as good a night of sleep as I can remember."

"Well now you have another skill to master. On a ship you make water or empty your bowels by hanging over the side." The smile evaporated like morning mist. "Come and I will demonstrate." We went to the bows and I chose the lee. I had crossed the sea enough times to know which side that was. I unfastened my breeches and made water.

I nodded close to the bow where a sailor, with bare buttocks hanging over the side was clinging on to the rail. The sailor called out cheerfully, "A fine morning, Colonel."

"And that is how you do the other."

Tom shook his head, "How long until we land?"

"Two or three days."

"I will wait, Colonel."

There was no hot food but George Smith had provided fresh bread, cheese, fruit and ham. Tom declined to eat the fruit, for obvious reasons. I ate some of it all. That done we ascended to the forecastle. It was the place we would defend if we were attacked but it was now deserted. "Lesson time, Tom."

We spent the morning in the language school of the **'Maryanne'**. I gave him the basic phrases and the words that would enable him to ask for food and drink. I knew that I was lucky. My mother had taught me French from an early age and the learning of languages seemed to come easily. German would be easier for Tom than French but he still managed to butcher the language. I just hoped that he would understand more than he spoke and his attempts to speak German would endear him to the locals.

We had enjoyed another cold meal when the lookout shouted, "Sails to the nor' west, Captain!"

We all turned to look. The lookout had a better view than we did for all I could see was something on the horizon. I looked at our sails. They were full and billowing but our ship was a trader. She was built for cargo and not for speed. The ships that hunted us, if this was they, would be lean and fast. I saw the hourglass being turned at the stern and I had a measure of time. When I saw that it was two ships the hourglass was about to be turned once more; I saw the ship's boy hovering close to the helm. We were being caught but they were not doing so quickly.

I headed for the stern. I knew that the captain would spend long hours at the helm until we were safe but I had been told by the mate that he had spent the night in his hammock. We needed a captain who was alert.

He had the coxswain on the helm and he stood with an unlit pipe in his mouth. He smiled, "I cannot smoke it but this gives me comfort."

"Are they the privateers?"

Sailors knew ships the way I knew different types of horsemen. I could not differentiate a ship but I could tell the difference between a hussar, cuirassier, dragoon, harquebusier or lancer across a smoke-filled battlefield.

"They are."

"Will they catch us?"

He chuckled, "They hope to. We are a prize that is worth a fortune in gold and an even greater fortune in the harm it will do to the Protestant cause. We have an advantage. These ships have travelled far from familiar waters. I know these seas and I know the wind. The wind is veering and soon will blow more towards the west. We will turn and make as though we are heading for the Thames. When darkness falls we will shorten sail and head south and east to Rotterdam. I hope that by the morning we are in Dutch waters and safe. The Dutch navy will be there."

He was a clever man and I hoped that he would outwit the Spanish.

There was nothing I could do and I returned to the schoolroom that was the forecastle. As I continued with Tom's lessons I continued to keep an eye on the ships. We changed course and the captain was proved prescient. The wind changed. By the time it was, by the turning of the hourglass, almost five o'clock and dusk was approaching, I saw the smudge on the horizon that marked the English coast. As much as I wanted food I was reluctant to leave the forecastle for we had a good view of the proceedings. As soon as we lost sight of the sails, confirmed by a call from the lookout, we reefed our topsail and changed course. When darkness was complete and another hour had passed, the sails were let loose and we sped up. We were not as fast as we had been but we were still speeding across the Channel to the relative safety of the Dutch coast.

We ate on deck and then retired to the cabin. We did not undress but we did take off our boots and jackets. I waited until Tom had successfully negotiated his hammock and then climbed into mine. Despite the fears in my mind I was soon asleep.

My sleep was rudely awakened by the sound of feet on the deck and orders being shouted. I rose. I donned my boots but did not bother with my jacket. Once on deck I saw that dawn was upon us but a pointing finger from one of the crew showed me a sail. That there was alarm was enough to tell me that it was not a Dutch one. I hurried to the stern and saw the captain, barefoot and with just a shirt and breeks covering him.

He shook his head, "This is not one of those that followed us, Colonel, it is another privateer. This one is French. She has the wind. Our only advantage is that as the sun has yet to fully rise she may not have seen us. We are closer to the mouth of the river. Let us pray that God is with us."

I asked, "Captain, they will have guns." He nodded, "What if they use the guns first?"

"Then we shall enjoy a fiery end but I think that the enemy, the Papists, know what we carry. There were too many people at the port while we prepared our ship for comfort. Not all were trustworthy. My crew are good men but their loose lips may have told the enemy what we would carry. We shall see." He was remarkably calm considering one outcome would be our total destruction.

I returned to the cabin. Tom had risen. "We need to dress and strap on swords. We will eat and then await the orders of the captain."

"Is there danger, Colonel?"

"There is a privateer closing with us. I have no intention of dying at sea. We will fight, Tom, although I wish we were on land."

I could have worn my breastplate but the thought of falling overboard and having a watery death did not appeal. By the same token a hat would not afford me any advantage. Nor would I wear a secrete, a helmet below my hat. I left my pistols in the cabin and strapped on my sword. I had two daggers, one in my belt and one in my boot top. Tom had his short sword. As we left the cabin I saw that the crew had each taken a weapon from the weapon rack. These were not soldiers and each one chose the weapons they felt most comfortable with. Some chose halberds or pikes. One or two chose boarding axes or hand axes. Others had short, curved swords.

I said, "Choose a weapon."

To my surprise he did not choose a halberd but a bow and bag of arrows. "You know how to use one of those?"

"My uncle was an archer and he taught me. It was too late for me to become as good as he was but he liked the bow for it was silent."

"Are you any good with it?"

He said, simply, "I hit that at which I aim."

"Then that is good. Stay close to me." I watched him string the bow. There was an art to it. He made it look easy. I then saw him go through the arrows and choose the best three. He put two in his belt and held the third next to the bow. "Now let us eat for we shall need sustenance before this day is out."

We ate and drank on the forecastle and all the time watched the French privateer draw closer to us. I knew that to the west of us would be two privateers and the Frenchman lay between us and the Dutch estuary we sought. Captain Stewart had to judge his moment to turn to perfection. One slip and they would have us.

It was not long before noon when the gap had closed to less than two ship's lengths. Leaving Tom at the forecastle I hurried aft, "What is the plan, Captain Stewart?"

He smiled, "To deliver my cargo, Colonel."

I nodded, "I am a soldier and I like to know what choices I have. What do you intend?"

"They will try to close with us and board us. Had they wished to stand off and dismast us they would have done so already. Unless we are very unlucky then we do not have the fiery death of hell ahead. They will take the sterncastle first and try to kill me. The helmsman is the weakness. If the helmsman and captain fall then those few moments can decide a nautical battle."

"And what other weaknesses are there?"

Captain Stewart pointed to the sails, "If the sails or the sheets are damaged and a ship loses way then the battle is lost. I will have men watching and guarding the sheets. If they take my ship then they will pay a heavy price."

An idea was forming in my head and I said, "Do not give up, yet, Captain, Tom and I will be at the forecastle. You need waste no men there, we two can hold it."

He clasped my arm, "You are a brave man, Colonel, and a noble fellow. I pray that God is on our side."

"As do I, but as I have learned, God likes a soldier who helps himself."

I returned to the forecastle and explained my plan to Tom. He shook his head, "Colonel, your good wife would not like you to take such risks."

I sighed, "Tom, if I do nothing then I risk death, my plan is no riskier than doing nothing."

He nodded, "I will do my part, Colonel."

After taking off my boots I took the coil of rope and climbed the ratlines to the lower foresail. There was a rope that enabled the crew to reef the sail and, holding on to the yard I worked my way halfway along. I fastened one end of the rope to it and then moved back to the mast. When I descended I secured the end of the rope to the gunwale. I replaced my boots. In the time it had taken me to do all that the Frenchman's bow was almost level with our stern and was heading closer to it. Some of our crew had bows but they were not archers and most of the arrows they sent fell short. The French ship had a couple of crossbows. They were deadly machines but slow to reload. The bolts slammed into the gunwale and one hit the mast.

I said, "Tom, wait until they are level with us before you loose. I want the helmsman and the French captain hit."

"Aye, Colonel."

I saw the French sailors with the grappling hooks. They would wait until they were level with us and then pour aboard us to flood our ship with men. The centre of the French ship was filled with men as was the stern. The forecastle of the enemy ship had few men. Timing would be everything if my plan was to succeed. What I was about to do I had never done before. More than that, I had never even contemplated the action. As their bowsprit drew close I untied the rope and pulled myself up onto the gunwale. The French helmsman turned the ship as the grappling hooks were thrown. So far the encounter was going the way that both captains would have expected. What they did not expect was a mad Englishman to swing, using the rope, across from our ship to theirs. It was a leap of faith and I threw myself across the gap, gripping tightly to the rope. The swing was exhilarating and as I passed one of the sheets holding the foresail I slashed. My sword was sharp enough to shave with and the rope parted with a twang. At the same time I heard the snap of Tom's bow. My swing took me a little higher and as I passed the sail I slashed across it. My swing was taking me back to our ship. I concentrated on timing my landing. I saw that while most of the grappling hooks had been cut by our crew, two remained near to the forecastle. I landed heavily and raced to the nearest one. Even as I slashed at it and severed it, a Frenchman with a boarding axe leapt aboard. A second stood ominously above me. Tom's arrow slammed into him as I ducked beneath the swinging axe to lunge at the naked middle of the French sailor with the boarding axe. This was no time for mercy and I tore my blade across his stomach. The tangle of guts and intestines flooding out told me that it was a mortal wound. It was only then that I realised that not only was there a gap emerging between our vessels but the Frenchman was drifting. The loss of the sheet and the slashed sail had damaged the ship but it was Tom who had done the most damage. He had slain the men at the helm. The cheer from the crew told me that we had won.

I went over to Tom and clapped him on the back, "You have saved my life, Tom. I thank you."

He shook his head, "No, Colonel, I might have saved the ship but I think you had the beating of the Frenchman I slew. You are a fearsome warrior and as brave as a lion. I am glad I am on your side." I nodded my thanks at the compliment. He pointed to the rope swinging from the yard, "Were you not afraid, Colonel?"

"Do you know, Tom, I was excited beyond words but let us never speak of it to Mistress Charlotte, eh?"

He grinned, "It is our secret, Colonel."

It took another two days to negotiate the river and reach Rotterdam. During those two days Captain Stewart made a great fuss of the two of us. The captain and crew had each played their part but they knew that we had won because of the two of us.

As the lights of the port drew closer Captain Stewart said, "I am indebted to you, Colonel, and I promise to repay that debt. I fear that I am putting you in more danger by asking you to ride to Mainz."

"I have to get there in any case, Captain Stewart, and after that encounter I will be less fearful. At least I can use my pistols ashore."

"Aye, well, I will get you the best horses that I can. I owe you that."

Lion of the North

Rommerskirchen
Cologne
Bonn

N

Koblenz

Griff 2025

Mainz Babenhausen
Schaafheim Marktheidenfeld

_____
12 Miles

Chapter 7

The captain was as good as his word. He went out of his way to secure us horses and by dawn we were heading along the road to cross, first, the Netherlands and then the complicated land of Germany until we reached the winter camp of the king at Mainz. Captain Stewart and the crew would just leave a watch aboard the ship for none wanted to be sleeping on a floating powder keg. The flag she flew marked her as a danger and those using the port would give her a wide berth. Wagons and drivers for the journey to Mainz would be sourced by the agent in Rotterdam. We put the problem of the powder behind us for we had a long journey ahead of us. The fastest that we could make the journey to Mainz and for men to be sent back to escort the powder was ten days.

We had two good horses. They were hackneys and I was told that their names were Anya and Bertha. The sumpter was a gelding called Hercules. I think he had been named as a joke. It was a good thing that they were all three fine horses for we had the best part of two hundred and fifty miles to travel and I intended to ride fifty miles a day. This would be a stern test for poor Tom who was still a novice rider, but the incident at sea and his success with the bow seemed to have given him great confidence. The praise from the crew went a long way to boost that confidence. I suppose the thought of riding a horse seemed safer than the risks of a battle at sea. We had avoided one but not by much. He led a single sumpter that was laden with our belongings, my armour and our weapons. The horses had been well looked after over the winter. The hackneys were as good as Jack and the sumpter had a broad back and a glossy coat that suggested he had been well rested since his last exertions.

As we rode I gave Tom another lesson, this time in geography. I explained our route, "There are places which are more Catholic than Protestant as well as the other way around. We must be wary until we know the affiliations of the people we pass. We say as little as we can and, if it is possible, we speak Dutch or German when in company. Your language skills will improve that way and make us blend in a little more. We are travelling through land which has been freed by our armies but that does not mean it is safe. There are bands of mercenaries who prey on the weak. As we are two lone riders we would be considered easy prey. I intend to be suspicious of any that we meet. We will stay, wherever possible, in larger cities and towns. It will be safer and there are likely to be Protestant troops stationed there. This is not campaigning season but men will be preparing to ride forth come April. Already King Gustavus will be planning what we will do to recover the last of the Protestant lands held by the enemy. I am afraid that we will be in the saddle for eight or ten hours a day until we reach Mainz."

He nodded, "I am finding it easier now, Colonel. The motion on the ship was not unlike the back of a horse. I am content."

He had changed immeasurably since that day on the Skerne Bridge. We also worked on his German and he was an eager student. He mastered most of the words quite quickly but his accent was atrocious. My mother, when she had spoken French to me, had always emphasised the accent. I did not mind Tom's failure to master the accent. For him it was all about understanding the words and being able to communicate. The ride east was one long lesson for him. Charlotte had taught him to read to better himself but my lessons were lessons in survival.

The route I had chosen meant that we would find no big city or town for almost sixty miles. I knew that the larger places would have spies. I was not an arrogant man but if men had come to England to kill me then I would try to hide whenever I could. That first ride was further than I had intended and we could go no further. The welcoming sight of the inn, in the village of Bakel, decided me. I did not relish sleeping in the open. Leaving Tom with the horses I went inside to enquire about accommodation, "Have you a room for two weary travellers, some food and a bed?"

I had spoken in Dutch and it made the man smile, "Of course, but we have no stables. I have a paddock at the rear with a gate and we have a dog." The dog would guard the horses.

"That will do." I said. I thought it judicious to introduce myself, "I am Colonel Bretherton."

The man's smile grew, "I thought I knew your voice and recognised your accent as English. Before I suffered this," he held up a maimed limb; I had not noticed that he had only two fingers on his left hand, "wound, I was a soldier in the army of Prince Maurice. You were not a colonel then."

"No, and I now serve King Gustavus."

"That is good. I fear that we might have lost already but for the Lion of the North." He turned to shout to the kitchen, "Helga, prepare the room and food, we have guests."

I nodded, "I will take our horses to the paddock."

"Pietr, go with the colonel and show him the paddock."

A youth came from the back room. It was clearly his son for the resemblance was remarkable. When we reached the back of the inn I saw that the paddock had good grass. I had acquired a bag of oats from the agent in Rotterdam. The rest, grass and the oats meant that the animals would enjoy their brief stay. We took the bags to the room. It had one bed and a straw paillasse was brought for Tom. We did not unpack but stacked the bags in the corner. The food was ready when we had finished and went back to the dining room. The meal was a simple stew enriched with sausages and beans. We had only eaten bread and cheese at noon and we were both starving. The Dutch made good ale and it did not disappoint. I felt replete when the plate was cleared and we had supped two mugs of ale.

The old soldier came to join us when we had finished. "I hope you do not mind me joining you, Colonel, but visitors are rare and I believe you know how the war goes better than I. The Spanish are more interested in Germany these days than the Netherlands but we are still wary of them."

I knew that the reason was not pure curiosity. The man, I learned his name was Cornelius, would have news to impart to other travellers. It would encourage them to visit again. Inns and taverns were the places to find out what was happening further afield.

"What is it you wish to know?"

"Will King Gustavus win?"

This was a soldier and he knew the strengths of our enemies better than any and I answered him honestly, "He is a better general than Prince Maurice." I wondered if my criticism offended him.

"Aye, you are right and King Christian, well-meaning though he was, could not defeat Count Tilly. Can King Gustavus?"

I nodded and told him of the battle of Breitenfeld. I know that others might have described the battle already but I had been there in the thick of it and he got the true version of events. I told him how we had almost lost but the brilliance of the Swedish general won the day. Poor Tom was struggling to keep up with the Dutch and when he asked for clarification on one point I said, "Tomorrow you shall have the English version. This tale is for Cornelius."

By the end we had consumed two more ales and I was weary. Cornelius nodded as we rose, "A fine tale, Colonel, and you are a modest man. I fought in enough battles to know that you did more than you said. It is an honour to have you as a guest."

The next day we were up before dawn and Helga gave us a good breakfast and packed a lunch for us to eat. She was quite scornful of the people to the east of us. I smiled as we took the food. It was the same in Piercebridge. Anyone who lived south of the Tees was untrustworthy and north of the Tyne were barbarians. I had learned it was true all over the lands I had travelled. People were parochial.

We stopped next in Rommerskirchen. There was no border as such but I knew, when we reached the town that we were in Germany. There was a medieval castle and it was large enough to have inns that sported stables. As we neared the city, which still had a wall, I said, "Here we are wary and cautious. The Dutch are Protestant through and through but here there may be Catholic sympathisers. I was quite happy to blazon my connections in Bakel, here I am James Bretherton a soldier of fortune."

"Will that not make people suspicious of you?"

"No, Tom. Mercenaries are rare in England but here they are commonplace."

The welcome in the inn was lukewarm rather than effusive. I understood that. Who knew if King Gustavus could hang on to his recent conquests? Men needed stability for longer than one winter before they trusted peace. When we ate I asked for a table in the corner but I still felt that we were being scrutinised. Men cast their glances at us. Our horses were good ones and I was well dressed. They marked me as a person of interest with or without a title. I saw groups of men studying us. Some were soldiers and I wondered if I had been recognised. Tom also understood the villainous nature of some of the glances.

When we reached the room he said, "I can see what you meant, Master. I saw men in that room who were the same type as those who came to Coatham Woods. I will sleep behind the door. They will have to push me from my bed to gain entry."

The scrutiny did not make for a peaceful night and we both rose early. We left as soon as the gates of the town opened. This time there was no basket of food to ease our journey and the breakfast was yesterday's bread and some indifferent ham. When we had saddled our horses I told Tom, as a precaution, to load his pistols. I did the same. Tom had two such weapons in holsters. I had two in my saddle holsters and two in my belt holsters. I was tempted to wear my cuirass but I knew that would weary my horse and speed was essential. We had covered more than one hundred and ten miles already. I hoped to make Koblenz by dark and that would leave just one hard day of riding. The horses would be in no condition to go any further but we would be in Mainz and our journey would be ended.

I said, "We have ten miles before we reach Cologne and another twenty-five to Bonn. When we reach Bonn I will be happier but Koblenz will mean we are almost at journey's end."

We had travelled just four miles when I heard, in the distance, coming from behind, the thundering of hooves. This was a land that had been devastated in the early part of the war. There were more deserted villages and houses than people. The fields were untilled and the only crop that was growing was an unwelcome one of weeds. It was February and in England and the Netherlands farmers had been preparing the ground for crops. Here it was like a graveyard. I primed two of my pistols. I could do so whilst riding. The cover pan on the wheellock was a good thing. Tom was still learning and he would have to prime his weapons when we were stopped.

"Let us ride a little faster, Tom. If the men behind are following us they will also speed up and if they do not then they are just travellers."

"Yes, Colonel."

We could not go as fast as we would have liked. The sumpter was laden and being led slowed down Tom's horse. He was becoming a better rider but leading a horse and riding were hard skills to learn. I was worried about the sound of the hooves and I turned in my saddle. I was really seeing if the men who galloped towards us, from the west, intended to catch us. There might be a perfectly reasonable explanation why the men raced along the road but I was wary. The men had not yet closed with us. Before we had reached Rommerskirchen I had given Tom his instructions in case we met danger. I hoped that they would not be needed.

When the sound of the hooves grew louder I turned again and saw that five riders were galloping harder towards us. They were clearly trying to catch us. There was no way of identifying them and no way we could escape, at least not with the sumpter. Flight was useless. I said, "Slow to a walk and when we stop, prime your pistols."

"Yes, Colonel."

I knew that he was nervous. He and his uncle had not used horses when they had been bandits but he knew the danger of footpads. I saw that our horses were sweating and I feared that we had ridden them too hard and to no avail. Tom had dropped the reins of the sumpter and I was pleased that he had remembered my instructions. If we had to defend ourselves he would need both hands. The sumpter was tired and would not run too far. I whirled my horse to face the men who approached. My primed pistols rested on my saddle within easy reach. My horse's head hid them from the five men. Tom was still a novice rider and it took him longer to turn his horse. The five men spread out. That was an indication that they meant us harm. They were, effectively, facing us on three sides, surrounding us as men might do on a battlefield. They were soldiers and knew how to overcome an enemy when they had superior numbers. I could see that their horses were poor ones. Our hackneys had the legs of them in a race. The sumpter, however, would have ensured that we were caught. I studied them as they approached. One wore a hat such as mine and one wore a pot helmet. The others wore woollen hats. They had swords but apart from the one with the officer's hat they were poor ones such as the kind Tom and his uncle had used. I saw that they had just one pistol each and it was jammed into their belts. They were not primed and I felt more confident. These were soldiers but poorly equipped ones. That alone was not a surprise. It was not yet campaigning season and many mercenary leaders let their men go over winter to save paying them. My men were all paid for the whole winter. I worked out that these men saw two men who had what they needed for the campaigning season: horses, weapons and armour. Soldiers were paid more if they had their own equipment. These five saw a chance to take from us. I worked out that they must have seen us in the inn and taken their chance to follow us and arm themselves at our expense. To do that they would have to kill us. I was back in the world of war.

They reined in just thirty paces from us and spread out further from each other so that they were in a half circle. We had spoken English in the inn and I took the initiative and spoke to them in German, "Now, what is it that you intend? Were you riding hard because you wished to return something we left in the inn where you spied us out?" I did not wait for an answer but shook my head, "I think not. It is more likely that you wish to take these horses which are better than the abattoir bound nags you ride and I can see greedy little eyes already viewing my cuirass peeping out from its sack. Do I have it right?" I knew that they had seen my holsters but they would not know that I was using wheellocks. It was an advantage.

The man with the hat spoke and it confirmed he was the leader. He was in the middle of the five. I could see that I had discomfited them. He said, "Just give us the horses and the sumpter. It is only a four or five mile walk back to Rommerskirchen and you look the sort who can buy more."

I nodded, "I can see that, from your point of view, that is the best outcome although I fear that once we have given you the horses and sumpter we will die. Isn't that right?" The look on his face confirmed my opinion. I kept my voice calm and reasonable, "Let me make a counter proposal. Turn around and ride back to Rommerskirchen and I will let you live, but if you are still here," I raised my two pistols and pointed them at him and Tom did the same, "by the time I count to ten then you are dead men." I pointed my right hand at the leader. "One, two…"

"Kill them!" The leader was relying on hesitation on our part. They could cover the distance between us quickly and if we were tardy in any way then they would be upon us. I think they believed we had matchlocks and there would be a delay that might see them close with us. My pistols fired simultaneously and I had them back in my saddle holsters before the smoke had cleared. Tom's two guns fired a moment later. I had my sword out in a flash and I dug my heels into my horse's flanks. The leader was down. The man next to him had been wounded and clutched at his shoulder. Tom had only managed to wound one of them. Tom drew his sword and bravely followed me. I slashed my sword at the unwounded man to my right. I caught his right arm for my sword was longer than his. The blow tore the sleeve of his coat and drew blood. I wheeled my horse around the back of the man I had wounded. The two men who thought that they just had Tom to face now made a cardinal error. They had two men left to fight and they hesitated, hesitation in battle is always deadly. I brought my sword to slash across the back of one of the men and Tom managed, through the distraction of the other, to stab the other in the arm. The four wounded men turned their horses and fled. One went to the north, one to the south and the other two went back along the road. They were saving themselves. I think they feared I would pursue them. Their attack had failed and their leader was dead. They were wounded and while three were relatively minor wounds, the slash across the back of one of them might be fatal.

I sheathed my sword, "Fetch the sumpter. You did well."

"I am sorry, Colonel. I did not understand what you were saying."

I nodded, "My fault. Your German lessons are incomplete."

I went to the dead man. I undid his jacket and tunic and saw the cross. His accent when he had spoken German told me that he was Spanish and the crucifix confirmed it. I lifted his purse and saw that it contained no gold, only one silver coin and the rest were copper. The men had been down on their luck. I took his sword and his sword belt. It was a good one. I tossed them to Tom.

"Here, a present for you. Now mount, we have wasted enough time."

Lion of the North

"What about the body, Colonel, and the horse?"

"The horse is not worth taking and the men will return when we depart. This man was their leader and he has good boots. They will look for his sword and purse too."

"Will they bother us again, Colonel?"

I smiled as I mounted the horse, "Tom, you were a bandit. If you were one of the men would you?"

He shook his head, "No, Colonel."

"And they will not. They will lick their wounds, find the horse and join the nearest regiment. These are the kind of men who will fight for any side, regardless of the cause."

When we reached Cologne I was relieved for it was a big city and friendly to the Protestant cause. Cologne had a cathedral revered for the bones of the Magi that rested within and, as such, was a place that the Catholics wanted. When King Gustavus had taken it he had placed a small garrison to guard the city on the Rhine. I headed for the Rathaus, close to the Alter market and found the officer in charge of the garrison. I told him of the incident. He knew me from the campaign before the battle and said, "I am sorry, Colonel. The war has filled the land with such parasitic lice. I will have men seek him but you are probably right. The rest of his scavengers will have picked his bones clean. Do you need an escort to Bonn?"

I did not want to draw attention to us by having men with us. If we were escorted to Bonn and left there then the same thing might happen. "No, we can manage."

We pushed on and we did reach Koblenz but it was well after dark and our horses were exhausted. I had to use my rank and reputation to allow us to enter the town after dark but when I recognised some of the officers who were quartered in the castle then I felt relief. We were close enough to Mainz to have some of our army quartered here to spread the load of the occupying army. We were almost safe.

It was from these officers that I discovered news of the war. Although both armies were in their winter quarters, that did not stop either the planning or the spying. The Scottish colonel who spoke to me was keen for conversation. I got to know him well in the early days when I had been bringing my company into some sort of order. Most of the other officers who were quartered in Koblenz were German or Swedish and the Scot was happy to speak to someone in a more familiar language.

"It has been a long winter for me, James. You were lucky that the king let you go home. For all the good that I have done I might as well have been at home."

Colonel Robert Lang was an older soldier. I had first met him earlier in the war when I had been serving with Prince Maurice. I did not think he had a family and it made me realise that I had something most of the other colonels did not.

"So, there has been no action."

"I would not say that. General Horn has invested Bamberg in Bavaria. It is a small nut but I hear that Count Tilly is preparing men to retake it."

"Then why has King Gustavus not mobilised the army?"

"Simple, laddie, he is waiting for powder and ball. The rumour is that the wagons bringing it from Peenemünde are delayed."

I shook my head, "They are not merely delayed. They are not coming from Peenemünde."

I told him about Captain Stewart and his face fell. "Then that is a disaster. We are far from Sweden and we need supplies. I fear that this will be the king's undoing. He is a great general but you and I know that without supplies an army disintegrates. I hear that many regiments have lost men to desertion over the winter and that disease has taken others. The empire now has shorter lines of supply."

"Tomorrow I shall reach Mainz and then I can tell the king where his supplies are to be found."

"And you shall have company. It is time to return to the army. I was given some discretion and your news is the trigger I needed. I tire of Koblenz and your news may well spark some action. I would be on hand."

"And your regiment?"

"They are camped outside the city. I will send my servant to tell Captain Dalgleish to mobilise them. They can march on the morrow too." He chuckled, "The advantage of command is that I can order others to obey my orders. The pace of pikemen is slow. I will enjoy your company. When the war starts I shall be with my men day and night."

Lion of the North

The colonel had a mixed regiment of pikemen and musketeers. The Scottish regiments had always been renowned for their schiltrons and Scottish pikemen were more familiar than the light horsemen I led. When I told Tom that we would have company he was relieved. The attack had shaken him. On the last part of the ride to Koblenz I had tried to make him feel better about his action for he had acquitted himself well but he felt he had done little. He had only hit one man and despite using two balls had failed to fell him. I knew he had done well but I suppose he saw that I had hit with every ball I sent. If he was trying to copy me then he was doomed to failure. War had honed me into a lethal weapon.

When we rode Tom enjoyed the company of the colonel's servant, Angus. Angus was also an old soldier and I knew that he would tell Tom the ways of the ordinary soldier. Tom was a servant but as a servant to a colonel, he needed to understand about soldiers.

The land through which we rode was similar to the land to the northwest of Koblenz. The marks of war lay upon it. Some villages and towns had escaped damage while others were ghost filled ruins with empty and untended fields. The bones of animals, butchered for food, littered the empty fields. The people who remained also had haunted and fearful faces. There were few smiles and suspicion was the order of the day. The war had lasted for fourteen years and while I knew that it might be over within the year, the people of Germany saw it going on well into the future with no peace in prospect.

Approaching the city from the north meant crossing the Main. The high ground overlooking the river afforded us a good view of the city. With so many men in his army the king had built his own pontoon bridge across the river, fording the island. It was a disconcerting journey for the boats appeared to be unstable. I know that Tom found it even more fearful than the swimming of the river. Once on the other side we made directly for the king. I had, before I had left Piercebridge, planned on going directly to my regiment. Captain Stewart had given me another purpose and I had to report to the king first.

The last time I had been in Mainz I had been with Sigismund and I had been a spy and had to sneak around to find his family. I could now move around the city freely. I had fame for I had fought with distinction in a number of battles. The result was that I was recognised as I passed soldiers who were still in winter camp and enjoying the inns of Mainz. We left our horses with our servants and entered the grand building flying the Swedish flag. We were waved through the various guards until I was spotted by the king's aide, Lieutenant Larsson.

"Colonel Bretherton, the king will be pleased that you have arrived."

"I fear that I have some dire news for the king." The smile left his face. "It concerns the powder and ball."

The lieutenant was a bright young man and he nodded, "Then come with me. The king is in conference with generals Banér and Torstensson." I knew both generals relatively well.

Colonel Lang bade us farewell and he left to find his brigade commander and report the arrival of his regiment.

I followed the lieutenant. The meeting was behind a closed door. He slipped inside and was there but briefly before he beckoned me to enter.

The king got down to business immediately, "You have news of the missing supplies?"

"Yes, King Gustavus." I told him what had happened and concluded, "They are waiting in Rotterdam."

General Banér shook his head, "I have said many times, King Gustavus, we need to root out these spies. It is bad enough that we are many hundreds of leagues from home with supply lines that can be cut as easily as a spider's thread but our enemies seem to know every move we make."

General Torstensson nodded his agreement, "You can bet that they are preparing their armies to meet us when we go to Austria."

The king smiled, "Gentlemen, can we deal with one problem at a time? Your news, Colonel Bretherton, is not as dire as you think. While the journey by road might necessitate a regiment to guard it, we have the Rhine as a road. I will send barges to Rotterdam. While horses and men need rest, barges do not. We will have our supplies within a week. Lieutenant," he began scribbling on a parchment, "take this to the port. I want two barges to head down stream and get to Rotterdam. Have a company of pikemen go aboard as guards."

"Yes, King Gustavus." Taking the signed and sealed order, he left us.

The king turned to his generals, "You are both right, we do have spies and to rid ourselves of them is all but impossible. We command a disparate army. We have allies and soldiers from many nations and while the cause for which we fight is a holy one, not all who fight have the same motives." He tapped his head, "The only plan which means anything is in here. Let Tilly and Albrecht von Wallenstein think that they know what I plan, the reality is that only I know. General Horn is the bait to draw the enemy to him and as soon as the powder and ball arrive then we will march to catch Count Tilly as he attempts to retake that city." He nodded to the two generals, "You have come at a propitious time, James, for General Banér and General Torstensson are due to return to their own armies and prepare them for the Spring campaign. They will soon be needed by me."

They waited for him to add more but he said nothing. Instead he turned to me, "And you, Colonel, will command not only your horsemen but also Colonel Friedrich's. Lieutenant Colonel Torsten Stålhandske will work with you. I intend for your brigades to be my eyes and ears." He smiled, "And as you will be commanding two regiments your rank is now Lieutenant Colonel. You will be paid accordingly." He smiled, "Cardinal Richelieu is still keen to subsidise us."

I nodded, "Thank you, King Gustavus. I will endeavour to live up to your expectations."

"You will, I do not doubt it." He smiled, "And did you enjoy Christmas with your family?"

"I did, Your Majesty, and I am grateful you afforded me the opportunity." I was about to mention my intention to leave his service at the end of the year but it did not seem appropriate. Sometimes a man must seize the moment. I did not.

General Banér said, as I neared the door, "Take your men out tomorrow, Lieutenant Colonel. Scout to the south and east. I have no evidence but I fear that the enemy will seek to dislodge General Horn from Bamberg. Look for signs of the enemy. We shall need your sharp-eyed soldiers sooner rather than later."

"Sir." I hesitated and then decided that I would be remiss if I did not tell him that which Isaac had imparted to me. I turned and said, "King Gustavus, I heard news, while in England, that the empire has hired assassins to kill you."

None of the three looked surprised. King Gustavus merely nodded, "I have my own spies and they have told me the same. I have to trust that God will watch over me. I have good men like Lieutenant Larsson, my bodyguard, Anders Jonsson and my page, Augustus Leubelfing, to watch me in battle." He smiled, "I thank you for the information. It is confirmation that you are a loyal warrior and I am happy that you serve me."

Chapter 8

It was getting on for dusk when we headed to the river. My regiment were camped on the island in the middle of the River Main. When I had first taken command of them they had been an unruly and wild bunch. They now had discipline and heart. I was proud of them for they reflected me. We were the only Anglo-Scottish regiment of horse in the king's army. The rest were Germans, Swedes or Finns. We were unique for we were light horse and were used for scouting. The Finnish Light Horse, the Hakkapeliitta, who could also scout were used more like assault cavalry. They were fierce fighters. My men were also renowned for their skills in battle but we were used more judiciously. They reflected me and my personality. I had appointed Alexander Stirling as the company captain before I had left. His deputy was Lieutenant Dick Dickson. We returned to cross the pontoon bridge and I asked the first man we met where Bretherton's Horse were to be found. He pointed to the western end of the island. "They are there and camped next to Colonel Friedrich's regiment."

I was pleased. Sigismund Friedrich had been my deputy and our spying trip to Mainz had resulted in his promotion to colonel of his own regiment. He had raised the regiment of Brandenburgers. I had yet to see them. As we rode through the other camps I was recognised and men waved. I had already spent time, on the road, explaining to Tom about the regiment. I wanted him to be prepared. When I saw my standard flying from the flagstaff, I reined in. The camp was neat and organised and a direct contrast to the one I had been given on my first arrival at King Gustavus' camp. I pointed to the flag fluttering above the command tent, "There is the camp, Tom. I shall ask Ashcroft, who was my servant, to take you through your duties. I shall not need you for a day or two. Familiarise yourself with the camp. I have another two horses, Marcus and Ran, so we will always have a spare horse. War takes its toll on horses."

He nodded, "I like Bertha and I am used to her." He smiled, "Do not worry about me, Colonel. I can get on with most people. It was my uncle who could start a fight in an empty room."

As soon as I was spotted by my troopers a cheer went up. I was flattered for the cheer grew as, nearing my tent, more men saw me. Tom said, "You are popular, Colonel."

"That will change once I have them digging latrines and they are going short of food."

I saw that the camp was well organised. We had used the names of animals for the companies. It was easier than using numbers and, as other regiments used numbers, it avoided confusion in the heat of a battle. We had camp followers who were married to a couple of the men and they had sewn standards. It was a small thing but I liked to think it made the men have a better sense of esprit de corps. The officers had their own tents but each company commander's tent was with their company. The exception was mine and I saw it in the centre of the companies, the flag under which we fought flying above it. The officers were seated at a table before the tent and I saw them stand as we approached.

Captain Stirling was a giant of a man and he had a grin that spread across his whole face as he roared, "Welcome back, Colonel! Now we shall see some action."

We reined in and Ashcroft, known to the rest of the troopers as Ashy, strode up, "I'll take your horse, Colonel." He looked at Tom.

I said, "This is my new servant, Tom of the Woods. He will need to be shown the ropes."

Ashcroft nodded, "It will be a pleasure, Colonel."

I knew that I was leaving Tom in good hands. My men were all good hearted. When in battle they could be terrifying but they were as loyal as anything when it came to their brothers in arms. Alexander made space for me at the table and Lieutenant Dickson handed me an ale. He said, "We are ready for action, Colonel. Sitting on our backsides for so long just makes us belligerent."

I looked at him, "Fights?"

"Nothing to get upset about, Sir, but aye. A few bloody noses. Nothing we couldn't handle." My two senior officers were strong men in every sense of the word.

"And is everyone well? I heard there were desertions."

Alexander Stirling shook his head, "In other regiments but we lost not a man, not to desertions anyway."

The lieutenant said, "We lost twelve men, Sir, but that was disease. Others lost more so we have more on the roll than most. Have you any idea when we will get some action? The lads need it. They are sharpened and ready to fight. If they don't get to fight the Papists…"

I understood. I drank some of the ale, "Well one reason we have not fought yet is because the king was waiting for supplies." I told them about my voyage. I saw the smiles spread.

Sergeant Campbell said, "Only you could make a voyage back to the front into an adventure, Colonel." When I told them about the attack on the road the smiles left their faces.

Dick Dickson said, "Then the lad you brought must be handy, Sir."

"He has potential but he has much to learn. I intend for him to be a servant rather than a trooper." I nodded to Captain Stirling, "Have you tried to recruit more men to replace those taken by disease?"

"We have but," he hesitated and lowered his voice, "Colonel Friedrich has managed to pick the best ones. You passed through his camp on the way here, Sir, and the only ones we found were unsuitable. He had rejected them already."

"Then as I am now Lieutenant Colonel Bretherton I will have to pull rank, eh?"

Both my comment and the promotion pleased them. We spent an hour just talking about the events of the winter. More men had taken wives and more of my men had become fathers. It would create a headache for me. Our army was not static. We moved around the land and I could not guarantee their safety. The women were tough and would not expect any consideration but I had expectations and I would have to ensure that they were safe.

When Tom returned with Ashcroft I saw that they were getting on and laughing. That was a good thing. Ashcroft said, "Tom was telling me how you met, Colonel." I had not intended on revealing Tom's past. That he had done so told me much about the young man. "You have done a very Christian thing, Sir." I nodded. I knew that the story would be spread through the camp before morning. I hoped that Tom had done the right thing.

The last thing he needed was for him to carry the burden of being a bandit.

I stood, "Well, Tom, show me to my quarters." I turned to the rest of the officers, "And tomorrow we will exercise the regiment."

Captain Stirling said, "And will you speak to Colonel Friedrich, Sir?"

"We will shake the wrinkles from this regiment first."

What I wanted was for Sigismund to hear of my promotion from someone else. He had been my deputy and obeyed my orders but he now had his own regiment and I did not know how that would change him.

When I reached my home on campaign I smiled. It was my old tent and felt familiar. The camp bed was more comfortable than one might imagine and I did not mind the lack of comforts like wardrobes and drawers. My clothes hung from a rope strung along the outer part of the tent. I knew I was lucky to have such a large tent. There was an outer part and an inner one for my bed. With the flap closed at night I was cosy.

Tom looked around the outer nervously, "Is everything to your satisfaction, Sir? Ashy told me how you liked it and…"

I held up my hand, "It is fine and your tent?"

Tom was also lucky. Most men shared a tent that held between four and six men. Tom's, whilst smaller and little bigger than a hovel, held just him. "It is comfortable, Sir. What do I do tomorrow?"

"We will be away all day. See to the horses. They do not need to be ridden but you should exercise and groom them. I will be riding Marcus and so you can get to know Ran. He is a big horse. Some would call him, like Marcus, a war horse. When that is done introduce yourself to the women of the camp."

"Women, Sir?"

"There are women who follow the troopers. Some live with them. There are families too. If you think your existence as a bandit was hard, Tom, then the life these ladies lead will show you real hardship. When we shift camp my men will ride but the ladies will follow in a wagon with the tents. They are good people and as loyal to the regiment as any trooper. They are the heart of the regiment."

I slept remarkably well but at the back of my mind was the thought that there were spies. That the king knew about them showed the character of the man. He did not shirk from danger. There were others who were two faced and pretended to support the cause. I was just glad that we had King Gustavus Adolphus to lead us. His plans were in his head. How could an enemy know what we were going to do when even the king had not concocted the plan yet?

The camp woke earlier than my home did. The fires were lit and men moved around while it was still dark. Another task performed by the women was to help Sergeant Wilson, the company commander of the Otters, to prepare food. We were an organised regiment. I suspected that Sigismund's Brandenburgers would be equally organised eventually for he had served with me since I had taken over the rabble that had been the regiment. He had seen what order did. I knew that other regiments were less well organised and food was cooked on an ad hoc basis. Tom hovered outside the tent. I wondered how long he had stood there. He was keen to impress.

By the time I was dressed the smell of cooking was drifting over and when the horn blew for reveille we were heading for the food. Two of the original camp followers, Jane and Gertha, curtsied as I neared them. I saw that Gertha was pregnant. Jane called out, "Did you have a good Christmas celebration, Colonel?"

"I did and you?"

She smiled, "We had snow and the land was so pretty and peaceful. Captain Stirling managed to get us a pig and we ate like kings."

I did not like to think how they had acquired a pig. I suspected that he had sent Peter Jennings and his Hunting Dogs to forage and find some Catholic farmer who still had a pig. One of the things we would do on this ride would be to find food. Our supply lines were stretched and starving men had a habit of deserting. My scouts would find what they could. The food was simple but good. Tom waited while I ate. I said, "Go and saddle Marcus. Take him to my tent and put my pistols in the saddle holsters."

"Sir." Eager to please he scurried off.

Lieutenant Dickson arrived, "I have checked the horse lines, Sir. All is well."

Before I could give him instructions Captain Stirling strode over; he was grinning, "A fine crisp morning, Colonel, and a good day for a little exercise. The horses need it." I nodded, "The orders, Sir?"

"General Horn is somewhat isolated to the east of us and we need to see if the enemy are moving."

Dick shook his head, "A bit early for campaigning, Sir."

"And yet we occupied Bamberg. We will just ride as far as the bridge over the River Main." I saw Lieutenant Dickson's eyes widen. It meant that we could be riding fifty miles. I smiled, "Since landing at Rotterdam I have ridden more than fifty miles a day on a hackney. We will ride to the Main at Marktheidenfeld and see what we can see."

By the time I reached my tent Tom had Marcus ready for me. When we were going into battle I would have six pistols but for this ride I would just use the two saddle pistols. Nor did I wear my cuirass. I just wore a buff coat made of moose hide. The king wore such a garment. He had to wear it because of a wound he had suffered five years earlier. I would wear it for comfort. I mounted and Murphy, my trumpeter, and Gilmour, who carried my standard, joined me. The three of us would ride together with Captain Stirling and Ashcroft.

I smiled, "Ready, Gentlemen?" Their happy expressions and chorus of '*aye*' told me that they were. "Then let us be about it."

We rode to where the eight companies were waiting. They looked splendid. The horses had good coats and considering they had endured a snowy winter that was amazing. The company guidons had all been given love and care over the winter and looked almost new. The breastplates of the officers gleamed and those with helmets had polished them.

"Lieutenant Jennings, we will head for Marktheidenfeld on the Main." He and the Hunting Dogs were my scouts.

"A long ride, Sir." There was just the hint of criticism in his voice.

I smiled, "If the land looks peaceful and there is no sign of any Catholic scouts then we will return earlier. Had you something better to do?"

He laughed, "No, Sir, my lads are eager to get back to work."
"Then lead on."

We would not be crossing the Rhine but keeping to the southern bank. It meant riding through the camp of Colonel Friedrich. His men had just risen and were at breakfast as we passed. Lieutenant Jennings and his company had alerted them. Sigismund was wearing just breeches as he washed. He called out, when we passed, "I did not know you were back."

"I arrived last night and General Banér wanted me to scout to the east. We will talk this night. Come to my camp."

He waved, "I will."

It was only when we had crossed the pontoon bridge to the Mainz side of the river that I realised I had given him an order. How would he take the summons?

Marcus had not been ridden since I had left and he was eager to open his legs. I almost had to fight him. The horses I had ridden in England and on the road east had all been relatively docile animals. Marcus was made for war. Alexander rode next to me with my colour party and the rest of his company behind us, listening for orders. We could only see the tails of the Hunting Dogs when there was a straight section of road. We had learned to use Lieutenant Jennings and his men to sniff out danger. It helped us to have the confidence to ride hard.

I said, "Were the men paid over the winter?"

Captain Stirling nodded, "Aye, Sir. The king is a fair man. I cannot understand why so many deserted. We had food. I mean, it was hardly a feast but it was winter and we ate better than the Germans did, not to mention that we were paid. The lads were happy enough."

John Gilmour said, from behind us, "I think some thought the war was over, Sir. We are deep in the heart of Southern Germany. Why, any further and we will be in Italy!"

"You may be right, John, but the war is not yet won."

Lieutenant Jennings stopped each time we came to a crossroads or a town. They were largely small places with no walls and no castles. He could speak German well and he had the ability to encourage locals to speak to him. In that way we gathered intelligence as we headed east.

Lion of the North

It was in Babenhausen that I found Jennings waiting for me. "Trouble, Lieutenant?"

He nodded, "When I stopped to water my horse a man sidled up to me. He did not want others to know he was talking to me for there are Catholics in his village. He said that yesterday he saw Croats to the southeast of us near the village of Schaafheim."

"How far away is it?"

"Just a few miles."

"Then we head there and we ride prepared. Have the men prepare their weapons." My men had, in the main, matchlocks but the officers all had managed to acquire one or, in some cases, two wheellocks. Some had snaplock harquebuses and they were good weapons too. I turned, "Ashcroft, tell the other officers that there may be Croats ahead. Be ready for action."

"Sir."

I primed my saddle pistols and regretted not bringing my other guns with me.

The nature of war in this part of Germany followed a pattern. While it was largely Catholic there were places that were Protestant. Our army tended to take from the Catholics although I knew that there were some regiments who just took regardless of the affiliations of the people that they robbed. The Croats were mercenaries and a fierce enemy. I guessed that Schaafheim was Protestant and the Croats would take all that they could before moving on.

Captain Stirling seemed to read my thoughts, "Croats are nasty buggers, Sir."

I nodded, "Luckily their firearms are not the newest."

"Aye, Sir, but they have those war hammers and their swords are heavy and stronger than the ones we use." He was partly right. My sword was the exception and I would weigh that against any Croat pallasch.

I saw the smoke rising from the village a mile or two outside Schaafheim. I could feel the tension rising inside me. I had planned on nothing more than a training ride which scouted out the land, as I had been ordered. That I had found a regiment of Croats within twenty miles of our main camp was disconcerting to say the least.

One of the Hunting Dogs rode from the trees to our right, "The lieutenant's compliments, Colonel, but he has found the Croats. They are camped in the village and they have piquets on the road."

If you used a dog to hunt then it was always advisable to heed their warnings. "Captain Stirling, bring the men along and have horse holders assigned. If they are in camp I want half the men to fight on foot."

"Right, Sir."

I led the other three and we followed Lieutenant Jennings' trooper. We walked rather than galloped. If the Croats were in camp they would be making noise but thundering hooves, as I had discovered on the road from Rotterdam, were always a warning. In addition, it did not pay to risk a fall. The lieutenant had dismounted half of his men. I smiled. They were all of my mind. I dismounted and Ashcroft took my reins. He and the other two stayed on their horses.

I walked forward to join Jennings who was standing behind a tree. He pointed and said, quietly, "There look to be about one hundred and twenty-five of them, Sir. They have already slaughtered the animals in the village. It looks like they are salting the rest. I reckon this is just a halt on a march; they are going somewhere."

I nodded, "Bamberg I'll be bound." Croats were used like we were, as scouts. These men had to live off the land. The general had been right to send us. I said, "Take your mounted men and get around the other side of the village. I will send the Wolves and the Foxes to join you. When you hear the trumpet then attack. I want prisoners."

"Right, Sir."

He hurried to mount his horse and they were gone in a flash. Alexander Stirling arrived, I said, "Send the Wolves and the Foxes to follow Lieutenant Jennings. He is coming to cut off the enemy." He hurried to obey me. Lieutenant Dickson rode up. He made to dismount but I shook my head, "Keep your Wildcats mounted. The rest of the regiment will fight on foot. Your company can stop any from escaping."

"Sir."

When all the men were dismounted and they each held a pistol or harquebus loaded and primed I turned to Murphy, "Sound the charge!"

I was already moving, with Alexander Stirling at my side, from the trees. A Croat sentry had been making water and when he stepped from behind the tree he picked up his war hammer and swung it at my head. My wheellock was raised and fired in a flash. He was so close that the ball smashed into his face and erupted in a messy mass of bones and brain from the back of his skull. I jammed the pistol in my belt and drew my sword. All around me weapons were discharged. This was a necessity of war. You took any advantage you could. We needed them to surrender and do so quickly. In my heart I knew that these fierce fighters would not surrender easily. Any prisoners we took would be wounded men. They were also the most skilled horsemen that I knew. If they reached their horses then even the wounded would be able to escape. The firearms made an immediate fog that hid us from the enemy. They would have no idea how many men were attacking them. It was an advantage for us.

I heard a Croat trumpet sound and saw an officer in his distinctive red coat and fur-rimmed hat shouting orders. Men ran for their horses. I heard the hooves of Lieutenant Jennings and his men as he led two and a half companies to cut off the escape. The Croats did not discharge their weapons for they were not loaded but they wielded their hammers and swords. My men took no chances. Troopers stopped to reload. They were used to working in pairs. One fired, the other reloaded and they protected each other. I levelled my second pistol to fire at the officer. He was thirty paces from me but my wheellock was an accurate weapon and I had trained myself to use it left-handed. I fired but luck was on the side of the red coated officer. One of his men ran between us. The force of my ball threw him around as he screamed and fell to the ground. The officer saw me. He shouted something and he and four men ran at me. I jammed the discharged weapon in my belt.

They were wild men and they knew how to fight with such weapons as they carried. The war hammer had a spike that could penetrate mail. The swords the Croats used were curved and could stab as well as slash. Apart from Alexander Stirling I had four troopers with me. I hoped that at least one of them still had a loaded weapon. One had because there was a crack from my left and a cloud of smoke. A Croat fell clutching his stomach. My hat and my sword marked me as an officer and the Croat officer came directly for me. I drew the dagger from the back of my belt. The Croat roared a challenge. I understood most languages but Croatian was still a mystery. The officer did not have a sabre but a Pallasch. It was a little longer than my sword and he swung it over his head intending to split my head in two. As that invited a slash to his middle I knew that he had to have some protection there. It would not be a cuirass but it might be a mail vest. Croats were, in many ways, old fashioned warriors. I blocked his blow with my sword and slashed at his middle with my dagger. It tore through the fabric and scraped along metal. I had been right.

He punched at my face with the sabre hilted sword. I moved my head out of the way but the edge of the guard gouged a long wound down my cheek. The officer seemed to take this as a victory. It was nothing. I lunged with my dagger, not at his middle but his upper right arm. My sword had a point and I pierced the thick fabric and pricked his arm. It drew little blood but I knew that I had marginally weakened his sword arm. I was aware that Alexander Stirling had slain his opponent and was leading his company to attack the rest. The officer and I were alone. I took it as a compliment that my captain thought I could defeat this officer. I needed to end it. I shouted, in German, "Surrender, you are surrounded."

I guessed that he could understand German. He clearly could but his answer was, I assumed, in the negative, as he renewed his attack. He drew his own dagger. It was longer than mine. He had the advantage now for he had two weapons that were longer than mine. My advantage lay in my experience. I knew his right arm was weaker. The blood flowing down my face would make him feel confident but the wound was not hurting me. I swung my sword and forced him to block the blow. I did so again. Each time I hit I was weakening him and that became clear for he forgot to use his dagger as he blocked my blows. I stabbed again with my dagger but this time I aimed at the top of his unwounded arm. My blade pierced the seam and this time did not merely prick but stabbed and he shouted in pain. I timed my next strike so that, when I swung my sword at his head, he was not able to raise his sword and the dagger that rose did not arrest the progress of my blade. I split, first his hat and then his skull. I had feared he was wearing a secrete beneath his helmet but he was not.

As I looked up I saw that some Croats had mounted their horses. They had lost too many men and with the officer and his trumpeter dead there was no way to rally them. I shouted, "Prisoners!"

Although my men strove to obey the order many Croats escaped and we took just five. They were all wounded. We treated their wounds and then bound them with their hands behind their backs. There was little point in asking questions as we did not speak Croat. King Gustavus had men who did. We had lost no men but eight of ours were wounded and they were also treated.

The villagers had suffered. Some of the women had been abused and many of the men had been butchered. We piled the dead Croats away from the village but we had no time to bury them. I knew that the bodies would be despoiled after we departed but we had no time to waste. We took the remaining horses, weapons, powder and ball and headed back to Mainz. Knowing the Croatian skill with horses each of the prisoners was led by a trooper. The horses we had taken, forty of them, were like gold. They would be used as remounts. They would have been well schooled by the Croatians. Along with the weapons it had been a good day but at the back of my mind was the worry that Imperial troops were within half a day of Mainz and our camps. The sooner the prisoners were questioned the better.

I let Captain Stirling cross the pontoon bridge to the camp while I went with five troopers and the prisoners to the king. When we reached headquarters I had the prisoners dismount and left them under the watchful eye of the captain of the guard. I sent my men back to the camp and headed for the king.

Our arrival had been noted and Lieutenant Larsson hurried down the corridor to greet me, "What happened, Colonel?" As we headed to the king I told him. He did not wait on ceremony but threw open the door and said, "King Gustavus, Lieutenant

Colonel Bretherton has returned with Croatian prisoners of war. I will find the men to interrogate them."

I shuddered a little. The king and the lieutenant were honourable and Christian men but the interrogators were another matter. They would use the wounds we had inflicted to their advantage. I saw that the two generals had gone and that he was with his aides. My heart sank when I recognised Prince Francis Albert of Saxe-Lauenburg amongst them. I did not like the man and I think that he hated me. I put him from my mind and told the king what had happened. He went immediately to a map and jabbed his finger at the village.

"I like this not, Colonel Bretherton. These villages are on the way to Bamberg. General Horn has less than ten thousand men. Has Tilly outwitted me and started the offensive early?"

Some of his more sycophantic aides chorused, '*No, Your Majesty*' or '*of course not, King Gustavus.*' He ignored them. He was not a vain man.

I said, "The prisoners will tell us more, Your Majesty."

"That they will. How are you and your men placed? Could you ride again on the morrow?"

"Yes, Your Majesty."

"This time take Colonel Friedrich's men. From what you said you outnumbered the Croats but as some escaped who knows how many men you might face."

Prince Albert snorted, "Careless, Bretherton, you should have taken them all and given the king an advantage."

I was going to reply but the king did it for me, "Prince Albert, until you have led men successfully in battle do not presume to tell a good leader like Lieutenant Colonel Bretherton how to conduct himself. I would also appreciate you giving my officers respect and use their title."

The prince coloured and said, "I am sorry, Your Majesty."

"It is not to me that you owe an apology."

The prince said nothing. A man like him would never apologise to someone he thought an inferior. I pointed to the map, "Here at Marktheidenfeld is a bridge over the Main. It was where I was heading when we heard of the Croats. I could take my brigade there tomorrow. If you sent some infantry to follow close behind us then they could bar the road to Mainz. If Count Tilly seeks to attack us here they could hold them up."

The king smiled, "You read my mind. Until we have all our men gathered then we are vulnerable. Do this."

Just then the lieutenant returned, "The prisoners are still being questioned but Count Tilly is marching on Bamberg with twenty thousand men."

"Then, Colonel, find him and shadow him until I can bring my armies to battle him."

The order seemed simple enough but I had enough experience to know that it would require us to take supplies with us. We would not be able to take tents and blankets would have to do. The powder and ball we had taken from the Croats would be a help but we would not be able to carry much food. We would have to live off the land and that meant taking from the Germans. Once outside I mounted my horse and rode back to the camp. Any thoughts of a slow readjustment to life on campaign had been shattered by those simple words, *'shadow him'*.

Lion of the North

Mainz

Babenhausen

Schaafheim

Marktheidenfeld

Würzburg

N

Griff 2025

6 Miles

Chapter 9

When I reached camp it was dark and I heard laughter from the fire close to my tent. I had dismounted at the edge of the camp and I walked Marcus to the fire. I saw Colonel Friedrich talking with my officers and there were bottles on the table. Tom must have been watching for me. Even as I neared the fire he rose and said, "I was worried, Colonel. Here, give your horse to me. I will clean your weapons later."

I nodded, "Thank you, Tom. Have the officers eaten yet?"

He shook his head, "They were waiting for you, Sir."

He took Marcus and I went closer to the fire. I was seen and a shout went up. Sigismund stood and walked over, "Once more I hear that you have gained glory this day."

I smiled, "Hardly glory, Sigismund. We caught them with their breeches down."

Alexander Stirling was a huge man but his size often made people fail to see how clever he was. He wanted to know what would happen next. He asked, "What did the king say?"

"The Croats were scouting for Count Tilly. There is an army heading for General Horn." I turned to Colonel Friedrich, "I have been given command of your regiment and mine. We have to leave tomorrow and shadow him. You know what that means?"

He nodded, "It means short rations, long days in the saddle and the danger of ambush." He gave a sad smile, "I had planned on celebrating with you but I can see that I need to warn my men." He held out his arm, "It is good to have you back."

I shook his hand, grateful that all appeared well between us.

I turned to Captain Stirling, "Officers' call." I saw Tom returning from the horse lines.

He turned to the other officers and said, "Warn your deputies what we are about and then join me at the colonel's tent."

As I walked to my tent, Tom trotting beside me, I said, "I am afraid, Tom, that you will be thrown in rather sooner than I expected. If you wish to remain in camp then I am happy for you to do so."

He shook his head, "If you are on the road then so am I, Sir."

"Then stand behind me and listen. We have busy times ahead of us."

We had various forms of seating. I sat on the empty barrel. Tom poured me some ale and handed it to me as the officers arrived. "Ashcroft, Tom, we will eat while I talk for time is of the essence." The two men hurried off to obey my orders. "We know where Count Tilly will be heading and that is due east of us, Bamberg. We can head south and east to intercept him. The Croats were obviously guarding his left flank as he advanced north. They will be replaced and the enemy will know that we are aware of their presence." I drank some of the ale. It had been noon when I had last drunk anything and I was parched. "The king will need to be kept informed each day. To that end each company will send a pair of riders back to Mainz with my messages: Wildcats first and Stags last."

Ralph Longstaff said, "You are assuming, Sir, that it might take us eight days."

The two servants arrived with platters of food. They handed the first four to the senior officers.

"I am assuming nothing, Ralph, but we have to plan. For the same reason I want each company to have half a dozen of the Croat horses we took today as remounts. Sergeant Campbell, see that each company has some emergency rations. If the Imperialists have already plundered as they marched we might be going hungry. We take all the ball and powder that we can. We need men to stay behind to watch the camp, the ladies and the horses. Choose wisely." We had some older troopers and some were married. Until the whole army marched to face Tilly then we did not need every trooper. I emptied the beaker and handed it to Tom. "Any questions?" I then began to shovel food from the platter into my mouth. I had forgotten how hungry I was.

Lieutenant Dickson nodded towards the Brandenburger's camp. "Order of march, Sir?"

I knew what he meant. I swallowed the food and said, "Colonel Friedrich's regiment will be behind us. That is for purely practical reasons. They are newly raised and this will be their first action as a regiment." I had wanted to speak to Sigismund about his men but Tilly had made sure that would not happen. "Hunting Dogs at the fore and Badgers at the rear." I looked around. I knew that I had an easier task than Sigismund. My officers knew what they must do. The men from Brandenburg would be keen to impress but would lack the experience to help their new commanding officer. "If there are no further questions then we leave before dawn. Gilmour, be so good as to let Colonel Friedrich know the orders." I smiled, "Let us eat the hot food while we can. We shall be on cold rations when we ride." My men finished off the food and wiped the platters clean with bread. We would be lucky to enjoy fresh bread when we campaigned.

When the officers departed Tom appeared with a second platter of food and another jug of ale, "And now, Sir, it is time you looked after yourself. Mrs Bretherton impressed upon me the need for food. She said the last time you came home from war you looked like a skeleton."

"I have eaten already, Tom."

"That was a sparrow's measure, Colonel."

I smiled. I had lost a little weight but I was hardly a skeleton. I knew that when I put on my cuirass the food I had consumed over Christmas would make it feel tight. "I will enjoy this repast, Tom, for you have brought it for me but we shall not be enjoying such fine fare for a few days."

I wolfed down the food and then, using the light of an oil lamp, studied the map. The bridge at Marktheidenfeld was vital for the alternative was Würzburg and I did not know who controlled it. Würzburg had a wall and a castle. Tom had cleared away the empty plate and refilled my beaker. I said, "Clean the pistols and sharpen my sword. I will need my four pistols tomorrow. You can have two." I knew that I needed to get more weapons for Tom. I preferred having six wheellocks. As Tom hurried away to obey my orders I shook my head. I knew that the best way to get such weapons was in battle. I was anticipating doing more than just watching the enemy. I knew that weapons would be discharged and men would be hurt. We had been thrown into the war before we were really ready.

I did not enjoy a deep sleep. My mind was already racing as plans and problems in equal measure rose into my head and I woke before the night sentry had roused Tom. He was still asleep when I rose and dressed. I made water and went to the fire where the night guards had prepared breakfast. The night guards would be the ones left to guard the camp.

Alf and Edgar were two old soldiers and I knew them well. They were solid and dependable. Both had been wounded at Breitenfeld but neither wished for retirement. The regiment was their life. Alf smiled, "I wish we were going with you, Colonel."

"As soon as you are fully healed then the Imperialists had better watch out, eh, Alf?" We both knew that it was unlikely that they would ever be able to come to war again. They would be camp guards but hope remained.

He smiled, "The wound is itchy, Sir, and that means it is almost healed."

"And almost is a world away from ready to fight, eh?" They both nodded, "I trust you will watch over my horses? We brought three more when we came."

Edgar said, "Which one will you take, Sir?"

"Ran, I think. Marcus was ridden today."

"Don't you worry, Sir, you are leaving the camp in safe hands."

Alf ladled some of the porridge into a bowl as Tom hurried over. "You should have woken me, Sir."

"I wouldn't worry, Tom, once we are on the road then your body will adjust." I had the bowl of porridge cleared quickly. Tom brought his with him as I hurried back to the tent. "When you are done, then fetch our horses. It would not do for the colonel to be tardy."

All around us the camp was coming to life. It was as though a nest of ants had been disturbed. I would need Tom to help me with the cuirass but I had everything else ready. By the time he returned I heard other horses being led from the horse line. Once he had fastened the cuirass I then began to put my loaded pistols in the holsters. I packed my maps into my saddlebags as well as a purse of coins. Sometimes we took and sometimes we paid. I needed to be ready for any eventuality.

I began to roll my blanket. I said, "I intend to wear my blanket en banderole. That means it will be wrapped around my breast and back plate. I do it so that the light will not reflect off my breastplate. If you do not wish to emulate me so then fasten it on your horse."

"I will copy you, Sir."

"And I will wear my cloak. It is still cold. Until we reach the month of May we will need protection from the elements." Having Tom with me was almost a burden. I was having to explain things to him that my troopers took for granted.

I mounted Ran and my horse stamped the ground, eager to be away. My colour party were waiting and with Tom bringing up the rear the four of us rode to where my companies were forming up. Gilmour said, "Do I unfurl the colours, Colonel?"

I shook my head, "Until we need to announce our presence I would keep our identity a secret if I can." I remembered Lieutenant Robert. Heinrich Holk would not have forgotten me.

There were no tears from the women left behind for some of their men were staying with them. They waved as we headed towards the pontoon bridge. As we passed Sigismund's camp he and his servant joined me. His deputy would follow on with the regiment. I knew, from Alexander Stirling, that he had fewer troopers than I did. My friend had yet to engender the spirit I had created in Bretherton's Horse.

He nodded east where the first hint of light appeared in the sky, "Back to war, eh, James."

I nodded. I did not mind informality when we rode but once I needed to then I would use command and formality. "Aye, are your men ready?"

He lowered his voice, "I think the next days will tell me that. We have trained and they seem keen enough but you and I know that it is when the balls fly and sabres clash that a man's mettle is truly seen."

"And that is why we will be wary of drawing swords. The king wants us to follow. He will not wish to lose men before the next battle."

"You mean he might allow Bamberg to fall?"

"The king is not worried about one small town. He has a war to win. I think that General Horn was the bait to draw Tilly north. Tilly has surprised the king by moving early but the king seems confident." He nodded and I asked, "What are your new men like? Your officers?"

"I was lucky to find some young Brandenburger nobles. They brought men with them. They are young and keen."

"But they will obey orders." I did not phrase it as a question,

He stiffened, "Of course. My regiment is young but soon will have a reputation like Bretherton's Horse."

I shook my head but said nothing. Reputation meant nothing to me.

We moved quickly along the road to Marktheidenfeld. Although we had no wagons we were a long metal snake that cleared the road of casual travellers. When one of my Hunting Dogs returned I wondered if there was trouble ahead. He said, "Lieutenant Jennings said there are a regiment of pikes and musketeers ahead, Sir, friendlies."

I was pleased. I had expected the foot soldiers to follow us but whoever led them was keen to impress. As the bridge was just a few more miles up the road then we would have the crossing of the Main secured.

I recognised the horse before I had identified the rider. I reined in, "Colonel Lang, I see that the king chose you."

He grinned, "Aye, laddie, my regiment arrived just at the right moment. I hear this was your suggestion." I nodded. "Then I thank you. I would rather be billeted in a town than a field." His men would be able to have a roof over their heads and fresh bread. Both were like gold to the men we led.

I saluted, "I shall see you anon."

The town before Marktheidenfeld was Esselbach and while there were no troops billeted there I was not sure of their loyalty. I left the Stags to guard the bridge until Colonel Lang arrived. Once we had crossed the Main then I let loose Lieutenant Jennings and his company. It would be the Wildcats who now rode in front of me and my colour party. With Captain Stirling and Lieutenant Jennings with me we had the three most experienced officers at the fore. We were in Bavaria and it was a Catholic land.

We stopped at Marktheidenfeld. It was a good place to stop although, when we reached there and Lieutenant Jennings pronounced it to be safe, we did not know that. We were weary and our horses could go no further having ridden sixty miles. We crossed the bridge over the Main. Here the river was narrower. It was just eighty paces across. We camped in the fields adjacent to the river.

The priority for us was the care of our horses. Cavalrymen without their horses were at risk. They were watered and then led to grazing. Our food was secondary. Sergeant Campbell had brought pots for cooking and some food. Men foraged for greens and took some vegetables from the fields. When Corporal Summerville approached with the two villagers I feared that it was a complaint of some kind.

The older man was dressed in sober black. Ralph must have told him my rank for he bowed as he addressed me, "Colonel, I am Klaus Riemenschneider and I bid you welcome." He smiled. "This is my son, Karl. You should know that this village is Protestant or, if we were allowed to choose, we would be. Bishop Philip Adolf, who was the Prince Bishop of Würzburg, imposed the Catholic faith upon us. That he died last year when King Gustavus retook the city is small consolation to us. We see you as liberators."

I shook my head, "We are not the Swedish Army, Sir. We are scouts. We will leave in the morning."

He looked disappointed, "King Gustavus Adolphus will not be coming?"

"He will come but we know not when."

The man looked determined, "Then we shall help you in any way that we can. You should know that the bishop in Würzburg conducted witch trials for the past five years and a thousand women were burned." He shook his head, "It has stopped now for the bishop is dead but my wife was one of the ones who was unjustly tried and executed. I tell you this not because I want you to take revenge for me but because the next town is Würzburg and it is a nest of Roman Catholics. We were always Protestant but Würzburg is another matter. They have no bishop but they persecute Protestants. It stopped when there was a Swedish garrison but they pulled out in October."

"Thank you for that and I am sorry for your loss." I knew that King James had also been a zealot when it came to witches. "Have you heard of Imperial troops in the area?"

He nodded, "There is a regiment of cuirassiers in Würzburg and I believe there is an army further south. Travellers crossing to the west have spoken of a baggage train."

I nodded, "Then I thank you and we will try to take as little as we can."

"Take what you will, Colonel, we want our home and our religion back and King Gustavus is our only hope."

When he had gone I wrote my report and sent two of the Wildcats back with it. They used two of the Croat remounts. They would have a rest back in our camp before rejoining us. I had a meeting with the officers from both regiments. "The intelligence I have just received changes everything. If there are cuirassiers ahead then we need to eliminate them as a threat. We have to find this column and ascertain where it is."

Colonel Friedrich said, "We captured Würzburg after Breitenfeld. I thought the witch trials ended then."

"Clearly while we might have taken the city it was not properly garrisoned. We will have to retake it."

"And you have a plan?"

I smiled, "Not yet, Colonel, but I will by the time we leave in the morning."

I sought out Lieutenant Jennings when the rest had gone. "Peter, you were at Würzburg were you not?"

"I did not enter the city, Colonel but I scouted it out."

"Do you think there is grazing inside the walls?"

He shook his head, "No, Colonel, it looked to be built up." He nodded towards our grazing horses, "They will do the same as we do and use the riverbanks. Cuirassiers ride big horses and they need good grazing and water."

"Excellent. Then this is my plan." I told it to Jennings to allow him to find flaws. I knew there would be some.

"Will you tell the others?"

"Aye, when I have sorted all out I will do so but you and your Hunting Dogs are the key to the success of this operation."

I went, first to Sigismund. This would be the first time he led his men into battle and I wanted him to be clear about what they would do. I had to allow him to lead his own regiment. For the first time I would be relying on another to obey my commands. That done I gave my battle plan to my officers. I was confident in their ability to carry it out. Once more it relied on my men having a shorter rest than most soldiers might expect. We had to catch the cuirassiers before they knew we were in the area. For the Hunting Dogs it meant leaving just after they had eaten so that they would be in position before dawn. With luck they would have nothing to do and would enjoy a rest for them and their horses. They were my guarantee of success.

Tom fussed over me. I knew he was tired beyond words already but he was determined that I would have enough to eat and drink. "I am content, Tom. How is your horse, Bertha, coping?"

"She is not as good as Cleopatra, Colonel, but the rest we enjoyed at camp over the last couple of days has helped. There is good grazing here and she and I get on well."

"And Hercules?"

Hercules was relatively unladen but he was there to carry my cuirass and the spare balls and powder. As I was wearing my cuirass he was having an easy time of it. "Loving it, Colonel. He has not much to carry. Our spare clothes do not weigh much."

"If all goes well on this raid then he will have to carry more eventually."

We turned in. This time Tom did wake me. The night guards had enjoyed just one hour of sleep. They were the Stags and were my reserve in case anything went wrong with my plan. The biggest flaw in my plan was that I was relying on information that was a year out of date. Peter Jennings had told me all that he had seen and he had good eyes but much could have changed in that year. We rode east on a morning which was frosty. The hooves of the Wildcats removed the rime of frost but the air was cold and the men who had cowls and hoods were grateful for the warmth they afforded.

We split into two at the tiny village of Höchberg. Sigismund led his regiment south to cross the road to Würzburg from the other side of the road and we would head to approach the bridge from our side. My plan was to surround the cuirassiers. The parting was where my worries started. We dared not use trumpets or horns to synchronise our movements. We had to rely on the sun and dawn as a signal.

One advantage of the frost was that the fields we crossed were hard as opposed to muddy. We took it steadily and when I saw the trees that marked the river line we halted. The Otters and the Badgers had been given the task of swimming the river. I did not envy them their task as the water would be icy. The river was not too wide but they would be wet and cold when they landed. Their task was to wait until we attacked before they took the gates and the bridge. As soon as we passed through the trees and reached the river the two companies left us to descend to the water and swim across. They did so without incident and I saw them on the other side as they loaded their pistols and dried themselves off as best they could. I waved to Seymour and Wilson as they led their companies south to the city and the bridge. Sigismund would have detached two of his companies to do the same. That done we walked, rather than rode our horses along the path that bordered the river. I led my colour party along with Captain Stirling and Lieutenant Dickson. Tom, to his chagrin, was relegated to the rear with the sumpter.

We heard the horses of the cuirassiers before we saw them. It was getting on for dawn and they were moving around at the horse lines. As soon as we heard them we stopped and sniffed the air. I could smell the fires of the night guards. The cuirassiers were in territory that had been captured by the Swedes and they would be wary. Klaus Riemenschneider had told us that there was a regiment of cuirassiers. That could be anything from a hundred men to a thousand. I did not think it would be the latter but until we saw them we did not know how many men we faced. I gave the signal to mount. I primed my weapons so that I had four pistols that I could use and then I waved forward my column. Behind us the men were four abreast. The path, with the river to our left, was wide enough for just such a number. Most of the men had only one pistol. This action would be determined by swords rather than black powder.

When I saw the trees thinning I held up my hand and the column stopped. I went forward alone to the edge of the trees. I could see the walls of Würzburg across the river. I did not see any sign that there were guards on the walls. Why should there be? They had a regiment of cuirassiers to protect them. I then turned my attention to the land to the west of the road. It was there I saw the small Imperial camp. There had clearly been a farm here at one time for I saw the half-wrecked building at the top of the bank. There were tents and I saw a rope pen with horses. It was not yet true dawn but there was enough of the moon shining for me to see that the camp ran along the river. I did a quick count of the tents. There looked to be about fifty. That meant anything from two hundred to two hundred and fifty men. We would need both regiments if my plan was to succeed. I saw the nearest sentries. They were not mounted and there were four of them about one hundred paces from me. That meant about eighty yards for us to cover.

I turned and, taking off my hat, waved for my officers to bring up the men. I did not speak. Words carried in the night. Instead I used hand signals. My officers nodded and did the same. Our men moved silently into position. I drew one pistol and then nodded to Gilmour to unfurl the flag. The first two companies were in place and the rest waited behind. I glanced to the city to the east of us. I detected a change in the sky. It was becoming lighter.

The horn when it sounded and the crack of a handful of pistols came not from my men or the camp on this side of the road but the far side, where Sigismund's Brandenburgers were supposed to be waiting for dawn and a joint attack.

Captain Stirling snorted, "Well, that has done it."

I nodded, "Charge but sound no horn, Murphy. The Brandenburgers have drawn the enemy eyes to them."

I urged Ran forward as horns and trumpets sounded in the Imperial camp. The guards I had seen ran to their horses. Their attention was to the other side of the road and not behind them. I holstered my pistol and drew my sword. The night guards had not seen us for their attention was on Sigismund's men as they charged into the camp on the other side of the road. The night guards wore breastplates but not backplates and our swords sliced into unprotected backs. I knew that the two companies on the Würzburg side of the road would be changing their plans too. My plan had been for them to be at the city side of the bridge before we began our attack.

We had a harder task now for some of the cuirassiers, realising that they were under attack, ran for their horses. The plan to capture a regiment of cuirassiers now lay in tatters. Had we been able to surround the camp and level pistols and harquebuses at sleepy men then my plan would have worked. We would have prisoners. I heard the crack of powder weapons as the Brandenburgers sought to remedy their mistake. My men were using cold steel but when a harquebus was fired at us then my men replied in kind. The air was filled with the acrid smoke from our guns and the camp was shrouded in smoke. The city, in contrast, was framed by the rising sun for the smoke sank into the river. The rising sun was borne of a frosty night and would not give much warmth until later but it did, at least, light the scene.

The road we had not used now became the flaw in my plan. I had thought they might try to enter the city but instead the horsemen who managed to mount fled to the road. They could then go south back to Bavaria. I sheathed my sword and drew my pistol. I still hoped for prisoners but I knew that was a forlorn hope.

By the time I reached the road more than half of the enemy regiment had escaped. Of the other half some had jumped into the river and were now heading away from the city. The rest had either been killed or wounded. I saw Tom leading the sumpter as he picked his way through the fallen horsemen.

"Captain Stirling, see to their wounded."

He raised an eyebrow, "See to them, Sir?"

I shook my head, "Take the weapons and their breastplates. We will let the people of Würzburg tend to their wounds. We have an Imperial Army to find. When you have done all that then join me in the city."

I galloped over the bridge with my trumpeter, standard bearer and Tom. Seymour and Wilson were waiting for me at the gates of the city. The gates were open and the four guards were bound. Sergeant Wilson shook his head, "That could have gone better, Colonel. We got a wetting for nothing."

"The best laid plans, Sergeant. At least our regiment didn't lose any men. Let us head through the city and let them know it has now switched allegiances." I took off my blanket and my cloak. I tossed them to Tom. "Ride at the rear, Tom." He obeyed. I did not want to risk him in the event of some hothead trying to make a name for himself attempting to assassinate me. Tom was safer away from me.

We rode through the gates under my banner. The king had made a mistake. Had he left a garrison here over the winter then the people would not have welcomed the Imperialists. This was Bavaria and it needed an iron fist. I had forty men with me and they were all armed. My cuirass was polished and without the blanket it glistened in the morning sun like silver. The blue feather in my hat would, when it rained, droop and look a little sorry for itself but now, at the start of the campaign it looked jaunty and bright. I rode one handed and my right hand was on the pommel of my sword. I knew that I might look ridiculous but I represented the King of Sweden and I had to strike a pose. People stared in silence. Klaus had been right. This was a hotbed of Catholics. I rode directly to the Rathaus, the town hall, and I turned Ran to ride up the steps. Ran was a good horse and I was a good rider. When I reached the top the door opened and the mayor and some of his officials appeared. I recognised the mayor by the chain of office around his neck. I ignored them and whirled Ran around to face the gathering crowd. They outnumbered my two companies but my men had pistols and swords at the ready.

I spoke in German, "People of Würzburg, I am Lieutenant Colonel James Bretherton and I am here obeying the orders of King Gustavus Adolphus of Sweden. He took this city last year and he rid it of your witch finder but I arrive today and find a regiment of Imperial cavalrymen camped outside. This is not a good thing and the king will be, as I am, displeased." I turned Ran around so that I was facing the mayor. I dramatically drew my sword and pointed it at him, "You have a choice, Mayor, either you and your people stop persecuting the Protestants or I will raze your city to the ground. What is it to be?"

I had terrified him, I could see that in his face. He put his hands together to implore me, "Colonel, I promise that the outrageous behaviour of Bishop Philip Adolf ended with his death. I swear that we will allow the Protestants to worship freely."

"Here and in the neighbouring towns, too."

"Of course."

"My men and I have work further east but we will be passing through on our way back."

"And you will be welcomed, Colonel." The man was now confident enough to smile.

"And one more thing, your people will feed my regiments. We shall leave the wounded Imperial soldiers with you. When they are healed you can send them on their way."

He hesitated and then the smile returned, "It shall be done."

Almost as though he was waiting for the order Captain Stirling led my regiment, followed by the Brandenburgers into the city. Any belligerent thoughts harboured by the people of Würzburg evaporated like morning mist at the sight of the soldiers and the prisoners.

I clattered down the steps sheathing my sword as I did so. Captain Stirling was grinning when I reached the bottom, "Sure, and you make a grand sight, Colonel."

I shrugged and said, "A little play acting was all. They are going to feed us. We will eat here in the square. It will make a statement and we can all fit here. Take charge and I will speak with Colonel Sigismund."

The smile left Alexander's face and he said, quietly, "He lost fourteen men."

"Fourteen!"

"He is not a happy man, Sir."

"Neither am I!" I turned to the colour party and Tom, "I will go and speak with Colonel Friedrich. Get me some food, Tom."

"Yes, Colonel."

I rode down past my men. They saw the food being brought out and knew what it meant. This was a good day for them. They had defeated cuirassiers, not lost a man and now food and ale were being brought out to them.

I saw that Sigismund had a fresh cut on his cheek and his standard bearer sported a bandaged arm. I reined in and waved away the ones who were close to the Colonel, "I wish to speak to Colonel Friedrich in private." My tone brooked no argument and we were left alone. "What happened?"

"A young hothead, the son of a count, disobeyed his orders and led his company to attack before I gave the order. He was seen by the sentries who opened fire. He died in the exchange and his men sought to avenge him. I am sorry."

I nodded. Nothing I could say would bring back his dead men. Sigismund was a friend but as an officer and a leader he was flawed. "Then learn from this mistake. You know the importance of discipline. Impose it and stop trying to be popular." The look he gave me told me that I had hit the mark. "We have a long way to go before we return to the king. I would like to take back two regiments, do you understand?"

His back stiffened, "Yes, Lieutenant Colonel."

As I wheeled Ran around I reflected that we had been friends but I suspected that it would no longer be as warm as it once was. I rode back to the rest of the regiment. Tom had found a table and a chair. He waved me over, I said, "I will be back soon."

I rode towards the far gate. The gate was open and there were guards there. I ignored them as I rode through. I shouted, "Hunting Dogs!"

Lieutenant Jennings led his company from the trees. When he reached me he had concern on his face, "We heard the firing. Did all go well?"

"It could have gone better. Did any leave?"

He shook his head, "A couple of horsemen tried to leave but when we rode from concealment they returned."

"Good. We are being fed. Bring your men to the square." He looked pointedly at the guards. I said, "I will deal with these."

"Sir. Right lads, we eat!"

They cheered. When they had gone I said to the town guards, "Close and bar the gates. No one leaves without my permission." The captain of the guard looked as though he might object and so I drew my sword and rode towards him. "The mayor has promised full cooperation. This sword is the guarantee that we will have it."

The man gulped, "Yes, Sir, it will be done."

I turned and rode back. Now I could eat and then, when I had sent another rider back to the king, we could continue to seek the rest of Count Tilly's army.

Chapter 10

It was eleven o'clock when we left the city. We had the Hunting Dogs out once more. Sigismund rode next to me. I think he was keen to make up for his mistake. He eagerly offered me a nugget of information, "One of the prisoners told us that Count Tilly is almost at Bamberg."

I turned in the saddle, "He told you willingly?"

The Brandenburger looked me in the eye, "The man was dying and he was promised a quick death."

I was not sure I believed him. He was giving me an answer that he knew I might find acceptable. "And why did you not mention this earlier? I could have included it in my report to the king."

This time, when he answered, I saw the lie in his eyes, "It only happened moments ago. I told you as soon as I knew."

Sigismund was playing games with me. I wondered if he had sent his own rider back to tell the king and garner the glory. It would not bother me but it would disappoint me. "Thank you and that changes our plans. Rejoin your command." My voice was cold.

He saluted and wheeled his horse around. Alexander Stirling and Dick Dickson had both been listening. Alexander said, "We head for Bamberg?"

"We do, Dick, ride ahead and tell Jennings of the change in plan. I want to approach the city from the west."

"Sir."

He galloped off. Alexander said, "We still shadow or do we harass?"

"We assess, Captain Stirling. The king put me in command, I think, because of my ability to make wise decisions. I am not reckless. If the city is under siege then we harass. If it has fallen then we watch."

"Fallen?"

"Aye, Captain. The general did not have huge numbers and General Horn is a canny general. He will not waste soldiers. The king sent him because of his judgement. Let us not speculate. We cannot reach the city today in any case." We had fifty miles to go and weary men riding into a battle was a recipe for disaster.

One good thing about the confession obtained by Colonel Friedrich was that we had barely deviated from the road to Bamberg. Lieutenant Jennings could use the main road which headed east.

We were just ten miles from Bamberg when we were halted. It was not just Jennings who waited for us but General Horn. Was this news of a disaster?

I halted the column and left Captain Stirling in command. I rode forward. I liked Gustav Horn. He was both clever and pleasant. More than that he was a good general and King Gustavus had made him his deputy. I saluted, "General."

He nodded, "I have told your Lieutenant Jennings to send out skirmishers. I have my men making a camp here. You and I need to speak. Let us use that deserted house over there."

"Lieutenant Dickson, have your men form a skirmish line."

"Sir."

Like many places in Germany there were houses and villages that lay untouched and others, like this little farmhouse, that was just a shell. As we rode towards its blast blackened walls I wondered who had fought and died here. The farmer and his family would have fled. Men would have fought and died and for what? No one would remember their little fight. We both dismounted.

"I have lost the city. I had but ten thousand men and Tilly more than twice that number. I left before he could inflict casualties. Your captain said that you managed to defeat a regiment of Croats and another of cuirassiers."

"We were lucky."

"A good general never disparages luck. I used my judgement and evacuated the city. I lost the artillery but I managed to retain most of my men. Now that I have yours I have something I did not have before, cavalry. I have sent a rider to tell the king of this misfortune."

I nodded, "And he knows of my progress."

"Then he will come."

I shook my head, "He may, General Horn, but it cannot be quick for he is waiting on supplies of powder and ball. Even if all went well then it will still be more than a week before he is supplied and he has gathered all his army." I saw the question on his face and I explained about the ship and the Spanish ships.

"So, you and I must do what we can." He looked at the shell of the building. "This can be our headquarters. We block the road to Würzburg although I do not think that Count Tilly will leave the walls of Bamberg. If he garrisons it and tries to move west then we now have enough men to defeat him. We will wait here and your brigade can make it hard for him to keep his men supplied. You can cut the road to Nuremberg. That city is, as you know, a Free City but that does not help us much as her people could support either side. Bamberg is Catholic and is another reason I left. The count will have supplies but if we keep him within the walls then they will soon run out. His horsemen will suffer." He smiled, "I am pleased that it is you who commands the cavalry. You have a brain and you use it well. I leave the harassment to you. Act independently but keep me informed. Between us we may be able to remedy this situation for the king."

"General." I rode back to my men. "Lieutenant, find us a camp to the south of the road. We are staying here." Dick was a good soldier. He did not waste time asking useless questions. He knew we needed water and grazing. We also wanted to have the ability to protect our horses. He galloped off, leading his Wildcats. "Murphy, officer's call." The trumpet sounded and my officers and Sigismund's began to arrive. I dismounted and handed my reins to Murphy. When they had all arrived I gave them the news and the orders. "Bamberg has fallen." I saw the shock on the faces of the Brandenburgers. My officers remained calm. "General Horn managed to extricate himself without losing more than his artillery. He intends to block the road to Würzburg, the Main and Mainz. Until King Gustavus arrives, and that cannot be for at least a week, then we hold."

Captain Stirling said, "Just hold, Sir?"

"No, Captain Stirling. We have been given licence to raid. We stop the enemy from foraging and the city from being resupplied. We do not risk our men." I deliberately looked at Colonel Friedrich when I said that. "But we are aggressive. Our aim is to make the retention of Bamberg untenable. When the king comes then the city will fall." I let the words sink in. "Colonel Friedrich, I want you and your regiment to ensure that the northern side of the city is ringed. Captain Stirling, you will take Wolf Company along with Badger and Otter. I want one company each day to ride to the east of the city. Lieutenant Dickson, Wildcats, Fox and Stag companies will watch the road to the south. I think that two companies will be needed each day. Rotate your men."

"Sir."

"I will command the Hunting Dogs and the Hawks." I smiled, "I will choose our task each day." I paused, "I am trusting you all to do the best you can. Now join your men."

Sigismund, as I had expected, did not hurry away but he waited for me. "You have given my regiment the least to do. I have a whole regiment to do that which you allocate for three of your own companies."

There was no point in lying and I said, "True, but as this morning showed, your men are not as well trained as mine. Remember, Colonel, the regiment I lead was partly trained by you. Do you think your Brandenburgers are as good?" For all our recent disagreements Sigismund was an honest man and he shook his head. "Then use this time I give to you and hone your men into a sharp weapon, for the real battles lie ahead of us."

I followed my horsemen to the camp. Dick had chosen well. There was a wood at the end of some fallow fields, and a stream that led to the Aurach provided water. The trees would afford protection from the south as well as kindling and hunting. By ensuring that not all my men were kept patrolling each day we could guard the camp and the men could hunt. The nearest village was Hartlanden and it had already been stripped of food by General Horn.

I saw that Tom and a couple of my men were building me a hovel. It was here that the nearby forest came in handy. Branches were cut and laid to make an open sided structure. With leaves and shrubs laid across the back and leaves as a bed I would be comfortable and, unless the wind was in the wrong direction, relatively dry. Tom knew of such things from his time in Coatham Woods. I led Ran to the horse lines. Tom would water my horse when he was done. I took off my hat and unfastened the fastenings on my cuirass. I had worn it a long time and it was a relief to shed it. Sergeant Wilson was already getting his cooks to prepare food. Alexander Stirling acted as an adjutant and I knew that he would have organised the watches. He would liaise with Dick but the watches would be manned by the companies not scouting. I hoped that Sigismund was as organised but I doubted it. From what I had seen his officers were glory hunters.

There was still light and as two troopers kindly brought over a log for me to use as a seat I sat and studied the maps. The River Aurach was not a major obstacle but it fed the River Regnitz which was. I worked out that we could easily make the Regnitz in under an hour. My first patrol would determine if it could be forded.

Alexander joined me to sit on the log. "How are we for powder and ball?"

Captain Stirling said, "Better than we might have hoped. We took from the cuirassiers and allied to that which we had from the Croats we are not in any danger of running out."

Dick sat on a small log, "Food is the problem."

I pointed to the woods, "Then we get the companies not on duty to forage. It is March and there may be early berries. There will be wild greens and mushrooms and we can hunt. There must be rabbits. Have the men make traps."

Dick nodded over to Sigismund, "The colonel is not happy, is he, Sir?"

Dick and Alexander knew the captain almost as well as I did. We were not being disloyal by speaking about him. We were worried. "I know. He raised the regiment and that means he feels an obligation to them. They are not the same quality as our men."

Alexander laughed, "Not as rough you mean? Aye, you are right. The Brandenburgers might know which knives to use at a table but our men know how to survive."

Dick said, "Give them time. They will either make it or they will break."

We had all seen many regiments broken and disbanded.

The captain said, "Where do you go tomorrow, Sir?"

"We will follow your company. You will have to cross the Regnitz and I need to see how easy it is. I intend to head south in case he is bringing reinforcements from Nuremburg but I want to know what the river is like."

Sergeant Wilson managed to make a good meal. When, like a conjuror, he produced bread that was not stale I looked at him in amazement. "Where did this come from?"

He grinned, "The people of Würzburg were so keen to see the back of us they did not notice my lads lifting the bread they thought they had hidden from us. Make the most of it. I cannot see us pulling off the same trick again."

Tom had made his hovel close to mine and he fussed around it to make sure it was as cosy as possible. "It is fine, Tom, and better than I expected. Tomorrow see if you can forage food. This is the sort of place you are used to."

"It is, Colonel, but Coatham was much smaller. I wish I had my bow with me." He shook his head, "Might as well wish for a goose feather bed. I shall make do with what we have and make the traps that kept my mother in food when we were hungry."

I knew I had been pampered. I had been born to a rich father and I had a noble woman for a mother. We had servants and growing up I had wanted for nothing. Even when I served Prince Maurice as a young officer I had not starved. Tom was like my men. He understood the true meaning of hardship and hunger.

We left after dawn and a breakfast of oats cooked slowly in water. I left my standard bearer and trumpeter in camp to help forage food and to guard our spare animals. If I had been the Imperialists I would be raiding my enemies. We followed Captain Stirling and his Wolf Company. I did not wear my cuirass and my cloak helped me to blend in with the trees when we passed through them to the Regnitz. We found a crossing that was just thirty paces wide. We only had to swim the middle ten paces and as the ground around was boggy I guessed that the river was always shallow here. Once across we headed south to find the main road from Nuremburg. That city had strong walls but I suspected the garrison had been stripped to furnish Count Tilly with his army. However, Duke Maximilian of Bavaria had an army and I deduced that they were at Ingolstadt. The Bavarian city lay south of Nuremburg. Reinforcements could be on their way north. King Gustavus Adolphus had over extended his lines and until we had more troops we were vulnerable.

Lion of the North

We found the patrol of horsemen in the village of Hirschaid. There looked to be a small squadron of them, fifteen men and, by their dress and equipment, they were mounted dragoons. The sentry at the end of the village must have been making water for when Lieutenant Jennings and I rode around the bend we just saw his horse. I drew a pistol and urged Ran on. Jennings and his Hunting Dogs were even faster to draw their weapons than I was. When the soldier emerged from the side of the house and saw us he shouted a warning and ran to his horse. Lieutenant Jennings' ball smacked into his back and the man fell, but his dying hand held on to the reins. As we entered the square we saw the other dragoons mounting their horses as they attempted to flee. I could not tell if they were on their way to Bamberg or were guarding the village. It didn't really matter. I aimed at the officer. I recognised his rank from his boots and his hat. I fired but Ran was galloping so hard that the ball merely plucked at his arm. I might have wounded him but I did not slow him. I holstered my pistol and drew my sword. Ball was too valuable to waste and the handful of men we faced were at a disadvantage. Our horses were galloping and they had to control, mount and then ride. My Hunting Dogs were soon amongst them. I heard the shouts from the dragoons and realised that they were Walloons. They had lost their own country to the Protestants and would not surrender easily. They were fanatics. As if to prove it a corporal turned and whirled his horse to face me. He had a heavy sabre in his hand and a pot helmet. He realised he could not outrun me and charged. It was brave.

I pulled Ran's head to the left and pointed my straighter sword at him. My sword was a handspan longer than his. He pulled his arm back for a slash. I was wearing gauntlets and I let Ran's reins drop as I lunged. I caught the sabre with my leather gauntlet. The blade cut into the hide but did not penetrate. The tip of my sword, in contrast, sliced across his thigh and raked his saddle. I used my knees to make Ran turn to the right as he pulled back his arm to slash at my head. I blocked the blow with my sword and I grabbed my reins and control of my horse. The blades sparked as they rang together. My movement had, effectively stopped my horse and the corporal's horse was stationary too. My Hunting Dogs and Hawks chased the other dragoons south. We were closer together now and that gave him an advantage for he had a shorter sword. He slashed at my throat and I barely managed to block it. What I was able to do was to twist my sword so that as he pulled back his arm he had exposed his left side. He wore just a woollen coat and when I slashed it was with such force that my blade cut through the wool and into his side. As I sawed it back blood spurted. He was brave and he stood in his stirrups to bring his sabre down to my unprotected head. I pulled on the reins to make Ran snap at the dragoon's horse. Ran was bigger and the dragoon's mount flinched. In battle the margins are very narrow and I slashed across his body diagonally. The tip sliced into his flesh and through his coat. His two wounds had weakened him and, combined with the flinching horse he rode, he was dumped on the ground.

There was little point in me joining the pursuit and I sheathed my sword and dismounted. The sabre had fallen from his hand but I kicked it away. I spoke to him in Dutch. He was a Walloon but he understood it, "Where is your regiment?"

A tendril of blood dripped from his neck. He smiled, "You are English, eh? I will not tell you, so you might as well finish the job and kill me. I will not talk."

I nodded, "For you are a corporal and a brave man but when we take one of your troopers, will he be as brave, do you think?" The man tried to rise but the effort proved too much. Bright blood spurted from his neck and he fell back dead. "Go with God." I knelt down and removed the pot helmet. It was not for me but Tom could use it as a secrete. I took the sabre and the long harquebus as well as the powder and ball. His horse would also be a good addition. Dragoon horses were sturdy animals.

I looked up as I heard hooves. My men returned. They had one prisoner and three horses.

Lieutenant Jennings reined in. "Two escaped. The rest are dead." He nodded at the dead man, "Did you learn anything, Colonel?"

I shook my head, "Just that they are Walloons. Ask the villagers what they know although I suspect they regard us as enemies."

I was proved correct. We headed back to the camp with a reasonable haul and a prisoner I would deliver to the general.

Alexander had also found a party of scouts. This time they were hunting for food and my men chased them back to Bamberg. Sigismund's men, too, found scouts and now Count Tilly knew that there was a ring of steel around his refuge. Count Horn had done the right thing. There was no point in making the lines of a siege around Bamberg for in such lines there was the risk of disease and death. We had a good camp and fresh air; well dug latrines and plentiful flowing water would keep our small army healthy.

That evening we also had news. My riders all returned at the same time. Although the message was for me I took the riders to report to the general. "The king is still waiting for his supplies."

The count nodded, "And by now he will have my news. He will know that we have lost Bamberg. We carry on the way we are, Colonel. Keep your men snapping at his scouts. Make them fear to leave their town."

While we ate I spoke with all my officers. "We maintain our noose. Corporal Summerville, tomorrow you will ride alone with your company. We need men with fresh horses and senses that are alert to danger."

Tom had enjoyed a successful day. He had found food and laid his traps for the rabbits that would graze at night. I gave him the pot helmet. He looked at it suspiciously, "It is only to be worn if there is a risk of battle but this," I tapped the metal, "can slow a ball and even stop one fired at distance. When shells explode it can protect from the pieces of metal that will fly. Mrs Bretherton will be happy knowing you have such protection."

It was two days later when they tried their sortie. Food must have been running short and they sent out a regiment of Croat horsemen to try to catch Sergeant Wilson and his Otter Company. They had clearly slipped out before dawn and they had studied the route we took when heading east of the river. Wilson did nothing wrong but he was unlucky. The Croats fired a volley from the safety of the woods and two men fell. I had drilled into my men the need for discretion. This was not the time for vainglorious bravery. He turned and, with his men, fled. We learned all this later but I was drawn into it. As luck would have it I was with the Hunting Dogs and we were heading south and east. I heard the musketry and immediately wheeled my horse to lead the company to the sound of the guns. I could hear the shouts and cries of the Croats long before I saw them. They were firing their harquebuses as they rode. We were heading across fields when I saw the guidon of the Otter Company.

I drew a pistol and shouted, "Skirmish line. Whoever is chasing our men, we hit them in the flanks." I was confident that the attention of the horsemen would be on the Otters. There was a fence at the edge of the field and then a piece of open ground close to the road. I saw the Croats for they wore brightly coloured and distinctive clothes as well as the red Imperial sash. The sunlight glinted from their swords and war hammers. Ran was a good jumper and took the low fence, intended to keep sheep safe, in one bound. As we landed I fired at the Croat who was just five paces from me. My wife's servant could have made the shot. He flew from his saddle. I wheeled Ran, my horse's hooves sparking from the cobbles as we turned. I replaced the pistol and drew the second one. This time I was behind a Croat. There were others behind me but the Hunting Dogs were amongst them. I fired at the Croat's back and his arms spread like a crucifix and he fell to the ground. The Otters, realising that help was on hand, turned and drove into the Croats. The light horsemen went from imminent victory to defeat in the blink of an eye. I drew my sword and slashed at the Croatian warrior who tried to turn and head back to Bamberg. He stood no chance for my sword sliced into his upper arm, shoulder and then his neck. There were a few moments of confused mayhem as our two bands of warriors slashed, stabbed and discharged pistols at one another. Then the Croats fled. The Otters were keen to follow but I shouted, "Hold! Reform!"

Sergeant Wilson rode up, "Bastards ambushed us. I left two men back down the road. Permission to find their bodies, Sir."

I shook my head, "You get your men back to the camp and we will recover the bodies. Briefly, what happened?"

"They were waiting in the woods. The wind was from the south and we didn't smell them. They fired a volley and Smith and Watkins fell."

"Collect the horses and weapons from the Croats and head back to camp. Have Corporal Summerville bring his men to join us."

I wheeled Ran and led the Hunting Dogs a mile or so down the road. We did not gallop. The sergeant had assumed that the men were both dead. So it was that we came upon the four men who were stripping the clothes from the dead. The horses of the four men were tethered with the horses of my dead troopers. My blood ran cold when I saw the long skinning knife held by one of them. They were going to mutilate the dead men. I did not hesitate but drew another pistol and led the charge. Our galloping hooves attracted their attention and they stood. The Hunting Dogs were angry and when twelve pistols all fired at once there was but one outcome. The four men fell where they stood.

"Hargreaves, get the horses. Find the dead men's clothes and dress them. Lieutenant, make sure there are no more of them close by."

"Right, Sir. Patterson, come with me."

I saw Bill Parr leap from his horse and run to the body of the Croat who had held the skinning knife. "What are you doing?"

The man was angry, I vaguely remembered that he had been the friend of Olly Watkins. "I was going to do to him what he was going to do to Olly."

"Put that knife down. We do not behave like animals. Now dress Olly and put him on his horse. We can bury them with honour and if you castrate that dead man there will be no honour!"

"Sir." My men were now disciplined and obeyed orders.

It was noon by the time our two companies rode into the camp. The Stags had helped us to recover the bodies. On the way back I realised that while I could not have prevented the attack I could have minimised its effect. After we had buried the men I had a meeting with my officers. "From now on we use four companies a day. Two go east to a mile from the walls and two go south, a mile from the wall. No more ranging further afield to see if reinforcements are coming. I want us to vary the routes that we take and from now I will ride with the trumpeter."

Hindsight was always perfect. It had cost me two men to realise my mistake. Sigismund learned from my mistake and he changed his routine. No one sortied again and no one tried to enter. However, a week after the attempt, the night guards at the camp of Gustav Horn heard noises coming from the town. He sent for me at dawn, "They are up to something. Take your regiment and investigate. This may be another trick."

When we reached the city the gates were open and there were no flags fluttering from the walls. Tilly had fled. I sent a rider back with the news and by noon Bamberg was back in our hands. The sullen faces of the citizens told us that they wished for the return of Count Tilly. We would need a garrison to hold on to the town.

Count Horn was pleased but he was too good a general to take it as a given that they had fled. "I will send a rider to tell the king. You and your brigade are to follow Count Tilly and discover where he has gone. I am guessing Nuremberg."

My brigade broke camp and headed south. The retreating army was easy to follow. Discarded equipment littered the road. We took everything that might be useful. Their feet had cut a swathe through the land on either side of the road. They had left Bamberg at night and they reached Nuremberg and were inside by the time we arrived. We camped outside and I sent a pair of messengers to tell General Horn that we would watch. I did not have enough men to surround the huge city and so I guarded the road north. My men scouted and foraged. It was my scouts who discovered, two days later, that Tilly had continued his march south. The gates of the city were unguarded and open. We entered the city and discovered that they had left Nuremburg shortly before dawn. I knew, without wasting horseflesh, that they would have reached Ingolstadt by the end of the day. My men and horses needed supplies and as Ingolstadt was where the Duke of Bavaria lived I guessed that Tilly would flee no further. He had food, powder, supplies and men. We returned, first to Bamberg and then, a weary two days later, Mainz. Our horses were exhausted for the fleeing army had devoured all the grazing on the road south. Sigismund led the brigade to our camp and I went directly to the king to report.

He looked pleased when I told him what I had done. He was a realist and knew that I could have done no more, "General Horn told of all that you did. I am pleased and now that the supplies are here we can take the war to Count Tilly. There will be no more shadowing, Colonel. We go to bring the enemy to battle.

Return to your brigade. My army is assembling and we shall leave to bring the enemy to battle in seven days' time."

Chapter 11

The first two days in camp were days of recovery. When you rode to war you had to check horseshoes, as well as the saddles and horse furniture. Our horses were vital to us and small injuries and wounds were tended to. Sergeant Campbell was a sergeant because he was the horse master. Weapons had to be cleaned and maintained. Action always resulted in damage of one kind or another and we had a bare two days to do so. My officers toured the camp to discover what needed repair or replacement. We also had more horses, for apart from the one patrol where we had been ambushed we normally took horses from our enemies. Some were little more than nags and fit only for carrying equipment while others were distributed between the companies. Sergeant Campbell did so equitably. The weapons that had been taken were also shared out. Every trooper now had a pistol and some had two. That they were not all the same was annoying but it could not be helped. Men swapped weapons so that if they had a pair they took the same calibre of ball. We had taken ball moulds when we had captured the cuirassiers and one task in camp was the making of lead balls for our weapons, pistols and harquebuses. We had taken many items from the Croats and cuirassiers. Some of the things were not military. The sashes and plumes might be used but we had taken crucifixes and coins from the dead. Before we returned home we might sell the jewellery but until then it was retained, banked if you like.

Three days after our return, and with the horses fattening on the better grazing, Sigismund and I were summoned to the headquarters. We took our servants and my standard bearer along with a sumpter. Mainz had a market and there were things that we needed. We would try to buy some flour to augment our supplies. While we were in camp we baked our own bread. Sergeant Wilson had made a bread oven. It saved the journey over the pontoon every day and the night guards enjoyed the warmth of the oven. We brewed our own ale but we needed cereal to do so. Here we could not raid and so we paid. I did not know Jurgen, Sigismund's man. He spoke no English and so Tom and John Gilmour rode and chatted together. From the number of horses that were being guarded it was clear that this was a meeting of senior officers.

"Tom, there is little point in waiting around here just to watch the animals. Go to the market and buy the items Sergeant Wilson requested." I handed him a purse, "Here is the money."

John Gilmour asked, "When should we return, Colonel?"

"The king is normally brief but we now have allies who like to hear the sound of their own voices. Have something to eat and return an hour after Sext. If we finish early I shall wait."

Sigismund nodded and said the same to his servant. I knew that John could speak some German. They would be able to communicate. We had left our pistols at camp but we wore our swords. In the absence of other signs of rank they, along with our hats, told strangers that we were officers. We were admitted and led to what must, in times past, have been an assembly room or Great Hall. There was a raised platform at the end with some chairs. It was empty apart from two halberdiers. Servants scurried around with trays of food, ale and wine. Sigismund and I took two ales. It was too early in the day for wine which tended to make me feel sleepy.

We were both recognised by other senior officers and they wandered over to talk to us. One was Colonel Munro. He led a brigade of Scottish mercenaries and I liked him. The other who came towards us beaming was Robert Lang, "My dear Colonel Bretherton, I heard nothing but good things from General Horn when he returned with us to Mainz."

"The general is here?"

"Aye, he left a garrison in Bamberg for King Gustavus summoned us all back here."

"How was your duty?"

He frowned, "This is not like Saxony. There we were liberators and here we are oppressors. It was unpleasant. My men did not take, yet we were shunned. Perhaps I should have allowed them to be like the other regiments and take what we wanted. We would have been viewed no worse."

Colonel Munro said, "Necessary though. We need to break the will of the Imperialists and Maximilian of Bavaria is a staunch supporter of Emperor Ferdinand."

Robert Lang was drinking ale too and he took a good swallow, "All I know is that we had to watch the locals when food was prepared. I had to hang two for trying to poison our food. Our men went in groups of ten to avoid being attacked."

I knew that they were both right. We had taken Mainz and there were enough Protestants in the city to ensure that we were not threatened as Colonel Lang had been, but once we headed into Bavaria then we would have to sleep with daggers beneath our beds.

The two sentries on the dais both banged their halberds and the noise in the room faded to silence. The king entered, like an actor on the stage. He was accompanied by Count Axel Oxenstierna, the High Chancellor of Sweden, and closely followed by his senior ally, Duke William of Saxe-Weimar with his brother Bernhard. His three senior generals walked behind the four of them. Johan Banér, Gustav Horn and Lennart Torstensson were all much better generals than the duke but politics was all. It was the coterie of aides who drew my attention. They flocked behind the generals like seagulls behind a fishing boat seeking to insinuate themselves as close as they could to power. There were more now than there had once been. The success of Breitenfeld had drawn them like wasps to nectar. I noticed that the only one I respected, Lieutenant Larsson, kept a dignified distance from them. He had no need to seek favour for the king rated him as highly as any colonel. When the generals and the three leaders were seated the aides jockeyed for position behind them. I noticed that Prince Francis Albert, the man who hated me, managed to ingratiate himself behind the king.

I was not the only one who noticed and Robert Munro shook his head and said, "I have no idea why the king keeps that popinjay, Saxe-Lauenburg, on his staff. You know at Breitenfeld when most of us had notched and battered blades, his sword still had the grease upon it. He had not drawn it. He is only close to the king when it is safe. In battle he lags behind."

Colonel Lang nodded, "The same could be said of most of them."

"Charles Larsson is a good soldier."

They both nodded and Robert Munro said, "Aye, he is but his father was a soldier. The rest are nobles who seek to recover land or, in the case of Saxe-Lauenburg, take as much land as they can get. They do not care for the cause and only worry about their self-interest."

It was then I saw the hooded and cloaked figure enter and stand at one side, partly hidden by a carved pillar. A man with a good sword stood next to him. He was clearly a man with a bodyguard and therefore important but he did not wish to be seen. Why? Who was he?

My speculation would have to wait for the king stood and we all stood expectantly listening for his words. The king was a practical man and he did not go in for flowery phrases. He was a soldier and he was addressing soldiers. "Thanks to General Horn, Count Tilly has been sent back into Bavaria to lick his wounds. Our resolute defence of the road to Mainz and the indomitable spirit of our horsemen has prevailed. However, it has shown me that before we take on Austria, we need to reduce Bavaria. If we can persuade, through feat of arms, Duke Maximilian to leave the alliance then Spain will be weaker."

There was a murmur through the hall. This was a clear change of direction.

The king waited until the murmur had subsided. "We now have our powder and ball. Thanks to our French allies we have money. The pay for your regiments will be awaiting your collection after this meeting."

We all fought for the cause but we were mercenaries and men who were not paid deserted. Thanks to our success we were able to augment our pay with what we took from the enemy but pay was always an inducement.

"Your individual orders will be with you by tomorrow, they are being written even as we speak." There was an air of anticipation in the room as we waited to hear the destination. "We will march to Nuremberg. I have intelligence that suggests we will take it easily with a show of force, for the Imperialist Army does not have enough men to garrison it effectively. Once that is done we head for the Danube. We have more than thirty-five thousand men and over seventy guns. Whilst Count Tilly is an able commander and will mount a stout defence, in General Torstensson we have the finest gunner to be found in any army. We will prevail. I do not know yet where Tilly will make his stand but we shall find him and bring him to a final battle that will see this war ended. Our redoubtable light horsemen, Lieutenant Colonel Torsten Stålhandske and his Hakkapeliitta along with Lieutenant Colonel Bretherton's brigade, shall discover where they are to be found. With your orders will come maps. Use them. There are many rivers we have to cross and it is important that every commanding officer understands our standing orders regarding river crossings. I will now hold a council of war to confirm our strategy. If you would wait here, your pay chests will be brought."

It was then that I noticed the shadowy figure and his bodyguard had departed. I had been so intent on the words that were spoken I had not been able to identify the man.

As soon as the dais was cleared the buzz of conversation rose once more. Sigismund looked particularly animated. As our brigade had been singled out he saw a future filled with promotion. Perhaps he saw himself as the commander of a brigade. I was happy enough with the command of two regiments and I wanted no more. I knew that I was smiling too for when we fought Count Tilly and, hopefully, defeated him, then I was that bit closer to leaving the army and returning home.

The pay chests were brought in singly. There were two of the king's officials, the chest was carried by two men and two others stood with drawn swords. This would take time. There was a hierarchy to the payment. The senior regiments of the allies would be paid first, followed by the Swedes and the mercenaries, mainly Scottish, English and Dutch, would be last. I waved over a servant for more ale. I listened to the chatter of Sigismund and the others as they speculated where we would fight. Such speculation was idle. We would know soon enough.

Lieutenant Larsson appeared at my side, "Lieutenant Colonel, the king would like a word with you." Anticipating that Sigismund would want to come too he turned and said, "The king wishes Lieutenant Colonel Bretherton to be alone. Perhaps you could watch his chest, Colonel Friedrich?"

"Of course." I think Sigismund was unhappy to be excluded.

I followed the Swedish aide out of the hall. I was aware that eyes were upon me. We were taken to an antechamber and when the door opened I saw the king was seated at a desk and next to him was the shadowy figure I had seen before. This time I knew who it was. The red garb and distinctive features meant he could be only one man, Cardinal Richelieu. He had brought the pay himself. I also saw that standing, with a grin on his face, was Torsten Stålhandske. The king had summoned his scouts.

"Close the door, Charles, and guard it."

"Yes, King Gustavus."

"Cardinal, might I introduce another of my talented officers. This is James Bretherton, an Englishman who leads the border horsemen that bear his name." The king was speaking in French and, thanks to my mother, I was fluent in it.

The cardinal nodded and said, "Like the colonel of the Hakkapeliitta, Colonel Bretherton and his men are known to me. The English are normally so dour and reserved, how is it that you have managed to lead your men with such flair and elan?"

The words came easily to me, "I was trained well by the Dutch in the early years of the war and, perhaps, because I was not trained in the ways of war I learned how to fight myself. It helps, as I know Lieutenant Colonel Stålhandske will attest, to have good soldiers." The Swede was clearly not as fluent in French as I was. He had understood what I had said but he just smiled and nodded.

"When this war is over, Lieutenant Colonel Bretherton, if you seek employment, you will find it in France. We have need of such leaders and their horsemen."

It seemed politic to do as the Swede had done. I nodded and said, "Thank you, Your Eminence."

The king said, "I have sent for you two because I want you to take your men before the rest of the army. Lieutenant Colonel Bretherton, you will take your brigade to Nuremberg and ensure that it has not been garrisoned. Lieutenant Larsson will be with you and you will send him back to me with the news. That done I want you to scout in the direction of Ingolstadt. I need to have intelligence about our enemies. Lieutenant Colonel Stålhandske, you will do the same in the direction of Nördlingen."

The Swede asked, "And if they are not there?"

"Then push on until you find them. Once you know where they are and what are their intentions then return to Nuremburg. I want you on the road by the day after tomorrow at the latest."

He sat back in his chair. The meeting was over. We both saluted and left. The lieutenant entered and the Swedish Lieutenant Colonel spoke to me, "Free ranging orders, my friend."

"And that suits me. My men do not like to be shackled to the army."

The Swede smiled, "You are right and my Finns are free spirits."

I nodded, "We found two regiments of Croats when we last scouted."

"They are nasty men, but, like you I think my men have their measure. And now let us collect our pay. My men will be eager to buy drink before we raid."

"I thought we were scouting."

"Raiding, scouting, it is the same thing."

That was where the difference lay between the two brigades. My men raided out of necessity and not as part of our daily lives. The Finns seemed to enjoy it. When we reached the Great Hall we saw that most of the officers had gone already. Sigismund waited with our two chests. Although two men had brought each chest I found that I could lift mine easily enough. We headed outside. Although there was no sign of our men I had heard the church bells ringing for noon while we were in the hall. We would not have long to wait.

"What did the king want?"

I detected a hint of annoyance in Sigismund's voice. I answered calmly, "We are to ride to Nuremburg and see if it is occupied. We then ride to Ingolstadt. Our task is to find the enemy so that the king can bring them to battle."

"What about our camps?"

"I am guessing that we are quitting Mainz and we will not wish to leave our camp followers so far from the army. I will have one of my companies escort my camp when the army moves. They can bring our remounts."

"You have more than we do." There was a petulant tone to his voice.

I did not state the obvious. Had his men obeyed orders we would have successfully captured a regiment of cuirassier horses. "I do not doubt that we will find more opportunities but we need to be warier than we were further north. The Bavarians are enemies. When we fought in Saxony we had friends to aid us. Here we do not."

Just then I heard a shout and saw our servants and John Gilmour approach. They had the sumpters but the one Tom led was laden. I would have to carry the chest. It was no hardship for we were not that far from our camp. When we reached Sigismund's camp I said, "I intend to leave by dawn. Make sure that you are ready."

"The men will have pay in their purses, they will wish to celebrate."

"And you command. You must give the orders. If you are worried about them objecting then do not pay them until we are at Nuremburg." I shrugged, "They are your regiment and not mine."

Sigismund still wanted to be his men's friend. I tried to be the friend of the men I commanded but I knew that ultimately I was their commander and I had to make the decisions and issue commands that they might not like. Tom and Gilmour delivered what he had bought to Sergeant Wilson. I took the chest to my tent. Alexander and Dick came over. I said, "We have our orders. We leave tomorrow."

Dick nodded and said, "And that is our pay, Sir?"

"It is."

"The lads will want to spend it."

I shook my head, "We cannot afford to have men out of camp tonight. No one leaves the camp from this moment on. Who is on duty?"

Dick said, "Davy Campbell."

"Go and tell him."

We had a table and Alexander and I went to it, "Fetch the books."

Captain Stirling, as Regimental Adjutant, kept the regimental books. The books held the names and dates of contract for each of the men. It also had their rate of pay. The problem we had was that the pay was in Swedish currency but, when I opened the chest I saw that it was in French, livres. I had a solution. "We will divide the coin into the piles determined by rank."

Lion of the North

Alexander nodded. We each had a different pay scale. Mine was the greatest, then his, the two lieutenants were next followed by the two sergeants and then the three corporals. Murphy and Gilmour were paid more than the troopers. It was relatively easy to work out the proportions. He said, "And your servant, Tom?"

"Pay him as an ordinary trooper. That is fair."

"Ashcroft is paid the same as Murphy and Gilmour."

"And he fights. Tom does not. Trust me, he will not be unhappy."

When the officers had been paid I gave Tom his money. He looked surprised, "You are paying me, Sir?"

"You work for me and why should you not be paid?"

He shook his head, "I am fed, clothed and have shelter. What more does a man need?"

"Tom, we are not bandits who take to survive. We are mercenaries who are paid to do a job. Take it. When this war is over and we go home you will have coins in your purse. What you do with them is up to you."

He looked at the coins in his hand and said, "I have rarely had coins. When we took money from men we robbed my uncle kept it. He gave me coppers when we went to drink in the ale houses but…thank you, Colonel, this was unexpected."

That done I asked Gilmour to summon the officers. They gathered around the table. Dick produced a jug of ale and he filled our beakers. They waited for they knew that I had spoken with the king and that we had orders. I had said nothing to the men but Gilmour and Tom had heard Sigismund and me talking. Word had spread.

"We leave at dawn for Nuremberg. We will have Lieutenant Larsson with us and if we find the city without a garrison then the king will bring the army there. Sergeant Wilson and Sergeant Campbell, you will escort the remounts and the camp followers. We still have a wagon do we not?"

Sergeant Wilson nodded, "Aye and a driver, Konrad." He smiled, "He likes our company and he does not eat much."

"Once we return to the king and tell him where the enemy is to be found then your companies will rejoin us." As I had chosen two companies Sergeant Wilson was not offended. I wanted his Otter Company to have time to recover from the loss of two men. While the rest of the regiment would not be able to leave the camp I knew that as the army would not be leaving for two or three days, at least, then they could hold a wake.

The last night in Mainz was a busy one for all of us. Tom would be travelling with the two companies left to guard our horses. He made sure that Marcus was ready to ride and my pistols were cleaned and maintained. He had learned the skill quite quickly. I had managed to get him a pistol from one of the dead Croats and as it had a different bore he would have to make balls for it. It would keep him occupied.

I said, "We will start with the Wildcats. Summon your men, Dick."

And so we paid the men. As word spread the other companies gathered. I was quite happy because I had nothing to hide and the men saw that everyone was paid fairly. That their officers had more was understandable. The officers generally gave some of their extra pay to their chosen man or deputy but that was up to them. There was nothing written down. Smith and Watkins were single men and their pay went to the company. The troopers would share it out equitably. Some companies kept the pay of dead men in a fund and shared it out at the end of a campaigning season. Breitenfeld had shown us that could result in a fortune. The pay from two dead troopers gave men a chance to toast the dead and have a wake to remember.

Lieutenant Larsson arrived in our camp an hour before we retired. He had with him a soldier, a mounted dragoon from the king's regiment. He smiled, "The king thought I needed protection. Axel here is my protection. When do we leave?"

"Tomorrow. So you need a tent?"

The young officer shook his head. He was a practical man, "No, we shall make a hovel."

That night I prayed, as usual, but the prayers seemed more relevant. We were embarking on a campaign that might bring the end of the war. For that we needed God's help.

We had one hundred and fifty miles to go. I planned on stopping in Würzburg. I wanted the mayor to see that we were back. We rode along a now familiar road. The difference was that this time we were actively seeking a battle. I rode with the lieutenant but that was because Sigismund chose to ride with his own officers. I suspected it was because he was cross with me but, to be fair to him, he might have been trying to create the same atmosphere as existed with my men.

I waited until Alexander had ridden ahead to see how the Hunting Dogs were faring before I spoke to the lieutenant about a delicate matter. "Charles, tell me it is none of my business and I will not ask again but some of the other aides…well, they seem to be about as much use as a two-legged stool."

He smiled, "You are right, Colonel, and the king knows it too."

"Then why keep them so close?"

"The king has a disparate alliance of soldiers. Some of the nobles hate each other almost as much as the Catholics. He keeps them close to make sure that there is peace and also to try to make them into closer friends."

"He risks much. I was told that some did not even unsheathe their swords at Breitenfeld."

"That information is correct, Colonel, and those of us who can be trusted and do draw swords have tried to tell the king. It is his weakness. He believes he can change any man."

I shook my head, "Some of them strike me as untrustworthy vipers."

The lieutenant shook his head, "I agree that some of them are ineffective but none, I feel, are treacherous."

I was not so sure. King Gustavus was vital to our cause. I had meant to speak to his deputy, Count Horn, about it but I had not had the opportunity. I would do so when the chance was presented.

We rode hard and reached Marktheidenfeld before dark. We camped by the river where there was good grazing. The Protestants in the town welcomed us and we were avoided by the Catholics. It was as I expected. We were used to sleeping on the ground but Charles found it harder. That night I spoke to him as well as my officers. "Tomorrow we ride through Würzburg. I know that when my banner is seen then hearts will sink. I want them to be fearful of us. The last thing we need is for them to try to hurt our supply lines. If they are afraid of me then they will just want to be rid of us and hope that I do not return."

Charles said, "But you are not a cruel man. Why would you give yourself an undeserved reputation?"

"Because, Lieutenant, we are far from friends and I do not want men to risk slitting our throats at night."

We rode through the gates of the walled city, our hooves clattering on the cobbles and echoing from the gatehouse. We rode directly to the Rathaus and reined in. Word of our arrival spread and the mayor hurried forth, "What is wrong, Colonel? We have obeyed your commands and there has been no persecution of Protestants."

I smiled, "Good. We came to ensure that you did so and to tell you that King Gustavus himself will be passing through these gates. It is he who will need a warm welcome."

"King Gustavus will come here?"

"With his army."

There was a smile on his face but not in his eyes, "Then we will fete him as he deserves."

"Good, and the other reason I came was to ask if you have been bothered by Croat horsemen?"

"Croats?"

"We both know, Mayor, the danger that they represent."

"No, Colonel, you are the first horsemen to pass through since your last visit."

I looked at his face as he spoke to me. Unless he was the greatest dissembler I had ever met he was telling the truth. My question had been unexpected and I saw the confusion.

We camped at Langenzen which lay a few miles from Nuremburg. I sent Jennings and his Hunting Dogs to scout it out and they returned after dark to tell me that while the gates had been closed, for it was night, and guards were set, it was just the town watch. The city was without a garrison of resistance.

We were so close to the city of Nuremburg that we were able to be at the gates when they opened. We waited, hidden, until they groaned open and then galloped through them. This was Bavaria and the city had welcomed Count Tilly. I took no chances and I had Colonel Friedrich take his men to secure all the gates into the city and to watch the boats on the River Regnitz. I already knew that there were many Protestants in

Nuremberg which might have explained why Count Tilly had not risked staying there. Certainly we were welcomed.

The Margrave of Nuremberg invited us to dine with him. I knew that we had to ascertain if we were welcomed and we accepted. When he asked if our men could be quartered outside of the city I became suspicious but when I said we had to keep one company in the city for close protection he did not mind and I relaxed. I chose the Stag Company and they were quartered in the barracks. While they would have to do a duty and some would be watching at night they would have beds and hot food. I worked out that they were sympathetic to the arrival of the Swedish army although I guessed they were a little fearful of the cost. I found time to speak to Lieutenant Larsson before we retired for the night and he concurred with my views.

"It seems to me, Colonel, that we might use the two companies you left at camp. While you scout out Ingolstadt they can return and secure the city."

He was a clever man and I knew that one day he would make a good leader. The next day he headed, with his bodyguard, northwest and my regiment, probably to the relief of the people, headed south and east. From now on we would be in danger and more likely to meet enemies than friends.

Colonel Friedrich joined me when we left the city. My Hunting Dogs were at the fore. I wondered if Sigismund had stayed away because Lieutenant Larsson had been with me. He said nothing at first and then, as we passed through the village of Wendelstein he suddenly said, "When will you give my regiment the chance to scout and to garner some glory?"

I did not rein in but my head whirled around, "Garner glory? What do you mean?"

"It was your men who surprised the Croats and the cuirassiers…"

I snapped, "You could have, as you say, garnered glory at Würzburg but, instead, your men ruined the chance to take a regiment prisoner. You and your men are still not ready. Your words confirm that opinion."

He whirled his horse's head around and galloped to rejoin his regiment. Our relationship became worse from that moment.

Chapter 12

When we reached Ingolstadt we could see that it was defended but I saw no evidence of a large army. We camped a few miles north and I used, as a sort of sop to his vanity, Sigismund's Brandenburgers as skirmishers. I saw no evidence that it had worked but I had tried. I held a meeting with Sigismund, Alexander and Dickson, "I believe that Tilly is not inside this city." They nodded their agreement. "However, we have to know and that means someone has to go inside the city."

Sigismund said, "I will go, Colonel."

I shook my head, "I was not asking for volunteers, Colonel. I will enter the city."

This time it was my two officers who objected, "You cannot, Colonel, that is madness."

"No, Captain Stirling. I have thought this through and it is a logical decision. I am the one who can speak French as well as Dutch and German. I have livres in my purse and I will play the part of a French mercenary seeking employment. Can any of you do the same?"

They both argued but I was adamant and I think that they knew I was right. Sigismund remained silent throughout until the two officers, realising that it was futile, gave up. Then the Brandenburger said, "And I will command the brigade in your absence."

I saw Dick and Alexander look at one another and I shook my head, "No, Captain Stirling will command my regiment and the brigade will remain under my orders."

His face showed me his anger but his voice was controlled as he said, "And what are those orders, Lieutenant Colonel Bretherton?"

His use of the full title was deliberate. "If I have not returned within two days then return to Mainz and report to King Gustavus." I waited until all three had acknowledged the order and then added, "Until then you make sure that no one reinforces the city."

The only one of my officers who seemed to have any understanding of my reasoning was Lieutenant Jennings. He and his Hunting Dogs were used to hiding in plain sight. I made sure that I just had two wheellocks and they were both French. I emptied my purse of every coin but French ones. I had a prayer book of my mother's with me and it was in French. Her hand, had written, *'pour mon cher fils'*. Everything else that I had was typical of a mercenary. I would not take my cuirass and I used one of the hats we had taken from the dead cuirassier officers. It had a red plume. The final act was to take one of the crucifixes we had taken from the cuirassiers and I slipped it around my neck. If we had the remounts with us I might have even taken a French horse to ride but Marcus would have to do.

I left the camp and rode with the Hunting Dogs as an escort. We reached the wood a little under two miles from the city before dusk. I knew that the main gate from the west was an imposing entrance called the Kreuztor. The Hunting Dogs came with me and their presence would ensure that I was able to enter the city. As we had ridden from the camp Peter Jennings had come up with an idea to help me get into the enemy stronghold. I agreed with the plan and we put it into operation. I left the wood and began to ride along the road towards the city. Ingolstadt was a much smaller city than Nuremberg but it would still have sentries watching from the towers. Peter and I were counting on them being watchful and alert. The wood we had used spread north and east a little and when I was about a mile from the walls, I left the woods and headed along the road. Peter and four of his troopers, shouting and whooping uncharacteristically in English, burst from the trees behind me. Two of them even popped their guns seemingly at me but, in reality, off to the left and right of me. I was ready for it and putting my head low over the back of Marcus' mane I urged my horse on. Marcus raced as fast as I had ever known. I saw that the gates were still open and the sentries there were encouraging me. Firearms were discharged from the walls. I clattered through the Kreuztor and reined in.

As the gates slammed shut, the captain of the guard strode over. To establish my identity I spoke in French from the off, "My God, that was close. Those damned Englishmen almost had me."

The captain spoke in German, "Who are you and why were they chasing you?"

I answered him in German but I used a French accent to do so. I dismounted and took off my hat to make a sweeping bow. I was playing the part of a Frenchman and the Bavarian would expect such grand gestures, "I am Jean Michel Jenet of Senonche and I am here to offer my services to Count Tilly. I am a soldier of fortune." I used my mother's name and a small town not far from Paris. They seemed to work for the captain did not frown nor did he question me further.

"The count and his army are not here. They crossed the Danube and headed for Rain. The margrave will need to speak to you."

I nodded and said, "Where can I leave my horse?"

"Bring him with us. There is a stable."

As we walked the Bavarian asked me more questions but none of them were about my identity. My use of French had been enough to fool him. He had seen what he expected to see. "Did you see any other Englishmen or Swedes on the road? We heard that there were some horsemen to the north of us."

"I saw some Finns to the west of here but those Englishmen came from nowhere. I was lucky to have such a good horse." After we had stabled the horse and the groom promised to feed and water him I was taken to the castle.

The man I was taken to was clearly a noble. He was about to enter his dining room when I was brought to him. I was whisked off to a small ante chamber. A soldier came with us and when the four of us were in the room the door was closed and a guard left outside.

The captain introduced me and told the story. I noticed that he exaggerated the numbers of men who had chased me. The five men became a squadron and the two discharged pistols became ten. The noble said, "I am Count Albrecht von Hepberg and I command here. The captain says you are a sword for hire. Where did you come from?"

He was more suspicious than the captain had been. I had fabricated a story in my mind that I hoped was plausible, "As you know, my lord, Cardinal Richelieu supports the Swedish king. I served in a French regiment and when I voiced my disapproval in the mess one night I was dishonourably dismissed. I have been a soldier all my life and if I could not fight for my country I could fight for my church."

The noble stood and came over to me. He pulled open my jacket and reached in to reveal my shirt. He saw the crucifix and nodded, "You appear to be telling the truth. I am afraid that we have no employment here but you can be of service. I will pay you and tomorrow I would have you cross the Danube and ride to Rain. There you will find Count Tilly. I will give you a message for him. Do this and there is a gold Reichstaler for you."

I stood straighter, "I would be honoured to do so for nothing, my lord."

He smiled for the first time, "No, you will earn the gold if you reach Count Tilly and thwart the Swedish king." He turned to the captain, "Take this man to the barracks and then he can dine with the garrison. I will send Christian with the message." The captain of the guard nodded. "He must leave before dawn and cross the river while it is still dark. Those English horsemen may still be there and watching."

"Yes, my lord, it shall be done.

The noble nodded, "And when you have delivered my missive to the count your service may be rewarded with a position in his army."

I was now seen as a friend and the captain was chatty as he led me to the barracks building. "I hope the Swedes do come here. We are not a large city but our walls are strong and the Danube means that we can survive any siege. Duke Maximilian has made it a fortress, albeit a small one."

"And where is the duke?"

"With Count Tilly. I think, my friend, that the count will snap up your offer of service. The Swedes have a larger army than we do and until the Duke of Friedland, Albrecht von Wallenstein, can bring his army we must defend."

I was welcomed into the barracks as though I was a hero. The sentries who had been on duty at the gate had added to the numbers of men I had evaded and I knew that the number would only grow as it was repeated. I felt a little guilty for I was deceiving these men who were both warm and friendly. I consoled myself with the fact that I would not be attacking them and what I did might save the lives of men I cared for more, my men.

The sealed letter was brought to me before I retired. It was in a leather case. It would keep it dry if it rained. I was told not to open it. I was taken to a dormitory and that night I enjoyed a bed. It was not a long sleep and the bells for Lauds woke me. The man sent to wake me smiled in the dark and whispered, "Good, you are up. There is some bread and ham and ale but you must be away quickly. It is the count's command."

"Of course." I was eager to be away. I knew that I had been lucky, thus far. I had fought many Germans but few Bavarians. This campaign promised to change that. Marcus had been treated well. The groom had given him oats and water as well as brushing his coat until it was gleaming. With the letter in my saddlebag I was led to the gate to the Danube. It was a wooden bridge and the sergeant who opened the gate said, "Walk your horse for I was told you had to leave quietly. The men at the far end of the bridge are expecting you."

"Thank you." I did as I was bid and when I reached the far end I mounted. I had to pretend, at least for a while, that I was heading for Rain. I knew that Rain controlled the crossing of the Danube. One problem I had was that as Rain was just twenty-five miles to the west of me, I had to cross the river again sooner rather than later. I headed down the road and as soon as I had passed the last building and before the sun rose I headed across the fields to the dark waters of the Danube. I would have to swim my horse. Marcus was a good swimmer but the Danube had a strong current. I found a place where I could see the northern bank. It looked to be less than one hundred paces wide and that was as narrow as I could have expected. The bridge at Ingolstadt had been two hundred paces wide. I let Marcus walk into the water and aimed him to swim diagonally north and west. The current would bring us further east. Once I felt him swim I kicked my feet from my stirrups and lay along his back. When his hooves found purchase I was just ten paces from the other bank and the sky to the east showed that dawn was on its way. I let Marcus shake himself dry and then headed to the woods. They were the same woods I had used the previous evening with

Jennings. I rode towards them and managed to reach them just as the first rays from the March sun splashed across the river.

I heard a movement ahead. My pistols would be useless and I drew my sword. Peter Jennings said, "Thank God you escaped, Sir."

I smiled and sheathed my sword, "I did not escape, Peter. I was sent forth with food and ale in my belly and a message for Count Tilly."

"Then he is not in Ingolstadt."

"No, he is twenty-five miles from here in Rain on the Lech. That is where we shall head."

The camp welcomed me although I think Sigismund was less than happy I had not only returned but done so promptly. "Break camp, we are heading west." I had already told Jennings what we intended and he was briefing his company so that they could lead the brigade. I went to the clothes I had left and changed from the wet ones I wore. I took off the crucifix and put it in my saddlebag and swapped my hats. Dick and Alexander stood by as I did so. We had no time to waste and I gave them the same information as I had Peter.

"The count is short of men. We could ride to meet the king and give him the news but I would rather go with accurate numbers."

Alexander said, "He will have left for Nuremberg already."

"He will be in that city before we reach it. This is the opportunity he has been waiting for. With von Wallenstein far from here Count Tilly is outnumbered."

We broke camp quickly and headed west. We followed the Danube to its confluence with the Lech at Marxheim. I had thought that the Danube would be the obstacle but it was clear that the Lech was an even sterner test. It was not one river but, I could see, that it was made up of many smaller streams and boggy ground. What I did see was a patch of bubbling water that suggested a ford or a part of the river that could be swum by horses. We headed for Donauwörth and as we did I could see that there were Imperial troops along the river and it looked to me as though Count Tilly had destroyed the bridge over the Lech. We reined in at Donauwörth. The view afforded from the back of my horse made it obvious that it was well defended. There were pikes and muskets there but the only artillery I saw were a couple of three pounders, falconets. We had been given the brief of scouting but I was tempted to lead my men and see if we could take the small town.

Jennings rode back to join us when we stopped. He had left half of his men to watch the road ahead. "How many men did you see?"

"No more than a hundred, Sir. They are guarding the bridge over the Danube."

"They saw you?"

He shook his head, "No, Sir."

Sigismund said, "Then we can take it!"

I turned to speak to Colonel Friedrich and I explained it to him as though he was a child, "Our one advantage is that the enemy does not know where we are. They have left the bridge intact and the one over the Lech is destroyed. We have not enough men to take the town and hold the bridge. We ride for Nuremberg. We have done what we were asked to do. We have found Count Tilly. I would not dream of spoiling the plans that reside in the head of the Lion of the North." The captain scowled in disappointment. He wanted glory.

We quickly found the main road north and headed along it. We managed the forty-five miles quickly. Our horses were not as tired as they might have been thanks to the longer rest they had enjoyed whilst waiting at Ingolstadt. King Gustavus had invested the city. There was a huge camp with an artillery park and horses were grazing on every piece of grass that could be found. As my men made their camp I was whisked to his side by a relieved looking Lieutenant Larsson.

"You have succeeded?"

I nodded, "Count Tilly is dug in on the Lech. He has destroyed the bridges and Donauwörth and the crossing of the Danube is guarded."

"The king will be pleased. The other brigade has yet to report but as you have found Count Tilly then it matters not."

It was just the senior generals and the Duke of Saxe-Weimar who were present when I reported. I handed over the letter I had been given. King Gustavus smiled, "You are a resourceful man,

Lieutenant Colonel, although some might say your action was reckless."

"A calculated risk and if I had not been fluent in French then I would not have taken it."

The king looked at his other leaders, "We garrison Nuremburg well. How many men does that leave us to take on Count Tilly?"

Gustav Horn had the information to hand, "Thirty-seven thousand men and seventy-two guns."

"Colonel, how many men does Tilly have?"

I sighed, "It would be a guess, King Gustavus. To ascertain numbers I would have had to reveal our presence. I can give you a figure but it was from the words of the men in the barracks at Ingolstadt."

General Torstensson said, "Often they give the most realistic figure."

"Give me an estimate, Colonel."

"No more than twenty thousand men and less than thirty pieces of artillery. He had to leave most of it at Bamberg when he fled."

"And at Donauwörth, did you see artillery?"

"A couple of regimental pieces that is all. There were no cavalry there. It was pikes and muskets that we saw."

"Then I have enough to plan. I thank you, Colonel. You may rejoin your men but by the morrow I want you and your brigade ready to scout. If the bridge over the Lech is destroyed then we need another way to cross that river. You and your men shall find it."

I saluted, "Sir." We made our way back out of the city and sought my standard. The two officers I had left with the baggage and the horses had chosen a good place. The camp, while we headed for a confrontation with County Tilly, would remain there. I would leave two companies to guard it and to act as replacements should we need them. The outcome of the battle, if there was a battle, would determine our line of march.

Sigismund's men were also camped close by, but as he had not left officers with them the carters had not chosen such a good site. His camp was prone to flooding. As we would soon be leaving it would only affect those at the camp. Tom looked pleased to see me and could not wait to tell me that our other horses were all in good condition. He took Marcus from me. "Get some clean clothes from the wagon, Tom, these will need washing."

"Yes, Colonel." As he went whistling off I saw the others in the camp smiling and waving at him.

Alistair Wilson came over. I said, "Any problems?"

"No, Colonel, it all went smoothly. We lost not a horse and having two companies meant we were mob handed." He looked at me, "We will be coming with you next time, Sir?" Although phrased as a question he was almost demanding that they come with us.

"You will although you missed nothing, Sergeant. We had no action to speak of. Your horses are rested and you will have enjoyed better rest."

"We would rather have been with you." He nodded towards Tom as he led Marcus to water, "He is a good 'un, Sir. He toils like a Trojan and never complains. The women have all taken to him and you know that is rare. If they don't like someone then they let them know."

I nodded. My wife had been right. Tom was a soul who could be redeemed. Ralph, Harry and Roger had been wrong. "Be ready to move soon; we are heading for Donauwörth. We have to winkle out the defenders before they can destroy the bridge, after that I am not sure. I will speak to the officers this evening after we have eaten."

His face broke into a wide smile, "And Davy Campbell has something special, Colonel. We found a wild pig in the woods. It was on its own. We managed to kill it without making a mess of the carcass. He has been waiting for your return to cook it. We will eat well tonight."

"Good."

I knew that this would be more than one meal. While we would enjoy roast wild pig the intestines and the guts would have been made into sausages that we would enjoy at another meal. The bones would be boiled up to make a soup that, with added greens and cereal, would keep those at the camp fed for a week. The bones would then be used to make tools or be carved into what rich men would call trinkets but we would call treasures.

The tents had been erected and I went to my tent where I stripped to my underwear. I called out, "Water, I wish to bathe." I knew that someone would hear me. It was Jane Brown, the common law wife of Paul White, who brought me the bucket of river water. She was not put out by the fact I was in my underwear. She had shared tents with up to eight men and had seen the bodies of more naked men than I had.

"Here you are, Colonel. I thought you might like to bathe so I brought some good soap and a freshly made swete bag. We passed some thyme and rosemary. It is too early for lavender."

She handed me a bar of soap and a cloth and placed the swete bag containing the sweet-smelling herbs on the bed. It was not the home-made soap my men and camp followers made. "Good soap, where did you get it from?"

She grinned, "If officers can't keep an eye on their possessions then they deserve to lose them. Some of those nobles who follow the king take too much on the road. I did them a favour by lightening the load of one of them."

"If you get caught you know…"

She laughed, "Lord, if I got caught by one of those preening princes then I should deserve to be hanged. Enjoy your bath, Colonel. When you are done leave the bucket and soap outside. I will collect them."

"Aren't you afraid that someone might take it?"

"From me? They know better than that, Colonel." As she opened the flap of the tent she said, "Ah, here is Tom, he can help you. He is a good lad, Colonel."

"I know, Jane."

I heard Tom call out, "Good day, Mistress Brown."

"And to you, Tom Wood. The colonel has water and soap."

He entered and said, "I will get you your clothes, Sir. When do you ride?"

"Probably tomorrow. I will take Ran this time but I had better have Anya in case I need a remount."

He began to lay out my clothes as I took off my underwear and prepared to clean the sweat and stink of horse from my body. "Will I be coming with you?"

I sighed, "Tom, I need you to guard the camp. I do not need a servant when I am fighting and the worry of what might happen to you might distract me. The women in the camp think well of you and I know that you can protect them." He nodded. I think he was beginning to understand his role.

I felt much better after I had washed, dried and donned clean clothes. I placed the swete bag Jane had brought beneath my breeches. I knew that the smell of horse would overcome the herbs within a few days but for now I smelled a little better.

The feast was a good one. I knew that the other camps would be envious as the smell of roasting wild pig drifted towards Nuremberg's walls. We still had ale and even some wine. We would not be leaving at dawn and I did not place any restrictions on my men. I knew they would not abuse the privilege. These were not the same men I had found fighting that cold New Year's Day a lifetime ago.

I did not drink too much for I had to brief the men. I think they all knew what we had to do but clarity was all. We had yet to receive our written orders but they would come. I was letting them know what lay ahead. When the food had finished and the troopers headed for their own campfires I sat at the improvised trestle table. "The king wants us to take Donauwörth. That means more than our brigade. I think that we will ride tomorrow but that does not mean immediate action. We will have to judge the moment we take the town well. We need the bridge."

Jennings said, "And then what?"

"Do you know, I have no idea. I doubt that it will be work for cavalry. General Torstensson has over seventy guns and he is a master of artillery. He may be able to pound them into a surrender."

Alexander Stirling shook his head, "When it comes down to it no matter how good the guns are men still have to cross the river. How will he do that without losing half his army?" My captain was right. It would not be us for we were scouts and not assault troops. The only solution that I could see was to build a pontoon bridge. Such a bridge built under fire would not be sturdy enough to be crossed by a large force of horses. They could be crossed by men but not cavalry.

We had just about finished when Sigismund and two of his officers joined us. "I wondered what the plan was, Colonel? I assume that we would be riding."

As I had already sent a message to that effect his statement was a little redundant. I shrugged, "We await precise orders from the king. We were discussing what might happen. The problem will not be the taking of Donauwörth, but what we do after."

"The king has said our brigade will take Donauwörth?"

I shook my head, "I am anticipating that as it was we who scouted it out that he will use us but I am as much in the dark as you are. All we know is that we must be ready."

One of the young officers, von Bulow, snapped, irritably, "We should know now!"

Sigismund flashed him an irritated look but said nothing. I said, "Lieutenant, the king is aware that there are spies in his camp. He does not wish an enemy to know what we plan too far in advance."

The young man coloured, "I hope you are not implying that I am a spy! I will not have my honour besmirched."

I stood as my officers began to murmur angrily. "Colonel Sigismund, take this whelp away from my camp before he learns about honour the hard way."

Sigismund was clearly embarrassed and he coloured, "Lieutenant von Bulow, return to the camp and remain silent." I think he realised he had gone too far. The other officer remained silent. Sigismund, however, could not let it go. "He used the wrong words, Colonel, but the young man had a point. Are we not trusted?"

"Colonel, the reason for our delay in leaving Mainz was that the news of the passage of the powder and ball was known to the enemy. Do you think that the king told the Spanish of the ship or was it more likely that someone in our camp told the Spanish? The honour of no man in either of our regiments has been besmirched. The king is being careful and I applaud that."

He bowed and the two left.

Dick Dickson shook his head, "Jumped up little cockerel. He needs a good hiding."

Alexander Stirling put his arm around his friend, "Dick, they are nobles and so inbred that their brains are addled. I thank God that we have officers like the colonel here who know their business. Do not worry about the Brandenburgers. We don't need them."

I said nothing. He was right but the king had decided to brigade us with them and that meant we had to work with them.

Sadly the interruption meant that the night ended on a sour note. We had all been happy and the mood had been a good one. As Tom prepared my bed he said, "You know, Colonel, I know that Colonel Friedrich is a friend of yours but those Brandenburgers are an unpleasant lot. When we were waiting to leave Mainz they caused more trouble than enough. I think that if we hadn't had the two sergeants there might have been violence." He lowered his voice, "They have no respect for women, Sir."

I nodded, "I wouldn't worry about the women, Tom. If they tried anything with Jane or the others I shudder to think what they might do to them but you are right to tell me. I am not sure how long we will be away but you, Konrad, and the older troopers will have to guard the camp while we are away."

His back straightened, "Don't you worry, Sir. I know how to deal with the likes of them!"

I knew he did and I nodded, "Good."

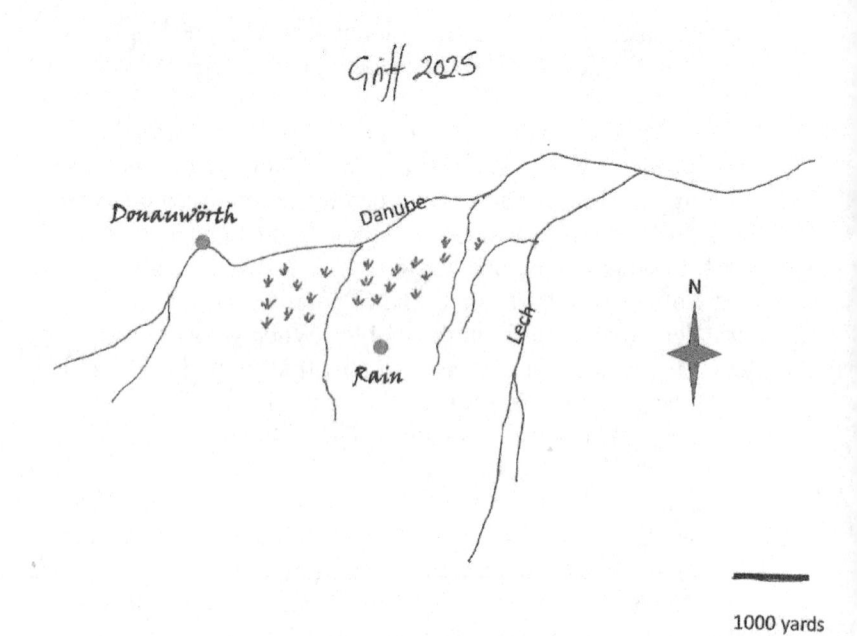

Rain 1632

Chapter 13

Rain, April 1632

The king must have had men up all night copying out his orders for they arrived as we breakfasted. I read them as I ate ham warmed on the fire from the night guards on yesterday's bread, now toasted and covered in butter. Both the order and the food satisfied me. The two brigades of light cavalry were to proceed to Donauwörth. We were to secrete ourselves by the river and when it was dark ensure that the bridge was in our hands. We had to have the bridge held by dawn. The main attack on the town would come the following day. It would take the foot soldiers all day to get into position.

I waved over Tom, "Saddle Anya, I need to speak with Lieutenant Colonel Stålhandske."

"Sir, do you need me with you?"

"No, I won't be long." I handed the orders to Captain Stirling. "When you have read them take them to Colonel Friedrich. We will have an officers' call on my return. I shall not be long."

I reached the Finnish camp and Lieutenant Colonel Stålhandske was reading the orders. I dismounted and he said, "You and I, it seems, are to be used to pick the Imperial lock."

I nodded, "How do you want to do this?"

"How good are your men and horses at swimming?"

"Fairly good." I was not sure about Sigismund's but my men were adept swimmers.

"Mine are not. I thought that if you and your brigade cross the river then they could take the Rain side of the bridge and my brigade the Donauwörth side."

Although we would have the harder task of crossing the river we would have, for once, the easier fight to take the handful of guards who would be at the safer end of the bridge. I nodded and shook his hand.

He grinned, "You and I have good men, Colonel, they can be wild but they get the job done. The king needs such men."

I mounted Anya and rode back. It was a good plan but it required us to move fast and find a good crossing in daylight. It would have to be far enough north of the bridge to avoid detection. I had maps but they were not detailed enough for this part of the world. I would have to rely on my Hunting Dogs once more.

The officers were all there when I arrived and I was succinct, "You have read the orders and Lieutenant Colonel Stålhandske and I have come up with a plan. We are to take the bridge on the Lech side of the Danube. That means a river crossing."

I looked at Lieutenant Jennings who nodded, "There is one, Sir, not far from the confluence of the Lech. The land on the other side, though, looks to be marshy and boggy."

"Good, for that means no people. We will be in position soon after dark and we take the end of the bridge. All that we have to do is to hold it." I looked at the faces and saw no dissenting ones. The Brandenburger officers looked, in the main, sullen but no one objected. "We ride in half an hour."

When the Brandenburgers had gone I said, "Corporal Summerville, rest your men here for the day and ride tomorrow. Bring twenty remounts with you."

While clearly disappointed he did not object, "Sir."

When we were on the road Captain Stirling said, "Why did you order Summerville to stay?"

He was not questioning the order but seeking the reasoning behind it. "The bridges over the Lech are destroyed and by the time we are in a position to assault, Count Tilly will have done his best to make the crossing difficult. King Gustavus does not waste men and I think that when we take Donauwörth the cavalry will be riding more than is good for the horses. Bringing remounts today would be of no use."

"Thank you, Sir, I knew there would be a good reason behind it. I am still learning."

With Jennings ahead I could relax a little and so I opened up to the Scotsman, "You should know, Alexander, that when we defeat Tilly and this war is over I intend to give up the sword and return to the bosom of my family."

He shot me a look of surprise, "Really, Sir?"

"That is why I want you to ask as many questions as you can. When I leave then Bretherton's Horse will be yours to command."

He shook his head, "I am not sure I am ready for such a command."

"It is not that hard. The king gives his orders and we interpret them. Besides, if the war is over then Bretherton's Horse may need a new employer."

"You think that this war will be over soon, then?"

"I think that now is our best chance. We outnumber Count Tilly and thanks to the king's decisions we have split the Imperial Army. One more major battle like Breitenfeld will see the empire sue for peace."

We rode in silence for a while, "Then without a war what would we do?"

"Oh, there will be a war. I began to fight in this war to stop the empire destroying the Protestant Cause in Germany. When that is over I will go home but the French, they want this war for a different purpose. Cardinal Richelieu seeks to replace a German empire with a French one. Really, we are fighting for France now. It is French livres in our purses. When King Gustavus goes home then the French will take up where he left off and with a battered empire he will soon prevail. He will employ the regiment."

"I am not sure that the men would like that."

"That is for the future and I am just making things clear for when I leave I do not want you to think I am abandoning the regiment."

"It will be strange to have the regiment without you at its head."

I laughed, "It is just April and this war has some way to go. First, we defeat Count Tilly and then von Wallenstein."

We did not follow the main road south as the Finns were. We used smaller roads and passed through forests as Jennings used both his nose and his natural skills to guide us to the Danube. We paused at noon for refreshment and to give our mounts some rest. We did so in a wood where we would not be seen but, in truth, we saw few people and as we saw not a single horse then word of our presence would remain a secret.

We were not seeking a ford, I knew there would not be one, we were looking for a narrow part of the river where my regiment could do as I had done when I had left Ingolstadt. We would swim the river. Of course, it would mean that until they were dried out our firearms would be of little use but as this would be a night attack then silence was imperative.

The place Jennings discovered was where a small stream joined the Danube. There was a farm at the confluence of the stream and the mighty river but the inhabitants wisely hid. The crossing of the Danube was just fifty paces wide. As the river and its tributaries joined the Lech not far from where we crossed then the current was sluggish. It would test the swimming ability of our regiments. Bretherton's Horse were all confident riders and swimmers but half of Sigismund's Brandenburgers were not. It helped my decision.

"Colonel Friedrich, take your non-swimmers and ride down the Donauwörth side of the river. If Lieutenant Colonel Stålhandske needs help then you can support him. I will lead your swimmers with me."

"Sir, I object to the orders, I should lead my own men."

"And if you come with me have you an officer who can command the others? Lieutenant Bulow for instance?"

He shook his head and nudged his horse closer to mine, "When this battle is over I will speak to the king. I wish to command my own men and not have to serve another."

I said, just as quietly, "And that is your right, Colonel. I am just obeying orders."

He rode back to his men. I put the spat from my mind. I could not afford to have my judgement clouded. If we failed then the bridge would be destroyed and King Gustavus would have another headache.

Jennings led and we waited until he and his men were in skirmish order on the other side before the rest of us crossed. One Brandenburger fell from his horse but Lieutenant Dickson rode his horse through the water to pluck the spluttering man from a watery end. We all adjusted our girths and then, after waving farewell to the rest of the brigade across the river, we walked our horses through the late afternoon. There was no point in reaching the bridge before dark and walking horsemen were harder to see than those who were mounted. Darkness had fallen and, by my estimate and the sound of church bells from the distant Rain, I guessed it was about nine of the clock. There was another reason we walked the seven and a half miles to the bridge. The land was riven with streams and bogs. Jennings had the knack of choosing the right path but we moved slowly across the land. As we did we could smell the woodfires from the braziers on the bridge. I knew that we were still almost a mile from our target. Taking Captain Stirling and my colour party with me I moved through the rear of the Hunting Dogs and when I reached Jennings I held up my hand. The snaking column of men stopped. We spoke quietly for sound travelled at night. "Lieutenant, choose your ten best men. You and I will scout out the bridge. We will do so on foot." He nodded and went to pick the men. "Captain, have men lead our horses. Wait fifteen minutes or so and then come but very slowly. We are a large body of men and noise travels." We had no means of measuring time except by counting but Alexander would judge the moment. I trusted him.

"You take risks, Sir."

"We are working in the dark and as good as Peter is, this needs my mind."

"Sir."

I handed my reins to Murphy. He would not be using his trumpet. I slipped off my cloak and hung it over Ran's back. I took my hat and tied it to the saddle. That done I joined Peter. Half a mile from the bridge we found an unforeseen obstacle. There was a stream barring our progress. We later learned it was called the Zusam. Once more Jennings' nose helped us to overcome the hidden obstacle. He found a small piece of dry land in the middle of the stream. There the water was shallow enough to wade. We had just ten paces to the dry land and then another eight to reach the far side where we could see the glow of the braziers of the night guards. Once across the stream, and hidden by bushes and scrubby trees, we drew our weapons. Jennings had got us here but now it was my turn to lead. I went to the fore with my sword in hand. Jennings and his ten men spread out behind me. We moved silently. A distant church bell tolled. It was midnight. The squelchy marshy land was behind us and the ground leading to the bridge was firmer. The going was easier and there were no slurping sounds. I could hear the guards talking. The Bavarian accent and language meant I could not clearly make out what they were saying but I guessed it was the same conversation night guards in any army had. They would be bemoaning that they had been chosen for the duty. They would complain about the officers and the food. They would chat about a leave and the doxies in the next town. What they would not be expecting would be mercenaries sneaking up from what they thought was the safe side of the river. We spread out and watched from behind some barrels that had been stacked there. I wondered if they were part of the defences. It did not matter yet but when dawn came it would be the time to investigate.

I knew that the lieutenant would be doing the same as I was and counting the men who were on watch. There were eight of them. One was dozing and I guessed that he was the one in command. Two of them stood watching the river to the east and west. That also made sense. The northern end of the bridge was guarded by men from the garrison and Count Tilly was in Rain. The others were huddled around the brazier. Two of them were smoking pipes and two were drinking from a jug.

I looked at Jennings and gave the signal to wait. Precipitous noise could be disastrous. The Brandenburgers' mistake at the cuirassier camp was still raw in our mind. The noise that came was not as alarming but just after they had switched the men watching the river there was a splash from the Donauwörth side of the river. In the grand scheme of things it was nothing but as the watch had just been changed the two men were more alert and they woke the sleeping officer. I nodded to Jennings and he and his men rose like wraiths. The attention of the eight men was on the other side of the river whence emanated the splash. We had our swords pressed into the backs of the sentries before they knew and I said, "Keep your hands from your weapons and remain silent and you will live. One false move or a noise of any kind and you die."

The officer, who was still dozy from his nap, nodded and they took their hands from their weapons. I did not need to say a word to my men who took their weapons and then, taking cords from their belts fastened the men's hands behind them. Captain Stirling and our men ghosted up from the dark. We could now speak albeit quietly. The guards had been speaking and those on the other end of the bridge would not be alarmed.

Murphy handed me my hat and cloak as I said to the captain, "Send the Wildcat Company to watch the Lech. I need to know what the land is like and have the Fox Company head downstream. We might as well know how the land is there."

He nodded and said, "No trouble then?"

I smiled, "Wet breeks was about the extent of the trouble."

I went to the barrels and taking my dagger prised open the lid. Inside lay black gold: powder. I nodded as I replaced it, "We came just in time. I think these were planned to be used to demolish the bridge."

Captain Stirling said, "I will get the lads to fill their powder horns before it is taken by General Torstensson for his guns." One thing my men always took were spare powder horns and the bounty we had found would keep us supplied for some time.

The next hours until dawn were nerve wracking. I hoped that the Finns had succeeded too but if they had not then we were isolated. The single splash we had heard was the only sound to disturb the night. As the sky became lighter I said, "I shall walk over."

"Are you sure?"

"We have to be certain that the northern end is in our hands."

I walked over the wooden bridge. I was gambling that sentries must cross the bridge at some time. As I neared the middle I saw a figure move from the other end. I kept moving. To my relief as the sun rose behind me I recognised that it was Lieutenant Colonel Stålhandske. He held out his hand as I approached, "Good to see you, Colonel."

"And you. We heard a splash in the night."

He nodded, "One of the Brandenburgers fell into the river. Luckily we had the bridge in our hands." His face creased into an evil looking smile, "The guards had their throats cut. My Finns are good at that sort of thing. How about you?"

"The splash helped us. Their attention was diverted and we took them prisoners. We also found powder. They were going to blow the bridge."

"And now we wait for the king. Good luck."

"And to you."

When I reached the other side of the bridge the land around the Lech was bathed in light. I could see the defenders on the

Imperial side of the Lech staring from a newly built redout. We had been seen but because they had destroyed the bridge all that they could do was watch us. I could not see them wasting ball and powder on a small brigade of cavalry.

"Captain Stirling, have the horses attended to. Have the Hawk Company and the Brandenburgers form a skirmish line between us and the Lech. I don't think that they will try anything but let us take no chances."

"Sir."

"Sergeant Wilson, get some food on the go." I had seen the cooking pot used by the sentries. It was well away from the powder.

"Sir."

That done we waited. King Gustavus arrived just after the bell for Sext had sounded from Rain. I realised he must have made his march in the night. I knew of his arrival when we heard guns firing. Lieutenant Colonel Stålhandske and his men would have had a better view than we did. We heard the cannons, the harquebuses and the shouts. When we could hear the distinctive sound of blades clashing we knew that the assault had begun and, eventually, when the Bavarian flag was lowered then we knew we had won. We had taken Donauwörth and the bridge. It was not a major victory but it opened the door for one.

With the bridge in our hands the king wasted no time and the army rolled across it. By the next morning we were marching the few miles to the banks of the Lech and the town of Rain. Having taken Donauwörth so easily the king was full of enthusiasm. I was sent north to scout out the crossings of the Lech downstream and the Finns were sent in the direction of Augsburg where, it was rumoured, there was another bridge. We knew that we would not be used in the assault. That was the work of infantry but first the redoubt that had been built needed to be reduced. It took three days for the guns and men to be brought over and for the engineers to build the redoubts that would assault the enemy defences.

It took us just two days to find a ford where we could cross the river and the many streams that made up the Lech. It would be a damp passage and infantry could not use it but we had found what the king had asked us to. I was there when

Lieutenant Colonel Stålhandske reported even better news. "King Gustavus, we have found an island in the middle of the Lech."

"An island?"

"Yes, King Gustavus. My men and I easily crossed to the island."

"I will come with you to inspect it." He sent for generals Torstensson and Johan Banér. He waved at me, "Come with us, Lieutenant Colonel Bretherton." He rode, with the Finn and with me and Lieutenant Larsson to inspect the island. The Duke of Saxe-Weimar and his brother Bernhard enjoyed the command of the whole army in our absence. The king knew how to use his allies. The German and his entourage rode up and down the lines marshalling men into position for an assault on Rain once the redoubt was subdued. Every Imperial eye was upon him and our small party was able to slip surreptitiously away. The island was about three miles from the town and, to the king's delight could not be seen from Rain's walls. He smacked one hand into the palm of the other, "This is where we have him. This is Tilly's Achilles heel. General Torstensson, could you build two pontoons of boats here?"

"We would have to find them, King Gustavus, but yes."

"Then this is my plan. We gather the boats and when we have them we build, under cover of darkness, two bridges. Lieutenant Colonel Stålhandske, you and your brigade, along with the Hastger Infantry Regiment, will cross the river and build earthworks to defend the crossing. I will make the count believe that when our artillery batters his redoubt we intend to cross there but, in reality, we will use this to bring our pikes and muskets to attack Rain." He turned to me, "Lieutenant Colonel Bretherton, could cavalry cross the ford you discovered?"

"I think so."

"Then, General Banér, I want you to lead two thousand cavalry to attack the rear of the redoubt. Lieutenant Colonel Bretherton will lead you to the right place. We fix Tilly's eyes on our seventy-two guns and then attack on two sides. We use our superior numbers to crush him."

Lieutenant Larsson said, "Do not forget General von Wallenstein. King Gustavus, the last reports we had was that he had almost subdued Saxony."

"I know, I know and that is why I want to take Bavaria. When that is secure we head north and finish off von Wallenstein. With God's help we will have our final victory and the Spanish will be forced to sue for peace and give up their dreams of a Catholic Empire from the Baltic to the Mediterranean."

We changed from scouting for food and river crossings to the gathering and fetching of boats. It took some days and each time we found a boat it was taken to be guarded by the Finns of the Hastger regiment. The king and his engineer planned to build the bridge in one night. I also spent some time each day with General Banér. He rode with me to inspect the ford and then chose his horsemen. He would be leading the whole division of cavalry but we would fight in brigades. My regiment was the only English one with the king. Colonels Munro and Lang were at Nuremburg. The bulk of the Scottish and English regiments were with the Duke of Hamilton and General Leslie in Saxony. General Banér chose mainly Swedish regiments and a few German ones. Colonel Friedrich was pleased that his regiment was chosen. I knew, from my conversations with General Banér, that it was only because he was part of my brigade that he had been picked to participate. His men had almost cost the Finns the chance to take the bridge and whilst I had said nothing his men's mistake with the cuirassiers had reached the ears of the Swedish general. I knew that this was Sigismund's last chance to redeem himself. If he did not impress in this action then his regiment would be reduced to escorting the supply wagons that would be increasingly necessary.

By the middle of April we were ready and the seventy-two guns began to bombard the redoubt. Count Tilly had built well and I knew that it would be slow work. Our regiments, lined up on the banks of the Lech cheered each time a ball smashed some of the wooden and soil defences. I knew that it was a feint but we had to keep it up to convince Count Tilly that King Gustavus was going to try to batter them into submission. The reality was that with the news of von Wallenstein's success in Saxony we had no time to waste on a long siege. The sixty-five thousand men that would be able to come to the aid of Count Tilly would outnumber us. The boats were continued to be gathered and the Finns at the river remained hidden.

It was on the fifteenth that the order was given. King Gustavus went with Lieutenant Colonel Stålhandske and his Finns to supervise the building of the bridges and the earthworks to defend the bridgehead. General Horn and the Duke of Saxe-Weimar were ready to lead the army the three miles south and cross the bridges as soon as the order was given. We waited, a mile or so to the north. I was just glad that we would be one of the first to cross the ford. That had been decided by the general on the basis that we knew the crossing best. The last regiments would have to cross a muddy morass. We waited for the rider who would race from the pontoon bridge to let us know that we could begin our attack.

I sat with my colour party, Captain Stirling and Lieutenant Jennings. Alexander said, "How does the king come up with such outrageous plans, Colonel? If this works then he must be the greatest general in history."

I nodded, "That is my view already for he seems to see war in a different way from other men. It helps that he surrounds himself with good leaders." I nodded towards General Banér, "He is a case in point."

The guns from our side of the river kept up a monotonous barrage. That we were winning the duel was clear because the return fire became more erratic. The rider who brought the message rode directly to General Banér. The Swedish general turned to me and waved his sword. Our horns and trumpets would be used to coordinate the charge. Crossing the river we would be vulnerable. My men spread out in a long skirmish line behind the Hunting Dogs. Some of the water we crossed merely came up to the hocks of our horses but, in places, it came up to our knees and thighs. The secret was to keep moving. We were far enough north for us to be out of sight of the walls of Rain. Tilly might have had a few small artillery pieces on the walls but nothing that could really hurt us. He had gambled and put his best artillery in his redoubt.

We knew when the king and the army had crossed the river and begun their attack on Rain. We heard the volleys as musketeers opened fire. We could not see it but when the clouds of smoke rose in the skies to the south we knew where the battle raged. When we were within half a mile of the rear of the redoubt we halted. We would no longer be at the fore. The general had his regiments of cuirassiers form regimental lines. We were a reserve at the rear. It made sense to me. The cuirassiers were armoured and rode massive horses. They would use cold steel. There was a regiment of lancers with them. Colonel Friedrich was less than happy to be relegated to the role of reserve. I suspect his young Brandenburgers had badgered him. It mattered not because he could not do anything about it. We would not be the ones who charged.

The horns sounded and General Banér led the charge. All that I could see were the backs of the horsemen before me but I could imagine the horror of the enemy who had been facing south and west being bombarded by our guns and now being attacked by King Gustavus and infantry. Suddenly, two thousand horsemen appeared at their rear. I did not see it but I heard the clash and clatter as the front ranks tore into the disorganised enemy. The Imperial Army was caught in a vice and attacked on two sides. The men who had crossed the pontoon bridge were infantry and with regiments like the Blue and Yellow, they were facing the best that we had. When the horns from the enemy sounded then victory was in sight. General Banér ordered us to reform and we were placed at the fore along with the other regiments who had not been involved in the attack. It was not before time for, as storm clouds appeared above us and rain began to fall the Duke of Bavaria sent in the only troops he had left, his cavalry. General von Scharffenstein led eight regiments to slow us down and allow the remnants of the Bavarian army to escape. These were cuirassiers and the torrential rain rendered the matchlocks of many of our men useless. My wheellocks could still fire but I would not be able to reload.

Murphy sounded the charge and we charged the cuirassiers. They were brave men and they rode fresher horses. The Brandenburgers were next to us and the command had been to ride in two lines and hit them simultaneously. Sigismund's lack of control became clear as they raced ahead of us and they did not use their firearms. Instead, they used their swords. They fought well but it was my men who halted at my command and those who could discharged their weapons. The fifty or so wheellocks made a hole in the enemy line and when I had Murphy sound the charge with swords drawn we were able to punch a hole in the enemy line of horsemen. The rain, the smoke and the confused nature of battle meant that it was hard to see exactly what was happening. Men just fought the enemy with the red sashes who were before us. It was a battle of swords and horses.

I suppose that we might have been able to defeat the enemy cavalry for our own cuirassiers now joined the battle. However, nature, in the form of a storm of Biblical proportions, came to the aid of the Imperial Army. The rain was now so intense that you could not see your hand before your face. Our firearms were rendered useless and, when the enemy sounded the retreat, they were able to extricate themselves on fresher horses as the mask of rain was driven into our faces by a wild wind. The churned-up ground and the bodies of the dead prevented an effective pursuit. We had won and taken the town, the enemy baggage and guns, but seven thousand of the enemy army had escaped.

Chapter 14

Munich May 1632
We had lost the chance to capture the Bavarian army but we learned that Count Tilly had been badly wounded in the battle, and even better news for the Protestant cause was to come. We learned that he had died of his wounds two weeks later. We had attacked, the day we heard the news, Ingolstadt which the Duke of Bavaria held. We did not besiege it. A siege was costly and besiegers risked disease and desertions. Instead, as we were in Bavaria, the king gave us permission to ravage the land around Ingolstadt which we duly did and Maximilian gave up Ingolstadt, withdrawing north of the Danube to await the arrival of the last Imperial Army led by Albrecht von Wallenstein. We took Augsburg in the last week of April where we were welcomed as the saviours of Protestantism. On the seventeenth of May we made a triumphal entry into the Bavarian capital, Munich. We took the treasury, the ducal art collection and one hundred guns without firing a shot. Of course, it had not all gone as well as we might have hoped. When we had approached Ingolstadt King Gustavus had gone too close to the walls and had a horse shot from under him. He was rescued by Lieutenant Larsson as most of the other aides, including my nemesis the German prince, had fled. Now, however, we had Bavaria and Duke Maximilian was no longer a threat.

As June approached I was summoned to a meeting in the Rathaus. All the officers were senior figures and I knew that it was an important one. As usual the king was with his senior officers and generals but there was a new one. Duke William of Saxe-Weimar was no longer with us. He claimed ill health but I believed he had not enjoyed enough glory. His men were now led by his younger brother, the eleventh son of Duke Johan of Saxe-Weimar, Bernhard. I knew that he was popular with the German soldiers and it explained his inclusion with the senior officers. It still galled me that the popinjays, as Alexander Stirling called them, still strutted behind the king as though they were responsible for our victories.

The king's face was grave and that was a warning. "Von Wallenstein has taken Prague and is heading for Bavaria." There was an audible gasp for he had an army of sixty-five thousand, or so it was rumoured. "Chancellor Axel Oxenstierna is heading with a relief force to Nuremberg."

I frowned. Our camp followers and remounts were at Nuremberg. It had not been deemed safe enough to bring them into Bavaria but with the Imperial Army heading for Nuremberg, they were in danger.

"I intend to leave a garrison here as well as at Ingolstadt. The rest of the army will march to Nuremberg where I hope to face von Wallenstein and end this bloody conflict once and for all."

There was a buzz of conversation. Who would be left here and at Ingolstadt and who sent to Nuremberg? I wanted to be with the king for Tom and our camp were there.

"Lieutenant Larsson has your orders of march. The designated garrison troops are also marked." The king looked tired. The euphoria of Rain and the death of Count Tilly had evaporated.

I took my orders and opened them. I was relieved to see that I was to go to Nuremberg. More importantly I was part of the cavalry element that would ensure that the ford at Fürth was in our hands. Sigismund, however, was commanded to be the cavalry element of the garrison. I knew he would be happy about that situation. He would enjoy the freedom of command. The infantry elements would guard the city but his Brandenburgers had licence to roam and raid. I was proved right. I did feel guilty for he thanked me as though this was my idea.

When I told my officers the situation then they were immediately concerned. Many had left their treasure at the camp for we trusted our people and the thought that the Imperial troops might have taken the camp was more than disturbing. They were all happy that we would not be tied to the army and would have the freedom to head north freed from the shackles of infantry and guns. General Banér was to command and we had our friends the Finns with us. We left on the first day of June.

I was keen to ride hard. Each day we delayed meant it more likely that our camp might be taken. The general kept a steady pace. Now that we were no longer brigaded with the

Brandenburgers our regiment felt closer. There had always been friction between the two regiments. The reason it had not ignited into violence was because of my officers. I was disappointed that Sigismund had backed off and not tried to help my officers. The Brandenburgers had learned that Captain Stirling and Lieutenant Dickson could use their fists as well as any trooper.

When we reached Nuremberg I was relieved to see that our camp was still standing. While the general went to speak to the commander of the garrison we went directly to the camp. It was still standing but that did not mean everyone was well. It was not until we saw the horse herd intact and the smiling faces of Tom, the women and the old troopers left to guard the camp that we relaxed.

Tom looked to have changed. It had been some time since I had seen him. I later learned that he had virtually run the camp. When some deserters had come to the camp it was Tom who had led the defence and accounted for four dead Imperial deserters before driving off the others. The women could not speak highly enough of the man who had been a bandit and come within a hair's breadth of being hanged. Charlotte had been proved right again.

"It was good that I was here, Colonel, but my place is by your side."

"Perhaps you are right, Tom, we shall see."

The decision was taken by the general to destroy Fürth. We galloped in one morning and drove out the small garrison of Bavarians who held it. The general then ordered the people to leave. It was not a cruel order. He intended to burn the town and thereby end the threat to Nuremberg. It was none too soon for we had news that von Wallenstein had taken Bohemia and was bringing thirty thousand men to join Duke Maximilian. The battle that King Gustavus sought looked to be imminent.

Having done what we had been ordered, the general allowed us some time in the camp while we awaited the arrival of the rest of the army. We were given the relatively light duty of scouting the land around the ford. It was as we did so that I discovered, close to the Regnitz and overlooking the ford, the ancient and deserted fort called by the locals Alte Veste, the old fort. We stopped to rest our horses on the top of its half-ruined walls. I realised that it was a good thing that the Imperialists had not fortified it or else we would have struggled to take it. That evening I rode into Nuremburg to tell the general about it.

"Well observed, Colonel. When the king arrives I will tell him."

"When is he expected, Sir?"

"He is ensuring that all the places we have taken are garrisoned. I expect him by the first week in July."

That was good news for us. It gave us time to hunt in the forests and to raid the Catholic lands and take animals and food. My men were also anticipating, when the Swedish chancellor arrived, the next pay. They had spent their last pay when we had reached Nuremberg. Mine lay in the chest. That gold and silver was for Charlotte, my son and a new child who would be born before I reached England.

We also found new recruits. We had lost men in the battle of Rain. There were not many but any loss was a serious one. In addition, some of the older soldiers had succumbed to illness. Forty was not old unless you were a soldier. Many had lead in their bodies. The king himself had a piece of lead in his shoulder, courtesy of a Polish sniper. Lead could be deadly. Other soldiers had not looked after themselves as well as they should and drink, tobacco, and whores accounted for some. That we had no desertions was a source of pride. I let my two senior officers vet the new men. I was the colonel but Bretherton's Horse was as much their regiment as it was mine. I would, I hoped, be leaving in October or November although I had the sneaking suspicion that the war might not be over by then. Count Tilly had been an aggressive leader but Albrecht von Wallenstein seemed to be more defensively minded and the rumour was that he would avoid a battle unless he had superior numbers.

The king arrived and the peace of a cavalry camp was shattered as the infantry regiments and the artillery rolled in. The garrisons we had left meant that we had fewer men with the king and we were awaiting the Swedish chancellor with much needed reinforcements. It was rumoured that the survivors of the men brought over all those years ago by the Duke of Hamilton and General Leslie had been brigaded into one unit and we would no longer be the only Anglo Scottish regiment. Colonel Munro and Colonel Lang's regiments were now garrisoning our conquests.

The king seemed to be distracted or out of sorts. By his high standards he was almost indolent. He did nothing about the Alte Veste. He changed, however, when the Imperialist Army arrived. General Horn had realised that the king was not himself and he initiated patrols. My regiment were not line cavalry but the general knew us to be scouts par excellence and we were given the hardest land to watch. The land was riven by rivers and streams. We were given the area due south of Nuremburg. We used a two-company system to cover as much land as we could and I was with the Hawk Company and the Fox Company as we headed for the confluence of the Regnitz and the Schwarzach rivers. Neither was a particularly big river. Both were nuisances. We stopped to water our horses and it was sharp eyed Sergeant Davy Campbell who spotted the enemy horsemen. What we had noticed about von Wallenstein was that he liked to make his men look different from us. His officers all wore red scarves and his men red sashes. We saw the flashes of red. They were to the southwest and clearly not cuirassiers for there was no sunlight glinting from either helmets or breastplates. We immediately primed pistols and I had the men stand to. It soon became clear that they were Croats. I recognised the red heavy coats and the fur lined hats. As they drew near I saw that they had an Imperial standard. It was a whole regiment and I estimated that there were more than two hundred and fifty of them.

"What do we do, Sir?" Sergeant Campbell was solid and dependable. He was not afraid of the numbers. Our horses were in peak condition thanks to the time we had spent at the camp before the arrival of the king.

"Our job is to scout and let us do that. These may be the head of a column or they might be like us, scouts." Croatian cavalrymen tended to be aggressive. I think that was why the enemy used them. Often just their presence inspired fear and flight in our men, especially the Saxons. "Make sure your weapons are ready."

Most of my men now had, in addition to their pistol, a harquebus, courtesy of the battle of Rain. Normally, they would be used whilst dismounted but the back of a stationery horse was almost as good, at least for my men. The small river was just eleven or so paces wide. The recent rains, however, had muddied the banks and we had moved to more solid ground when the Croats had been spotted. I waited to see what they would do. One of the Fox Company troopers, Nosey Nesbitt, who was named for his huge misshapen nose which had resulted from a fight as a youth, shouted, "Sir, cuirassiers and infantry." He pointed south. This was the army.

I was about to give the order to fall back when an order was shouted in Croatian. We had been spotted. Half of the enemy horsemen dug their heels in their horses. I gave the only command I could, "Fire!"

I had six pistols and I picked up two and fired. The target was a mass of men and aiming was unnecessary. I holstered them and then drew two more. There was a pall of stinking smoke before us. My men fired their second weapon and then I heard their swords as they were drawn. I fired my last two pistols at the red coated Croats who appeared before me. They were thrown from their saddles. "Fall back." The command was easy to give but less so to obey. We were aided by the bank we had muddied when we had watered our horses. We had emptied thirty saddles and the riderless horses milled around. It slowed the others and they struggled to get up the bank. One officer made it and he swung his war hammer at me. Had he connected then I would have been a dead man but my sword was longer than his hammer and I slashed across his arm, my sword biting through to the bone.

Sergeant Campbell shouted, "Move it, Sir!"

I realised that I was the only one left, the rest having obeyed my orders and I wheeled Marcus around as Sergeant Campbell fired his last pistol at the Croat who had spotted the target of my inviting back. His body fell into the river. We galloped hard and after a mile I turned and saw that they had given up the chase.

The news energised the king. The enemy was coming and that meant he could have his battle. He was also encouraged by the news that the Swedish chancellor was bringing reinforcements. The loss of Bohemia meant that there were men who could bolster our numbers and ensure that we were supplied. We had captured one hundred guns at Munich but we did not have enough powder. Supply was always a problem. The reinforcements could guard the wagons that brought it. The news that the Imperial Army was heading for Schwabach also made us move our camp to the eastern side of Nuremberg. Our camp lay on the route the cavalry took each day as they rode to watch them and when we went to face them in battle then all peace would be shattered. We had to shift our camp. The move took a couple of days and enabled us to assess the condition of both horses and saddles. A battle exposed weaknesses in both.

It was in the middle of July when our army was marched to Schwabach. Von Wallenstein had a good army and it was the same size as ours. This would be a good test but we were confident that King Gustavus would prevail. We drew up before them but they made no attempt to leave the walled city. We tried for a week to induce the Imperial Army to move but they refused battle. As we waited and attended daily officers' calls we debated the reason. In the end we decided that von Wallenstein did not have enough supplies and feared the Swedish king. When, in August, the king headed back to Nuremberg I had a different theory. In our new camp I sat with my dispirited officers. The whole regiment had wanted a battle. A battle meant the chance for loot as well as the potential end to this war. It had been many months since Rain and my men liked victory.

"I think that this Imperial general wishes to wait until winter. When King Gustavus retires to a winter camp then men will desert and it is then that they will take back the lands we have conquered." The thought depressed me for I would not be allowed home. King Gustavus was no fool and if that situation arose he would want his army and his officers close to hand.

When the Swedish chancellor arrived in late August we had more men and more supplies. We also had parity of numbers. We settled into a routine. We had one day every two weeks where we were the regiment watching the Imperialists in Schwabach. It was not an arduous duty but it was a necessary one. We had water from the river and we always chose a new camp from the one occupied by the regiment we had relieved. We were due to go on our second duty when the disastrous news came that the enemy had left Schawabach. The German regiment sent to watch the city had been lax and were not vigilant enough. They were part of the reinforcements brought by the Swedish chancellor. It was their second duty and they had, probably, expected the same boring twenty-four hours. They sent messengers back as they sought the enemy. The enemy could head back to Rain and recover it or even retake Munich. Another fear was that they could threaten our supply lines. Every regiment of horse was sent to find them and it was the Finns who did so. The wily Wallenstein had headed for Fürth. The deserted town was occupied and Alte Veste invested. We had an enemy within sight of Nuremberg. I was glad that we had moved our camp.

I had rarely seen the king angry but he was that day. Had the colonel of the regiment sent to watch the enemy been more vigilant then we could have caught the enemy on the road. The delay had enabled the Imperialists to dig trenches and to build redoubts and abatis. Even worse was the news that they were improving the abatis and defences during the long hours of August daylight. The king had General Torstensson move our guns so that they could be used when we attacked. The problem we had was that the old fortifications protected Fürth and the site was elevated. We had to take Alte Veste before we could use our guns to bombard Fürth.

The king challenged the enemy to battle. He did so by forming up our regiments in battle order but battle was refused. He even used the old-fashioned method of a personal challenge but von Wallenstein refused. As August ended and September approached, our army of almost forty-five thousand, not to mention the camp followers and others, began to run out of food. The local farms had all been raided and there were neither crops nor animals to be had. That the enemy was also suffering did not help. Von Wallenstein refused battle. We were beginning to starve and people were dying of disease. Worse, some soldiers, mainly Germans began to desert.

On the first of September we were summoned to meet with the king. He had devised a battle plan. He had been forced to do so by the enemy's refusal to fight us in open battle. I could see that General Torstensson was far from happy with the plan and the other generals also looked less than enthusiastic. When he explained it to us I could see why. He intended to make an assault on foot and take Alte Veste. That we had to take it before we could invest Fürth was clear but our strength lay in artillery and well used cavalry. It had brought us success. General Torstensson would be forced to use the smaller infantry artillery which could be used closer to the obstacles and that would endanger his gunners. Half of the cavalry were to fight dismounted. We were not one of those regiments. We, like the Finns, were light horsemen. We were to fight with the cavalry reserve. Once the old castle was taken and the enemy fled back to Fürth, then we would descend upon them. That part of the plan seemed to me sound. It was just the first part that would see many men slaughtered. Between the two camps the Imperials had forty-four thousand men.

The attack would take place on the third of September. As with any battle, the night before we fought saw men paying off old debts. It did not do to go into battle owing money. Others gave their coins to the ones who would stay in the camp. Our women were trusted. Tom was selected by many men, especially my officers, to guard their money. He was both honoured and annoyed for he had asked to come into battle at my side. He could not do so while he was the custodian of their treasure. It pleased me for many reasons. I wrote a letter to Charlotte and William. I had done the same before Rain and the other battles. The letters were never sent but Tom would keep it and if the worst happened and I died then he would take it, with my belongings and treasure, back to Piercebridge. It was not maudlin to do what I did. It was practical. I did not expect to die but a man who did not plan for his death invited it.

We rose early and said prayers before we ate. We always made peace with God. We were not Papists who confessed to a priest but we each spoke to God in our own way. After a good breakfast I rode, at the head of my men and mounted on Marcus, to the higher ground to the east of the Regnitz. The king already had his massed infantry battalions ready by the river. The enemy knew we were coming and would be ready. Linstocks would be smoking and weapons would be sharpened and to hand. Thirty-seven regiments, three hundred and six companies would make the attack and there were nine regiments of dismounted cavalry ready as a reserve. It looked impressive and I know that the king expected to win. I prayed that he was right.

Lion of the North

General Torstensson began the battle with a bombardment. The smaller artillery pieces he was using sounded too light to do much damage but he was a master gunner and I saw the balls crashing through the trees that had been used as an obstacle. After a bombardment which I thought was too short, the order was given to attack and the vaunted Swedish infantry began to march. Few men used pikes these days. They were too cumbersome. Many had cut down the long weapons to make a shorter weapon which could be easily wielded in a trench. Swords were popular but most men carried at least one pistol. The musketeers were the ones who might make a difference. They were well trained and disciplined. The problem they had was that the enemy battalions were not standing in lines before them as in a normal battle. They were in their trenches and behind abatis. The normal slaughter they inflicted did not manifest itself.

We had a good view of the battle for the wind took away the smoke after each volley and we were able to watch the painfully slow progress as the infantry tried to move up the slopes. We watched as the infantry attack was blunted. The battle had raged for five hours and we had barely claimed a fifth of the defences. King Gustavus ordered his reserves to attack. Bernhard of Saxe-Weimar led the dismounted infantry. I could see the logic behind this attack. Some of those attacking had breastplates, they were cuirassiers and they had more protection. We watched as our reserves moved through the retreating wounded and men returning for more ball and powder. There was disorder and that was the moment when the battle was lost, for von Wallenstein launched, from Fürth, his cavalry reserve. Even as we were ordered to go to the aid of our comrades I knew that it would be too late for some. The Imperial cavalry included lancers and Croats. They fell upon our dismounted horsemen and began the slaughter.

We were in the second rank behind some cuirassiers. My standard fluttered behind me and Murphy had the horn. Bretherton's Horse would join the charge that was the only hope for the men trapped on the slopes of Alte Veste. My men each rode with a pistol in their right hands. Once the cuirassiers were engaged I would lead my men to fire at the second enemy regiment. My men could use swords but the weapon that the enemy feared us using was the pistol along with the harquebus. We would send a wall of lead at the enemy. We heard the wail as the enemy horsemen fell amongst the men who were now trapped by abatis and trenches on one side and enemy horsemen on the other. The clash of steel as the cuirassiers hit was so loud as to be almost painful. We wheeled to the right and I shouted, "Halt!" The horn sounded and my men obeyed instantly. The Imperial dragoons who were before us were also armed with pistols but the difference was that we were ready to fire and they were not. They were moving and we were static. Even as their commanding officer ordered them to wheel I shouted, "Fire!" I discharged one pistol and even as the volley rippled down the line I had drawn a second and fired that one. I shouted, "Charge!" Saddles had been emptied and the lead balls had cleared a path through the enemy dragoons. When we charged and used our swords the dragoons who survived fled and allowed us to attack other horsemen in the rear. There is little glory in war despite what poets write. We slashed and stabbed at the backs of men who thought their rear was protected by a regiment of dragoons.

    It was little enough that we did but our attack forced the Imperial cavalry to turn and face us. When they came at us I had time to order a second volley. We sent another regimental volley and it was so unexpected and at such close range that even breastplates were no protection. The cuirassiers rode around us and when I heard the horns from King Gustavus sound the retreat we were able to fall back in good order. We had empty saddles but the cuirassiers who had gone before us had lost more men. We returned to the banks of the Regnitz and reloaded but the enemy had done enough. King Gustavus had lost. By dawn the next day the last survivors reached us and we had the butcher's bill. We had lost not only two thousand five hundred men but General Torstensson was amongst the prisoners taken. We had lost our master of the gun. Alte Veste was a disaster.

    We were the ones now on the defensive. More men deserted and this time some of them were the Swedes. None of my men did but every company had suffered losses. I was just pleased that none of my officers had died. Davy Campbell had a nasty wound to his left arm and Lieutenant Jennings had almost lost an eye and had a disfiguring scar on his face but he was philosophical about it. He was alive.

This was when we were at our lowest ebb and the king sent men to sue for peace. It was refused. By the second week in September we had lost almost ten thousand men to either disease or desertion and when General von Wallenstein broke camp to join Heinrich Holk in raiding Saxony we were forced to march north and follow him. If Saxony fell then we would lose our most important ally. We had lost Bohemia and the loss of Saxony was not to be contemplated. It was a dispirited army that left Nuremberg for the long march north. The march cost us more men as disease took some for whom the autumn rains were too much and for more men who chose to leave the army. As we trudged north, wrapped against the wind and the rain, I reflected that my dreams of a return home for Christmas lay in tatters. Spirits were so low that men spoke more of defeat than victory. I was a realist and knew that the king was still a good general. If he could raise more men then I believed we had a chance. My only surprise was that half of the young nobles who were his aides had stayed. Surprisingly the only German one to stay was Prince Francis Albert of Saxe-Lauenburg. He must have been promised land by the king for I had yet to see him use his sword in battle. I noticed, however, that he had added to his retinue and he had with him a huge man who would not have looked out of place guarding Isaac the Jew. He had eastern features and was clearly a bodyguard. It partly explained why he had not left with some of the other Saxon nobles.

It was in the middle of October, as we trudged up yet another road filled with mud and the detritus of an army moving ahead of us that Tom, who had taken to riding next to me, voiced what I knew in my heart but had kept hidden from my head. "We shall not be home for Christmas, Colonel."

I shook my head. I did not want to say the words. I said, "You could go. You could take my letter and the gold I have in the chest. There will be others from the regiment who wish to enjoy a life of peace."

He shook his head, "I will stay so long as you do, Colonel."

"War in winter is a miserable thing, Tom. More men will die in camp. It will be like Nuremberg all over again."

He was a cheerful and optimistic man, "Fewer of our men died from disease than other regiments and none deserted."

I nodded, "But there are men who have served as a mercenary for more than ten years, some fifteen. Even the best of them want to have a life back in England or Scotland. There is peace there."

"I will stay, Colonel. You cannot dissuade me."

I was secretly pleased. I would do my best to ensure that he came to no harm but I was happy with his company. He was not a friend, not in the true sense of the word, he was closer. He had been my chamberlain when we had stayed in inns. His tent guarded mine. He brought me all my food and helped to dress me for war. I needed Tom. My wife had shown foresight.

Chapter 15

We trailed behind the coat tails of the Imperial Army as it headed for Saxony. We were often the ones sniping at the rear of their baggage train. Von Wallenstein was heading for Leipzig for he wanted to close the bridges over the rivers and seal Saxony off from our army. It was depressing for the Imperial Army cut a swathe through the land and the grazing was poor. Food was scarce. We had more supplies than some other regiments, especially the infantry, for we had raided but belts had to be tightened.

We managed to have some success too. It was not the joy of a victory in battle but it resulted from my men's skill and courage. One late afternoon Lieutenant Jennings, with the sword wound to his face now blackening but still angry, reported that two of the enemy wagons were somewhat detached from the rest. We had followed them long enough to know that the men who guarded them were a company of musketeers and pikemen. There had been a squadron of cavalry but for the past three days they had been off foraging for food. The enemy were short of supplies too. The complacency that had been shown by our horseman at Schwabach was now displayed by our enemies. We had not attacked their rearguard and they saw no reason why we would now. We were close to the village of Schleiz and I knew that the head of the column would already be camping and cooking their evening meal. I made an instant decision. "Badger Company and Hawk Company, stay here. Captain Stirling, take your company and the Wildcats, head up the western side of the road. The rest of you follow me. We will attack from both sides. We will use swords. I do not want them to hear pistols." I turned, "Tom, stay here. You might get in the way." He did not like the order but he nodded his obedience.

I dug my heels into Ran and with drawn sword galloped off. We left the road and the earth of the fields that were adjacent to the road dampened the sound of our galloping hooves. The rumbling wagons would be making enough noise to cover the sound of our approach. Lieutenant Jennings was next to me and he pointed his sword at a gap in the trees. I followed his lead and we found ourselves cutting off a loop in the road. We could get ahead of them and surprise them even more. The wagons were being pulled by bullocks and it was a slow progress that the enemy was making. Men led them and the guards flanked each side. Once we neared the road I saw the men trudging next to the wagons. Their heads were down. They were weary, inattentive and just waiting for their beds and food. Everything that they did doomed them. They were not ready and did not expect to be attacked.

I reached the leading wagon of the two and saw that the main convoy of wagons had disappeared around a bend already. My men were right. The wagons were detached and could be taken. I wheeled Ran and pointed my sword at the wagons. My men copied and suddenly my four companies smashed into the side of the musketeers and pikemen. Captain Stirling had timed his approach well and his men slammed into the other side of the wagons. The musketeers had no time to prime their weapons. If they had been using harquebuses then they might have had a chance but a musket needed a stand and a linstock. The pikemen were just slow to bring their weapons around. More than half of the guards, along with the drivers, just ran. They tore up the road discarding their pikes as they fled. I had to use my pistol to fire at the officer who tried to rally his men. I disobeyed my own order but it seemed to work. I am not sure I hit him but when the smoke cleared from before me he and his horse were not there. I did not even have to bloody my sword for when I pointed it at the musketeer who still had his musket, he dropped the weapon to the ground and held his arms above his head. Murphy picked up the musket and nodded, "Empty, Sir. They had no time to load." It was over so quickly that I could scarce believe it. The single pistol shot might have alerted the enemy though.

We had eight prisoners and ten of the men who had protected the wagons lay dead. "Lieutenant Jennings, take your men and Fox Company. I want you to escort the wagons back to the column. The rest of you load and prime your weapons and form a skirmish line." My single shot might bring men to investigate and if they did we would be ready. We all knew that when the survivors from the rear reached the next wagons then retribution would follow. They would not want to lose two wagons. Sure enough, by the time we had all loaded our weapons and I sat with two primed pistols, we heard hooves as Imperial horsemen galloped down the road in a column of fours. I waited until they were twenty paces from us and then gave the command, "Fire!" Each of my men discharged a pistol or harquebus. The lead balls scythed through the head of the column. "Fire!" The second volley sounded. It was not as loud for half of the first volley had been from harquebuses. Smoke filled the road. Men shouted and horses neighed.

The Imperial horn sounding the retreat was heard through the smoke even as we reloaded and when the gun smoke disappeared we saw a dozen horses and two dozen bodies littering the road. "Otter Company, take the loose horses and bring the weapons from the bodies. The rest of you reload and be ready in case they come again."

That the enemy did not come again was testament to their fear of us. I liked the Finns but they were wild men and had they been in the same situation then they would have charged after the other wagons and ignored orders. My men were light horsemen but I had managed, with the help of Alexander Stirling and Dick Dickson to instil discipline into them. In the grand scheme of things it was a petty victory but as my men had the purses from the dead, their weapons and horses not to mention the first pick from the wagons, there was an air of euphoria in our camp that night. It had been a long time since we had felt that way. The bullocks would have made a good meal but the wagons were needed and the supplies they contained would help to feed the whole army. We managed to butcher the carcass of one horse so we ate meat.

That was our victory but news from ahead was discouraging. We heard that Leipzig had fallen to the enemy and that was hard to bear. A year ago King Gustavus had been heading to winter quarters at Mainz and I had been heading home. It was now clear the Imperial Army would winter somewhere in Saxony. We would also have to winter close by and the king chose Naumburg, thirty miles away from Leipzig. That the king had not given up on the hope of victory was clear for Naumburg controlled the bridges over the Saale. The journey to our winter camp was cold and it was miserable. Once there we made our usual camp and chose the best site that we could. We made hovels but these makeshift dwellings would have to keep us dry in a cold Saxon winter. The king was forced to use his personal guards to prevent men from deserting. For my regiment it meant having to forage every couple of days. We were chosen because we had many remounts and had endured the fewest losses. It was a hard duty because we were foraging in land that was filled with our allies. I decided that we had to take risks.

The night before we were ordered to find food I gathered my officers. "The enemy will have his own scouts and foragers out and they will be closer to Leipzig. My plan is to ambush those men. That way we hurt the enemy and still keep our army supplied."

Davy Campbell said, "Risky, Sir."

I nodded, "But no more so than taking from the people who are, ostensibly, our allies. If it fails then I am open to suggestions but we have been tasked with finding food and that is what we will do."

It meant dividing the regiment up into pairs of companies but we were now comfortable with that system. I rode with the Hunting Dogs and the Stags. Murphy and Gilmour, as well as Tom came with us. We did not need the standard but the horn could prove to be invaluable for we would be close to each other.

We found some enemy cavalry raiding a small hamlet called Thiessen. They were a regiment of harquebusiers and when the Hunting Dog who had spotted them reported to me, I knew that they were newly raised. He said that they had their regimental flag with them and their saddles and guns looked new. These were small things but to us they were important. A newly raised regiment still had much to learn and that they had brought their standard with them was telling. The Imperial harquebusiers had dismounted and their lack of experience was shown when they did not use horse holders but tied up their horses. We saw the animals off to the right, unguarded and trying to graze. We also dismounted but one man in four stayed with the horses. We then headed over the fields and through the trees on three sides of them. We did not want to risk losing a man to friendly fire. I had a pistol in each hand and Tom was behind with two more. I was much more accurate than he was and his skill would be in reloading quickly. Murphy and Gilmour flanked me like bodyguards.

There was noise ahead. The Germans were showing their inexperience and their officer allowed them to shout. They had also failed to use sentries. There was no order to the raiding. When we raided we had purpose. We sought food, firewood, animals and, if we had time, then buried coins. However, we always had sentries to watch for an enemy. These men did not. We heard their glee as they discovered treasure in the hamlet. That could have been anything from maidens to coins, chickens to beer. There were shots fired too. That was a mistake for the ones who fired would have no chance to reload. There was rarely a need to use pistols when taking a village and the threat of a gun was often enough to cow villagers. A man did not waste powder and ball. The noise that they made also hid our approach. Surprise was a deadly weapon. The one thing we could not legislate for was when we would be seen. All it took was a man to look up at the wrong moment and see one of us. As it happened the one who did see us and shouted was not heard immediately because of the noise and screams in the village. We managed to get five paces closer before he raised his harquebus. Before he could fire, for I saw him raise his weapon, I shouted, "Fire!"

My men all knew my voice and every pistol and harquebus fired. We did not aim at any of the men who were close to the villagers. It meant that instead of taking out most of the raiders, more than half survived. One was the leader and seeing so many of his men lying dead or dying he shouted the order to run. Some of his men fired their weapons hurriedly as they fled and they did little damage. My men had taken aim and ensured that their weapons were level and steady. A gun fired in haste could send a ball into the ground or into the air. Luck meant that only one of my men was hit. I saw Harry Burns clutch his arm and curse.

"At them."

My men knew, as I did, that if we could hurt this regiment we would be hurting their army. Horsemen were valuable as were their horses. The gunfire had spooked some of their horses and they had managed to tear themselves free from their hitching post. As the riderless horses galloped off it added to the confusion as some troopers saw their mounts disappearing into the distance and they had to hurry to the nearest animal. I saw my men taking prisoners. It saved a lead ball and these men were beaten. The officer managed to escape with twenty or so men. There were others, I knew, who would have escaped over the fields and through the trees but we took thirty prisoners and captured forty horses. This was the second village that they had raided and we took the supplies that they had already taken. We also took their colours. The standard bearer had more courage than his officer and he died defending them.

When we rode into the camp we discovered that the rest of the regiment had managed to take supplies from other raiders, although our horse count was higher and we were the only ones to have a colour. The supplies were a drop in the ocean but we had them and the Papists did not. The next day the Finns did the raiding. We had a day in camp and we shared out the treasure we had taken. I never took any despite the pleas from my officers. I did not need it. I was well paid and we had been paid again when the Swedish chancellor had arrived. I was told that another shipment of gold would be arriving soon. Cardinal Richelieu was keen to hurt the Spanish and his gold paid for Germans and Swedes to die in that cause rather than Frenchmen. He was a clever man.

Tom had also profited. I let him take from the men I had slain. His speedy reloading had helped me. He was almost embarrassed to take it. As we had ridden back he had told me that he had more in his purse from that one day than in a month of robbing with his uncle. "You know, Colonel, he should have come over here and volunteered. He was a nasty man but this war would have suited him."

I shook my head, "Tom, you have served with these men, would your uncle have fitted in?"

He shook his head, "They would have tired of his ways, Colonel. I could have joined up, though."

"Tom, I was fated to find you. You would never have managed to get over here on your own. My wife was right to redeem you. This was meant to be."

I had wondered, however, if we were both doomed to spend the rest of our lives here in Germany, fighting a war that showed no sign of ending. We were now as far from victory as we had ever been. When we had ridden into Munich I had thought the war was over. How wrong had I been?

Our camp was not the happy place it had been when we had been close to Nuremburg. We had lost men to battle and disease. One of the women, one of the camp followers, had also died and Bertha had been popular. The children who were with the women were also suffering. My men always ensured that they had the first of the food but childhood was a parlous time for all. When a two-year-old died, to my men it was as though we had lost a major battle. The whole regiment were there to bury the boy. I saw hardened veterans weeping. It was one thing to lose a comrade in battle but for a child to die in such circumstances tested their faith in God. My officers did their best but they were fighting a losing battle. It was November and we were still in the field. A year ago they had been in a winter camp in Mainz and spending pay in the German city and I had been with my family. We had just enjoyed a huge victory. Now the victories of Breitenfeld and Rain seemed to have happened in another century. All that we could taste was the defeat at Alte Veste.

The enemy had taken Leipzig and they now occupied it. Our scouts and the spies that were used to watch the enemy gave us accurate information and we knew that von Wallenstein outnumbered us. As much as the king wanted a battle he would not risk losing to a man who had bested him once before. If we had parity of numbers then we might seek a battle. We needed a battle because feeding our army was hard. The enemy had the advantage of a large city as their base and the lands they had conquered. The Saxons were suffering under the Imperial boot.

The momentous day that preceded the great event of that year saw us in the saddle. Once more we were scouting and my Hunting Dog Company spotted the huge column of troops leaving Leipzig and heading north and west. We headed across the fields to use the trees to shadow them. My men were spread out in a long line of pairs of riders and without metal to reflect light and wearing dull clothes we were hard to see. We had two companies on patrol and I sent a rider from Badger Company to report to King Gustavus and tell him what we had learned. I did not give him numbers for I did not have them. Nor did I speculate on what they were up to. I had learned that the king and his generals just liked to be given facts unadorned by opinion. We would keep them in sight and try to estimate their numbers as we rode. They often disappeared behind trees and around bends but I was able to identify the flags of regiments. After an hour of shadowing the column I was able to estimate that there looked to be about five thousand men. It was not a threat to our lines for our army outnumbered this column by four to one but it was an intriguing move. Most of the men were infantry and, with their wagons, it meant that they were moving at a snail's pace. Their direction suggested that they were not trying to outflank us. That had been a worry. Lieutenant Jennings had good eyes and it was he who recognised General zu Pappenheim. We had met him before and I knew him to be a good general. He was a popular leader for he was usually successful. The news was vital for he had been recently recalled by the emperor to help von Wallenstein. The two men were the best leaders the Papists had. It showed how much they feared King Gustavus. We kept trailing them until, by the end of the day, their destination was clear. They were heading for Halle. The town still had a Swedish garrison and the walls would prevent zu Pappenheim from an easy victory. He had no guns with him. Von Wallenstein was spreading the load of his army whilst threatening the road from the north.

When the column continued to pass Halle I wondered at the move. I turned to Sergeant Seymour, "What is zu Pappenheim up to I wonder?"

"I thought he was going to try to take Halle, Colonel."

I shook my head, "That is too big a nut for just five thousand men who have no artillery to crack. It has walls and a castle not to mention artillery." Swedish artillery was good. I reached for my map. "It is a long way but he could be on his way west to ravage Lower Saxony and Cologne." If he could threaten the Rhine and the Protestants' lands to the west of it then it would be almost a victory in itself.

As darkness fell so the enemy camped. We returned to Naumburg where I reported to the king and Duke Bernhard of Saxe-Weimar. It was late when we arrived back at the king's headquarters. As I was admitted by Lieutenant Larsson to the building used as a headquarters, I could hear the king talking, "Cardinal Richelieu thinks that because he provides money he can influence the direction of this war. We are preventing French losses and it is Swedish soldiers who are dying for France."

Duke Bernhard of Saxe-Weimar said, "So long as he provides the gold, King Gustavus, then he can think what he will. Our path is well chosen."

They turned as I entered, "More news, Bretherton?"

"Yes, King Gustavus, the corps which has been detached is zu Pappenheim's. They have no guns with them and they have passed Halle. It appears to have a mixture of infantry and cavalry alike."

The king went to the map, "Then they head for Saxony."

"It confirms what we were told. This is von Wallenstein's winter camp and he does not wish a battle. Pappenheim goes to threaten the west." The duke was a more energetic leader than his older brother. I liked him and the Germans rated him as highly as King Gustavus.

The leaders there looked at me and the king said, "You are sure that it was zu Pappenheim?"

I had learned to trust my men and to be positive in my reports, "It was, King Gustavus."

"Then we outnumber the enemy. Duke Bernhard, I want to break camp and be on the road to Leipzig before dawn. We will have our battle with von Wallenstein. God is with us!"

Doctor Jacob Fabricius was the king's chaplain and he was often present at these meetings. He clutched his Bible and said, "God is with us. Victory is at hand."

The king smiled at him, "Let us pray so, Doctor."

As I left I saw Prince Francis Albert of Saxe-Lauenburg. Unusually for him he was not near to the other nobles and aides but was conferring with the man I had seen before. I was closer to him this time and could identify more features. He was a mercenary and, by his dress, a Pole. He looked to be a Cossack. His features were almost oriental. Their heads were together and they were so engrossed that I had almost passed by them on my way back to my camp before they saw me. The prince snapped, "Are you eavesdropping, Englishman? Be away with you or I will have my men end your worthless life here."

When I had first come to Germany and met the man I had been intimidated by him and his rank but now, after years of war, I saw him for what he was, a blowhard and a bully who had not an ounce of courage in his miserable pampered body. I turned and said, in German, "Nothing a coward like you says is worth listening to and if this man works for you then he is also a…" I searched for the word and remembered the Swedish one I had heard spoken by Torsten, "a nithing." They both knew what it meant. It was someone so without worth that they were irrelevant. I saw their hands go to their weapons and I laughed. "If your honour is besmirched then let us settle it here and now. I know my skill but your sword, Prince Francis Albert of Saxe-Lauenburg, as far as I know, refuses to be drawn when battle nears." I saw him take his hand from his weapon and he shook his head. The Pole took his hand from the pommel of his sword too. "I thought so."

As I turned he said, ominously, "When the guns crash and the battle rages, watch your back, Englishman."

The gloves were off. If he was able he would try to kill me in the heat of battle and now he had a bodyguard to do the deed so that he would not have to soil his own hands. I was not particularly worried as I had a regiment and Tom to watch out for me and I also knew that this was a man who would hide from danger and I would be close to it.

For my men the news of an impending battle was both good and bad. We would be going to war but we would be leaving our camp and our women behind. This time Tom would not be with them. He would ride with me for I might need both of my horses in the battle. I would ride one and he would lead the other. We had some way to march to reach Leipzig and the last thing I needed was to ride a weary horse to war. I did not take all of my men. There were some still sporting wounds and others who had been laid low by illness and disease. Such men were a liability. We left them at the camp. They were led by Harry Burns. If we lost, and I did not rule that possibility out, then when we fell back they could defend our treasures. King Gustavus did not approve of having gold in camp. He thought it encouraged theft as well as gambling and fights. However, as he knew that men had to be paid, he turned a blind eye to the practice of hiding coins. Men buried their gold in the camp. Tom hid mine. I never thought I would die but it paid to be prepared. Tom hid the gold so that if I fell then he could return with it to Charlotte.

We had a bare two hours of sleep for we were roused by the third hour after midnight and broke camp. We had a cheerless departure. There was no hot food and we were all well wrapped against the cold. We headed east towards Leipzig. We still had eight companies but none of them had full numbers. What we were filled with was a determination to end the war that November.

As we headed along the road to the ford over the Rippach I wondered just what we would find. The Saxons in the area had been more than helpful. They told the king of the best route to Leipzig and the one that would avoid the enemy. They reported that while there was a cavalry detachment guarding the ford it would not be able to stop our army. That showed the difference between soldiers and farmers. When I was told the news, by Lieutenant Larsson, I knew that a determined defence at a ford could slow or even stop our advance. He also had more unwelcome news, which he confided to me. The Saxon leader, Hans Georg von Arnim-Boitzenburg, had forbidden the Duke of Brunswick to bring his two thousand men to bolster our numbers as ordered by King Gustavus. The lieutenant shook his head, "I know the Field Marshal did great service at Breitenfeld but he did serve with von Wallenstein and I wonder if this is treachery."

He had to hurry off to give orders to Colonel Dodo zu Innhausen und Knyphausen, who was third in command. I was disappointed that the three generals who had been the rocks on which we had gained our victories, generals Johan Banér, Gustav Horn and Lennart Torstensson would not be leading us. Johan Banér and Gustav Horn had been given commands to protect the parts of Germany we had secured and our master of the guns still languished in Ingolstadt.

The ford was defended. The farmers had been wrong and the cavalry detachment had been reinforced. The king ordered the army into battle lines and placed regimental artillery in the village of Poserna. While the other light cavalry, the Finns, were on the right, we had been attached as scouts to the Duke of Saxe-Weimar's cavalry on the left, close to Porsten. Muskets popped but the enemy appeared to have no artillery. The stream looked fordable but there were bogs and marshes on both sides. We needed a safer way to cross. A local farmer approached the general who commanded the cavalry. I was too far away to hear what was said but I was summoned to his side, "Colonel Bretherton, take your regiment to the mill." He pointed to the watermill to our left, "This man says there is a ford there." He shrugged, "A ford to a farmer may not be of any use to an army. Investigate and if it is true then send word back to me."

"Sir."

I waved my sword and my regiment followed me in a column of fours. As we neared it I saw that it looked to be a ford but we would need to ride across it to be certain. I sent Lieutenant Jennings and his men to cross first. When I saw them on the other side, waving that it was safe, then I sent Gilmour back to the general. Our cavalry could cross. It was as I began to cross that I saw the cuirassiers forming up on the slight slope above Lieutenant Jennings. His men had their firearms out but I could not allow one company to be charged by what looked like squadrons of heavy cavalry. "Murphy, sound the charge!"

If nothing else the trumpet would tell Jennings that we were coming and might make the Imperial horsemen halt. My decision to use a column of fours proved wise as the ford was not wide enough for more men. I heard the guns of the Hunting Dogs as they barked and as we left the ford I waved my sword and ordered Murphy to sound 'form line'. I sheathed my sword and drew a wheellock. The Imperial horsemen were galloping down the slope towards my men. Our volley was a ragged one but even a ripple of lead balls found some flesh and when my men drew their second weapons and fired another ball the enemy halted and drew their own weapons. They wore breastplates and had an advantage but when I heard the horns behind us I knew that we had reinforcements. I shouted, "Hold them! Help is at hand!"

The arrival of another one thousand cavalrymen was enough to make the cuirassiers flee. The general took the time to form the cavalry into lines. He said, "Colonel, secure any prisoners and horses. You will be our reserve."

"Sir." I was happy with the order. We had spent the day in the saddle the previous day and had less rest than any. The chance to sit and watch the skirmish unfold was a welcome one. I let my men obey the order and, with my officers and colour party, we watched the attack. There were bridges over the Rippach but they were all small ones. We had taken an unguarded ford on the flank and we were now able to roll up the enemy from their right. We saw the small artillery pieces pound the enemy and then watched the commanded musketeers as they fired volley after volley to clear the banks. The Croat horsemen retreated to the top of a small hill but using the small artillery pieces Oberst Graf von Erbstein and his commanded musketeers cleared them. We had risen and marched at four o'clock in the morning but twelve hours later we were only just across the Rippach. By the time the field was cleared the king ordered a fortified camp to be made close to the village of Röcken. The king was close enough to have his battle.

Chapter 16

Lützen November 1632

In our camp my men were in good spirits. We had taken the breastplates from the captured and dead cuirassiers. We would not use them but they would be sold to those who wanted more protection and the proceeds shared amongst the companies. The weapons and purses were also equitably distributed but the horses were put into our horse herd. We would need the remounts. Thanks to our extra service and the news we had brought the king we did not have to stand a watch and we ate relatively well. For once we all enjoyed a full night of sleep. I had a feeling that we might need it and I was proved right.

We were roused before dawn although dawn was hard to see for we awoke to a thick fog. There was a change in our orders. Lieutenant Larsson came to deliver them, "The king wishes you to be brigaded with the Finnish horsemen." He hesitated, "The king would like you and your men on the right with the Finns but he says that if you do not wish to be commanded by Lieutenant Colonel Torsten Stålhandske he will understand and you can remain with the Duke of Saxe-Weimar."

Unlike Sigismund I was not precious about my rank and I knew that Stålhandske was a good officer. "No, I am happy to serve there."

The lieutenant looked relieved, "That will please the king. It is he who will lead the attack on the right."

We mounted our horses and left the remounts in the camp. The handful of men who had suffered slight wounds the day before would remain with them. We walked our horses across the camp to join the Finns. It was slow going as it was so foggy that it was hard to see your hand before your face. This would delay the start of the battle. We were greeted as old friends by the Finns. As well as light horsemen there were also Finnish cuirassiers. Some of the light horsemen had also bought breastplates from our men so that they looked even more like a disparate amalgam of men. It just showed that one should never judge a man by the clothes or uniform that he wears. It is what is in his heart that counts.

Lion of the North

The fog meant that it took some time to cross the Flossgraben Canal although, gradually, the light improved. It could not be helped and the enemy did nothing to try to prevent our crossing. I wondered why. As the Blue Regiment, the elite of the Swedish infantry took their place in the centre of the line, I asked Torsten Stålhandske why they were allowing us to move without hindrance.

In reply he pointed to the far left. I saw, with sinking heart, the standards of zu Pappenheim's horsemen. The delay at the Rippach had allowed zu Pappenheim to be recalled. We no longer had superior numbers and von Wallenstein had showed that he was as wily an opponent as we had ever met.

The king must have seen the arrival of zu Pappenheim. While the gunners prepared their weapons he rode to our fore and addressed us, the Swedish and Finnish flank. "You true valiant brethren! See that you do valiantly carry yourselves this day, fighting gravely for God's Word and your king which, if you do, so will you have mercy of God and honour before the world: and I will truly reward you; but if you do not, I swear unto you that your bones shall never come in Sweden again."

Everyone cheered although, to me, the last part seemed unnecessary. Perhaps it was part of the Swedish philosophy.

The king then headed to the German soldiers commanded by Duke Bernhard of Saxe-Weimar. It was hard to hear all the words but phrases drifted over including one that struck in my mind, "Run not away and I shall hazard my body and blood with you for your best."

Again, when he finished, then there was a huge cheer. In contrast there was nothing from the Imperial Army. They just stood although once the king had finished, a regiment of Croat horsemen galloped towards us, clearly intent on mischief. Our horsemen all had pistols at the ready and we opened fire, dispersing them. Only a couple of the enemy were unhorsed but it was a small victory and we cheered and jeered as they retreated.

It was then that von Wallenstein set fire to the city of Lützen. The castle was still manned by his soldiers but the Imperial field marshal decided to prevent it from falling into our hands.

Although the sun had cleared the fog, that fog was replaced by smoke. The smoke was worse as it made men cough.

The king then ordered his trumpeter, Jöns Månsson, to play Psalm 46, *'God is our refuge and strength, a very present help in trouble'* and Psalm 67, *'God be merciful unto us, and bless us'*. The king and most of the Swedes all sang along with the trumpet. He had done the same at Breitenfeld and Rain but this was the first time that I heard the words as clearly as I did. Perhaps it was the smoke that was drifting before us to make it even eerier, I don't know but the words stuck in my head. They made me think of Charlotte and I turned to look at Tom.

Some of our guns opened fire and they began the battle. The smoke from the city and the guns obscured the result but when the Imperial guns opened up we suffered our first loss. A young French officer had a piebald horse and the ball killed the animal instantly although the officer was unhurt. As far as I know that was our first casualty.

The men and their leaders all knew the plan and the line of infantry began to move forward as the guns belched forth their foul smoke. The king came over to speak to Lieutenant Colonel Torsten Stålhandske. I was close enough to hear him as he ordered us to attack, not the skirmish line of Croats, but the Imperial cuirassiers in their black coated armour.

"I will do so, King Gustavus."

The king rode back to his place at the centre of our line and I saw the aides flock like gulls around him. I saw the Prince of Saxe-Lauenburg and his Polish friend. Both were as close to the king as they could be. Was this a change in the German noble? Did he intend to actually win some honour? I put him from my mind.

So began, for me and my regiment, the Battle of Lützen. I did not see the battle fought by Duke Bernhard of Saxe-Weimar on our left for the smoke from the batteries, added to the smoke from the burning city, obscured it. I saw the battle on the right and the centre.

We had with us some small regimental guns called falconets. They were light but mobile. The gunners rode horses that pulled the little guns and we were assigned to protect them. We also had musketeers with snaplock muskets to add more protection. My regiment would give mounted firearms that could fire over the heads of both the gunners and the musketeers. We moved north towards the enemy and as soon as we did so the Croats fled. We reached a relatively flat piece of high ground. It was not a hill but we had passed up a gentle slope and the ground before us was fairly flat. It was as we neared the cavalry that I saw something I had never seen before, civilians and camp followers arrayed as regiments. I wondered at that for a brief moment but as our horses approached they fled. They were a von Wallenstein trick to make us think that they had more men than they did. People said that the Finns were wild horsemen and they could be but under the steel hand of Torsten Stålhandske, they could show discipline too and they did that day. Once the Croats had fled along with the false regiments of camp followers, the cuirassiers prepared to charge. We were ordered to bring up the guns and his Finns drew their firearms.

"Bretherton's Horse, prepare weapons."

We had a double line. The front line would fire and they could reload when the second line advanced. I knew that we might not even need to open fire. The Swedish gunners were good. The artillery pieces that they used were made of bronze and fired a three-pound ball. The heavier artillery guns were used to break down walls. These guns, operated by a two-man crew, were to break up an attack. The cuirassiers charged us. If they did the same as they normally did they would charge to within pistol range and then open fire. The regimental artillery had a greater range.

The corporal in command of the guns, there were ten of them, looked at Oberst Graf von Erbstein and raised his hand. I watched the black cuirassiers as they approached and when they were fifty paces from us the Oberst said, "Fire!"

Already there was smoke drifting over to us not only from the guns that were firing but from a burning Lützen. The ten guns added to it and I could not see the effect of their cannonade. They had been commanded to fire by the Oberst and now my men waited for my command. I drew my first wheellock and when I saw the shadows appear through the smoke shouted, "Fire!" The rest of the cavalry with us also fired and the scene before me disappeared, as a fog as thick as the one we had trudged through that morning enveloped us. The regimental artillery and the musketeers fired again and again as fast as they could. They were firing blindly through the smoke.

Lieutenant Colonel Torsten Stålhandske's commanding voice yelled out, "Cease fire!" We all stopped and my men reloaded. The gunners with the regimental artillery swabbed out their guns and waited. You did not put a fresh charge into a hot gun barrel. As the smoke cleared we saw that the survivors had fallen back and the ground before us was filled with the dead and the dying. It was pitiful to see the dying horses as they tried to raise themselves.

Tom nudged his horse next to mine to help me load the wheellocks, "Is that it, Sir, is it over?"

Gilmour laughed, "No, Tom, that is just the preliminaries. The cuirassiers have been hurt and we threaten their flank. Look at the baggage train." His words were for me rather than Tom for as the smoke cleared we could see that half of the Imperial baggage train was being looted as the other half was trying to get away.

I looked to my left. The Imperial Army had a ditch before it and guns protecting it. I saw that two of the king's elite regiments, the Swedish Regiment and the Yellow Regiment had taken the ditch and guns that lay close to them. Even from this distance I could see the mound of bodies that told me it had been an expensive assault.

It was then that we saw, through the drifting smoke, the cavalry of Count zu Pappenheim. I recognised the standards and the uniforms. They were coming for us and trying to turn the right flank of our army. This time they meant business and they were in a line and charging. I saw that one of the regiments was made up of cuirassiers but the rest were harquebusiers or combinations of squadrons cobbled together. In all there were about fifteen hundred horsemen although the smoke made an accurate count all but impossible. We had less horsemen but with the commanded musketeers we outnumbered them. Zu Pappenheim had a company of lifeguards, his Rennfahne, and he rode amongst them. I was close enough to Oberst Graf von Erbstein to hear his words to the falconet gunners, "Aim at the leading company!"

Lion of the North

We waited for the musketeers and the falconets would fire first. We had all reloaded and even Tom had a pistol at the ready. When the falconets and the muskets fired, a wall of smoke arose. A freakish breeze that came from I know not where suddenly swept the smoke away and I saw that most of the lifeguards and zu Pappenheim had been scythed down. Lieutenant Colonel Torsten Stålhandske shouted, "Fire!" It was at extreme range but it proved to be the correct command. The Imperial cavalry stopped and then, as the body of the commander of the cavalry, zu Pappenheim, was carried from the field, his cavalry went with him.

Up by the windmill I recognised the standard of Heinrich Holk and his men as he organised the cavalry. The batteries by the windmills were vital to the Imperial line and they had to be protected. Holk might have been the one to send the killers to take me. I had to put all thoughts of vengeance from my mind. My regiment had a job to do.

We were winning and I had the sudden thought that we might emerge victorious. Lieutenant Larsson galloped up, "Lieutenant Colonel Stålhandske, the Småland Regiment has been cut to pieces and the musketeers have been hurt. He needs horsemen."

Torsten turned to me, "I must watch Holk. Lieutenant Colonel Bretherton, take your regiment and go to the aid of the king."

"Murphy, sound the horn." I drew and waved my sword and shouted, "Column of fours." It was the best formation to use and I led my men across the battlefield to follow Lieutenant Larsson. The smoke was even thicker closer to the ditch and the fighting around the guns. We had to pick our way through bodies, both Imperial and Swedish. Ahead, as Lieutenant Larsson raced to get to the side of the king I saw that the king was beleaguered and surrounded by enemy horsemen. He still had his page and one of his bodyguards but they were in danger of being overwhelmed. This was no time for caution and I shouted, "Murphy, sound the charge! Drive these horsemen from the field."

To my surprise I saw that Prince Francis Albert and his Polish mercenary were also riding to the aid of the king. The rest of the aides were not to be seen. Perhaps I had misjudged the German. The swirling smoke and the mayhem and chaos of battle meant that I lost sight of the king. My officers each led their companies to do what they did best and kill Papists. I had just my colour party and Tom with me. I saw the king clutch his arm as a cuirassier fired at him. The thought flicked through my mind that the king should not be here. I saw many bodies around him and at least half were the Småland Regiment.

It was then that I saw treachery of the highest order. Lieutenant Larsson, his pistol held before him gallantly charged towards the king to save him. The Pole with Prince Albert deliberately drew his own pistol and fired it into the back of the gallant Swede. The range was less than ten feet and the ball would have shattered his spine. I was still fifty paces away but through the smoke I saw the king turn and as he did so a Croat fired his harquebus at the king, but the ball that ended his life came from the wheellock of Prince Francis Albert of Saxe-Lauenburg. The king fell from his saddle. I had seen him hit by at least three balls.

"Murphy and Gilmour, stay with the king and his bodyguards!"

"Yes, Colonel."

The two killers, prince and Pole, raced off in the direction of the burning city of Lützen. Ball and canister flew around us but the two men seemed to lead charmed lives as they galloped away. I had left my command but I could not allow the attempt on the king's life to go unpunished. I had no idea if we were winning or losing. To be truthful, if the king was dead it mattered not.

I saw the German prince glance over his shoulder and say something to the Pole. The mercenary wheeled his horse and I knew he was coming to kill me. I had a pistol already drawn and primed. I realised that the Pole did too. Marcus was racing. This was when he was at his best with the smell of battle in his nostrils. I knew that I could drop the reins and he would continue to charge. The Pole fired first. As I saw the flash I jerked the reins to my left. The ball caught my hat but my manoeuvre had worked. I was just five feet from him when I fired. The ball tore into his neck and his arms spread. He let loose the reins of his horse and it moved, not away from me but towards me. I had to swerve to avoid it. As the Pole fell I saw that the prince was getting away. The mercenary's attack had moved me from my path. The assassin was escaping. It was as I turned to follow him that I saw Tom was still trying to stay with me but his horse was struggling. Marcus liked battle, Tom's horse did not. My comfort was that being behind me he was safer.

I holstered my spent pistol. I determined to close with the prince and use my sword. A pistol would do the job but I wanted the satisfaction of seeing the face of the king's assassin as I slew him. I knew that Alexander and Dick would not approve. They would just want him dead the quickest and safest way possible. Perhaps it was a flaw in me. It was as I headed after the killer that I saw the Yellow Regiment, one of the most experienced regiments, slaughtered by point blank Imperial musketry. They did not even get a ball off and the Imperial infantry, seeing the gap, headed for our reserves commanded by Dodo Freiherr zu Innhausen und Knyphausen. He was the last defence before the baggage train. If we lost the baggage train then the battle and, perhaps the war, would be lost. Along with it we would lose our own camp and the ones we had left behind. I had now set myself a course which meant I could do nothing about that. I had to get the prince and end his life.

He had a good horse but mine was better. I began to gain on him. I knew he feared me despite all his bluster when we had met. It was something I had seen in his eyes and that fear now manifested itself as he kept turning to see where I was. I used that to my advantage. When he looked back I moved Marcus so that I was on the opposite side to where he had looked. His head began to jerk from side to side as he sought me. He should have concentrated on riding the horse and the result was that he lost even more ground to me. When I kept my horse directly behind his it was too much for him and his horse faltered. The prince knew how to ride and he kept his seat but only just. It allowed me to close with him and I raised my sword. For the first time since I had met him he drew his sword. I brought mine down to end his life instantly with a blow to the neck. He blocked it but only just and the edge of my sword shaved off the metal crowns he wore on his shoulders. Marcus snapped at the prince's horse which jerked away taking the prince out of range of my weapon. I dug my heels in and Marcus leapt forward. I slashed at him as he tried to control his horse and he flicked his sword at mine.

This time the blow was even weaker and my sword sliced through his reins.

He screamed, "I will surrender!"

"No, you will not." I stood in the stirrups and brought my sword down diagonally to hack into his neck. I bit deeply and as I sawed the blade back he fell from his saddle.

What I had not noticed, in this long chase, was that I was now amongst some Croat horsemen. Four rode at me. I dropped my reins and drew an unfired pistol. I barely managed to raise it and hit one. The other three would have me. Suddenly, from behind me, I heard the crack of a pistol and a second horseman fell. Even as I slashed at the third another pistol sounded and the last man fell. I turned and saw Tom, with two smoking pistols. "Enough, eh, Colonel? Mistress Charlotte would be most unhappy."

I sheathed my sword and, as more Croats came to avenge their friends, wheeled Marcus, "You are right. Let us get back to Murphy and Gilmour."

I drew a pistol from my waist holster as we headed back through the fog of war. It was as we did that I saw the Blue Regiment suffer the same fate as the Yellows and the whole Imperial Army headed for our reserves. Our fate now rested with Dodo Freiherr zu Innhausen und Knyphausen for I saw that Duke Bernhard of Saxe-Weimar had been pushed back and some men were routing. What was happening on the right? There we had been within a handspan of victory. I saw that Imperial batteries at the windmills on the high part of the Imperial lines were still sending ball after ball to decimate Duke Bernhard's Green Regiment as they bravely tried to end the battle.

Finding our way back to where the king had fallen was easier said than done. Men loomed up out of the fog and we had to wait to see if they wore a red sash or not. It was lucky that I had spare pistols and that they were primed. The only way I found the king was by my standard, planted in the ground by the body of the king. Murphy and Gilmour lay dead, butchered and despoiled. All had been taken from them and the king was in an even worse condition. I saw a wound to his forehead and his clothes had been stripped from him. If it was not for the old wound to his shoulder I wouldn't even have recognised him. Someone had ensured that the king was, indeed, dead. I dismounted.

I looked up as Torsten Stålhandske and a regiment of Finns rode up. He threw himself from his saddle and knelt by the body. He shook his head, "I should have sent more men. It has all been for nothing." He seemed to see my two dead men, for the first time. "And these men died as valiantly as the king's bodyguards." He looked at the bloody shirt which was the only garment covering the king's upper body, "They gave him no honour in death. They will pay." He turned to his men, "Take the body to the church and stand guard over him. The rest of you, come with me. We have vengeance to exact."

I picked up the trumpet and hung it from my saddle. "Tom, pick up the banner and, when you have climbed on your horse, wave it. Today you become the standard bearer. I need my regiment."

"What about Ran, Sir?"

"You have led my spare enough this day. I will change horses."

There appeared to be a sort of lull. The odd gun popped off and the smoke still poured from the burning city but wounded were being taken to the rear and officers were rallying their men. The battle hung in the balance. I did not know who would win. Duke Bernhard and Dodo Freiherr zu Innhausen und Knyphausen commanded and both were solid soldiers but they were not the Lion of the North, they were not King Gustavus Adolphus. Men headed for the waving standard. Some walked, some trotted and one or two led horses. My heart sank for there seemed to be far too few of them.

Dick Dickson still had at least half of his men with him but he sported a bandage around his head. It covered one eye. He glanced down at the bodies. The king's had been taken but the rest remained where they had fallen. He shook his head, "Poor buggers."

I said, flatly, "The king is dead."

He just stared at me. More men arrived and the companies formed up. They came from all over the battlefield. One of the aides who accompanied Lieutenant Colonel Stålhandske rode up, "Lieutenant Colonel, Colonel Stålhandske's compliments and he would like your regiment," he glanced around, "what remains of them, to join him on the right."

"We will join him as soon as possible."

I saw the remnants of our cavalry with the Swedish leader and saw Thurn and Henderson's brigade forming up on the flank of an Imperial position. Captain Stirling appeared. His left arm hung down at his side. He, too, was wounded. I said, "Captain, roll call. How many men remain?"

"Sir." He began to call out the names, first of the officers and then their deputies. All the time more men were arriving, seeing us gather, and they all loaded their weapons. Alexander rode over, "Sir, we have one hundred and thirty men. Sergeant Wilson, Corporal Longstaff and Corporal Summerville are all dead." He shook his head, "Their men told me that they saw them fall."

"How is the arm?"

"Useless, Sir, it was a ball to the elbow. I reckon I am a cripple now and my days of soldiering are over. This will be my last battle whether I survive or not." He saw the question on my face. "I can still fight."

"Otter, Hawk and Stag companies, I shall lead you now. Can any of you blow a bugle?"

Paul White rode up to me, "I can, Sir."

I handed him the bugle, "Then you shall ride with Tom."

He nodded and said, "Don't worry, Sir, I will keep an eye out for him. Jane would have my guts for garters if anything happened to him on my watch."

I had already changed horses and seeing that Nosey Nesbitt was too badly wounded I handed Marcus' reins to him. "Make your way back to the camp, Nesbitt, and let them know…"

He nodded. "I will, Sir. Good luck."

"Bretherton's Horse, I know not what the outcome of this day shall be but we will end it together. We have brothers in arms who lie on this field, they fought for God and King Gustavus and we will honour them by securing victory."

They cheered and I dug my heels in Ran's flanks. I was now the best mounted. Ran had ridden as much as any horse in my regiment but he had not carried an officer in a breastplate.

We rode to the right to join the remnants of the cavalry led by Lieutenant Colonel Stålhandske. When I arrived he nodded, "You have more men left than most. Colonel Thurn and Colonel Henderson are going to attack those Imperial guns. Take your regiment and support their attack." He pointed to the Imperial cavalry led by Colonel Piccolomini, "They may try to stop them. I will keep an eye on Holk. My horses are weary and I must preserve them. This battle hangs in the balance and we owe it to the lion to try to salvage a victory from it."

"Sir."

We rode over to the two regiments. John Henderson's regiment had less than eighty musketeers and no pikemen. Jacob Thurn's had just forty pikemen and one hundred and twenty muskets. A full regiment of Imperial musketeers along with pikes held the ditch. The guns appeared to be without gunners and that was good news. I saluted. I was aware that, technically, I outranked both of them but as I commanded fewer men I would defer to them. "Lieutenant Colonel Bretherton with Bretherton's Horse. We are here to support you."

Colonel Thurn returned my salute and nodded, "Just keep those Croats from us and we will do the rest."

"Follow me!" I led my men to the right of the infantry who were ready to move. I saw the Croat cavalry ahead. "Two lines, Tom and Paul, behind me." As the infantry moved I ordered, "March!"

We were moving at the same speed as the infantry and that was easy for the horses. The ground was flat. All of those thoughts ran through my mind as we headed for the ditch. We would not charge the ditch. That might prove disastrous. Infantry could negotiate the obstacle better than we could. I was watching the Croats.

Both sides were short on powder and ball. In addition, barrels were fouled and that limited the range. I knew that instead of closing to a healthy eighty paces, the two regiments would wait until they were twenty paces from the ditch. The Imperialists would have to do the same. When they halted I saw the muskets raised. It was then that the Croat harquebusiers charged. I was ready and I shouted, "White, sound the charge. May God be with us." Ran leapt forward, eager to go to war. The horn sounded. I wondered if Murphy would hear it as his soul ascended.

We had one advantage. The Croats would want to stop before we made contact to fire their harquebuses. If they fired them at the gallop then they would waste ball and powder. The other advantage we had was that while we were charging them, they were trying to hit the flank of Thurn's regiment. Even as we closed with them I heard the sound of the muskets as the musketeers opened fire and a pall of smoke filled the ground to our right. The wind was still bringing the smoke over from the fire at Leipzig and within moments a light fog filled the ground between us. I had no time to worry about that. I had a pistol levelled. I was the leading rider. Ran was a good length ahead of the next men, Tom and Paul. The troopers from Otter Company could not keep up with me either.

I saw the Croats appear through the fog of war and realised that four of them had seen me. I worked out, later on, that the smoke hid the men behind me and they thought I was alone. I watched as they wheeled towards me. Two held harquebuses but two had curved swords. I aimed at one of the swordsmen. One of the harquebuses belched smoke and the ball flew over my head. I fired when I was just five paces from the first swordsman and I struck him in the chest. I holstered my pistol and was drawing my sword as the second swordsman slashed at my body. If he had aimed at my head I would be dead but he struck at my chest and the blade scraped and scratched across my breastplate. A pistol sounded behind me and I saw him fall from his saddle. I wheeled my horse and rode at the fourth Croat. The barrel of the weapon looked as big as a cannon. I saw him pull the trigger and waited for the black oblivion of death. I was already raising my sword and I brought it down. The pistol sputtered but misfired. It had been hastily loaded and badly primed. My blade ended the shock on the man's face.

The musketry was so intense that the smoke became a wall and it was a test of a man's nerve. If the Croats got through our pitifully thin line then the musketeers and pikemen would die and our right flank would still be threatened. Success might not bring victory but failure would ensure that Duke Bernhard's men, advancing to the windmills, would be attacked in the flank and that would bring defeat. One thing I had learned in my time in these wars was that a man just did his part. You could not afford to worry about victory or defeat. You obeyed orders and did what you could.

"Close ranks!"

We needed cohesion and I slowed my horse so that the Otter Company was able to close with me. My back was watched. I knew that I had either Tom or White to thank for the ball that had killed the second swordsman. I used my sword to great effect. The Croats had nasty curved swords but my blade was longer. Three men had fallen to it when the Croat with the war hammer rode at me. For a Croatian he was very big and I realised that he would strike me before my sword could hurt him. I jerked Ran to the right. It allowed me to strike at his left side and as he readjusted his war hammer I stabbed at his thigh. It did two things: it wounded him and made him scream and that made his horse move away. The hammer head of the war hammer struck me but it was a glancing blow on my cuirass. It would need the attention of a blacksmith but I had survived. More importantly it allowed me, as my horse passed the rump of his horse, to slash at his unprotected back. From the blood pumping from his thigh I had struck something vital but the blow to his back, delivered with all my force, cut through to his spine. This was a confused melee. We did not need red sashes and scarves to know who we fought but you only saw your opponent at the last moment. This was a time for the quick and the dead. If you were quick then you might live a little longer and if you were slow then you died. It was as simple as that.

Tom had his wits about him and he shouted, "Sir, the musketeers have taken the ditch and they are turning the guns."

"Keep at them, men. We are close to a victory."

Tom's words and the news they brought gave my men the impetus and when the guns ceased and the smoke thinned, the Croats saw that they had lost and fell back to Holk at the Windmill. Lieutenant Colonel Stålhandske and the cavalry had still not moved but their presence pinned the enemy to the guns. If they left then we would take the Imperial battery that had caused so many deaths.

"Reload and reform lines. Take the wounded to the rear."

Lion of the North

I saw that Captain Stirling was still with me, his bloody left arm hanging useless at his side. "Sir, Davy Campbell is dead. It was a war hammer. He never knew what hit him. It was quick."

Quick or slow it mattered not to Davy; he was still dead.

I watched the musketeers as they turned and loaded the Imperial guns and aimed them at the artillery close to the windmills. The Imperial Army had withdrawn every soldier they could to protect the guns. I saw von Wallenstein and Holk there with the other leaders. Duke Bernhard was bringing his best regiment, the Green Regiment, with all that remained of our musketeers and pikemen up the slope to the windmills. Darkness was not far away and I knew that a battle in the dark would be a bloody affair. Jacob Thurn gave the order for the captured guns to fire. Within a dozen shots one of the big artillery pieces was upended. Equally important were the balls that bounced and slew some of the brigade commanders. It allowed the Green Regiment to close with the enemy. Many of the Imperial leaders lay dead and when our captured guns destroyed two more guns then we were able to assault them. Lieutenant Colonel Stålhandske led the rest of the cavalry to attack and we followed behind. Even Ran was now weary and it was the Finns who pursued the fleeing Imperial Army.

I was not sure if we had won or not. We held the field but our dead were so great in numbers that the word victory seemed hollow. It took some hours to fully clear the field and to capture loose horses and take weapons before we could trudge wearily back to our camp. I was alone with my thoughts. I had lost half of my officers and more than half of my men. Bretherton's Horse was a shadow of its former self. My plans to return home also lay in tatters. I was doomed, it seemed, to stay here in Germany and, without the Lion of the North, I did not think we had a chance of winning.

Epilogue

Pappenheim's regiments reached the battlefield too late to affect the outcome but were in enough numbers to ensure that von Wallenstein was able to retreat successfully to Leipzig. The day after the battle we buried our dead. More of my men had survived than I had thought. Some had been unhorsed and wounded. They had, eventually, wandered back to the camp. The women wept at the dead. We shared the treasure taken equitably. With the king dead I was not sure how things stood. Lieutenant Colonel Stålhandske came to see me two days after the battle. He had been ordered to go into Saxony with Duke Bernhard. As von Wallenstein was quitting Leipzig that city would be in our hands for winter. Already the seriously wounded were taken there to be cared for in the hospital.

The Swede put his arm around me, "I am not sure what your plans are but know that I would be happy to fight alongside you at any time."

I asked, "Will Sweden continue to fight?" We had lost six thousand men, a third of our army and the majority of them were Swedes.

He shrugged, "Gustavus Horn and Johan Banér are good generals but it is now the chancellor who commands. Who knows? My Finns wish to fight and so long as they do then so will I. Farewell."

Our camp was a depressing place. That the war would continue was clear. The Chancellor of Sweden was already raising men to replace the thousands who had been lost. The men in the camp had mixed feelings. Some wanted vengeance for what they thought of as the murder of King Adolphus. Tom had told them the story and they were appalled. Others could no longer fight. Alexander Stirling's arm meant he would not be able to do what he loved. The night after the battle he told everyone that when things had settled down and he had made his arrangements he would be going home. He had saved his coins and would buy and then run an inn. He had even picked a place out although he did not tell us of its location. I think he feared that someone else would seize his idea. That was because there were others who had decided that they had endured enough. Paul White and Jane now had children and they did not want them to suffer. The two-year-old who had died was an event that had made their mind up before the battle. Like Alexander they had money. It was not as much as my captain but it was enough so that they would have a life. All in all with wounds, disease, injuries and a desire to return to England or Scotland, more than half of the company made that decision. I said nothing for I still had mixed feelings.

A week after the battle, and as those leaving were making plans to travel together to Lübeck where they would take ship, I was summoned to the headquarters building where the Duke of Saxe-Weimar now commanded. I took Tom who would wait with the horses. When I arrived I saw some faces I recognised but there were more Germans than Swedes. I also noticed some scowls cast in my direction and that I did not understand. I was directed to an antechamber. The door opened and Gustav Horn came out. He looked serious, "Lieutenant Colonel. I am pleased you survived."

There was something in his tone that worried me, "What is amiss, General? Something does not feel right."

He sighed and took me to the side, "Colonel," he smiled, "James, I like you. The king liked you and you are a brave man."

"I sense a but coming, General."

He nodded, "Tell me, what happened when the king died?"

That was easy and I took him through the events. I told him of the Pole and my chasing of the prince across the battlefield.

He nodded, "I can tell that you are speaking the truth, however, the prince has friends and they are on the staff of Duke Bernhard. They wish you to be put on trial for the murder of Prince Francis Albert."

I think my mouth dropped open, "He killed King Gustavus."

"His friends dispute that. They say that the prince tried to save King Gustavus. We only have your word for what happened. The others are all dead. If he was alive then he could be questioned."

I gave a wry shake of my head, "He was a slippery snake and his friends would believe him. My servant knows the truth. He was there, too."

"I hardly think the word of a former bandit would carry much weight. Johan and I believe in you and we will do our best. Come, face these charges as bravely as you fought at Breitenfeld and Lützen and all will be well."

We entered and I saw a table behind which the duke sat. Next to him were men I recognised as aides who had served on the staff of the king. The duke apart their faces were already set. General Banér stood at the side. He smiled at me. Gustav joined him and, hat in hand, I faced what amounted to a court.

The duke smiled, "First of all, Colonel Bretherton, I should like to commend you and your men for your actions in the battle where we won a great victory."

I said nothing but I knew it was barely a victory and certainly not a great one.

He said, "However, there are charges that you must answer." He held up a piece of parchment. "It is alleged that you murdered Prince Francis Albert of Saxe-Weimar. What do you say?"

"I say that while it is true that I took the life of that man I did not murder him. I fought with him because he had killed King Gustavus."

One of the Germans stood and yelled, "That is a lie."

The duke said, "Sit, Graf. If you cannot control yourself then leave."

The man sat down. I looked at him and said, "Were you there or were you with the other aides who fled and left the king to fight with just his page, squire and Swedish aide?" I stared at him and then switched my eyes to look into the duke's, "Duke Bernhard, you are a brave man and I like to think that I am too. Has anyone ever seen me do anything which was not honourable? Have I not always obeyed the orders that were given to me? I will swear on any number of Bibles in any language you choose as to my innocence but what I would prefer is to face my accusers," I looked at each of the other men in turn, "with sword in hand and let God decide who is right."

The looks on their faces confirmed what I already knew, they were all afraid of me. I saw a hint of a smile on the duke's face although he quickly hid it with the back of his hand. "It will not come to that." He sighed and put the parchment face down on the table. "It seems to me we have an impasse. You are right,

Colonel, all the witnesses to the murder both of the king and the death of the prince, are dead. All except you." He looked at the Bible that was on the table and put his hand on it. He closed his eyes. He was silent for a moment and then he opened them and said, "I have come to a decision. It is one I make in the best interests of our cause. Lieutenant Colonel Bretherton, your men may remain in the army for they are brave men and we need such men but you are no longer required. You should quit the army and leave Germany before the end of December." The man called Graf looked as though he was going to object for he put his hands on the table and half rose. The duke said, his voice heavy with threat, "I do not think it will do anyone any good to let this matter leave this room. The colonel will be paid what he is owed and he will leave. There is an end to it. Agreed?"

He looked at each of the men in the room, including the two Swedish generals. They all nodded.

I was not happy and said, "And what about my agreement?"

The duke stood and held out his hand, "Your agreement is not necessary, Colonel. You are a mercenary paid by the alliance and your service is no longer needed. I wish you well."

I shook his hand. Almost as an act of defiance I put my hat upon my head and then put my hands on the table. I looked at the prince's friends and I said, "I doubt that I shall ever see you again for I return to England, but should any of you ever cross my path again then we will cross swords." I put my hand on the Bible. "That I swear." I stared down each one of them in turn. They were terrified. I said no more but left. When I reached Tom he saw my face and said, "Colonel?"

I shook my head, "I am angry, Tom. I will speak when I am calm, if that day ever comes."

I was still not settled even when we rode into the camp but I knew that I had to speak to my officers. I sent Tom to bring them to my tent. There were four of them but only three would be staying in Germany. When they arrived I opened a bottle of port. "Tom, bring glasses and one for yourself." He knew I was upset and obeyed but I saw the looks on the faces of the others. I waited until the port was poured and then lifted my glass, "Bretherton's Horse and our dead comrades!"

"Bretherton's Horse and our dead comrades!"

"King Gustavus!"

"King Gustavus!"

I downed mine in one. Alexander Stirling said, "What is wrong, Colonel?"

I shook my head and then decided that they deserved the truth. I told them all. Dick Dickson stood, "Let me find the bastards, Sir, then they will see a murder."

I smiled, "No, Dick. I have threatened them already but they are not worth it. They did nothing to save the king and they are looking for a scapegoat. I am that scapegoat. Besides, you will have to get on with them if you are to lead my regiment, Captain Dickson."

"Captain?" I nodded. "And the regiment?"

"You deserve both the rank and the regiment."

"I am not sure I want either."

Alexander said, "Dick, you know men will want to stay. There are men who have yet to earn enough to go home. You owe it to them."

I nodded, "Alexander is right, Dick."

He downed his port and poured himself another one, "Aye, you are right."

Peter Jennings said, "I was torn but this has made my decision for me. When you travel home, Colonel, I will travel with you."

It proved to be not only Peter who no longer wished to stay. Only forty men remained with Dick and Corporal Seymour. With camp followers and children there were almost sixty of us who headed up the road to Lübeck. We took a wagon and Konrad came with us to drive it. He had become as much a part of the company as any. General Horn ensured that we were paid before we left and the night before we did the company had a party where old debts were paid and toasts were drunk. Dick and David knew that it was the end of Bretherton's Horse as we knew it and we were mourning the end of something special. There were tears as we left for we had spilt blood together and buried friends. Those memories never leave.

As we rode north Tom said, "Well, at least Mistress Charlotte will be happy. She shall have you home for good."

"Perhaps, Tom, and I thought I was ready to leave the world of war but to leave like this…I hoped to be content but now I wonder if I shall ever be."

The End

Glossary

Bidet - another name for a nag or poor-quality horse
Gott mit uns - God with us (the Swedish password)
Haliwerfolc - The men of the saint (Cuthbert)
Knacker's yard - horse abattoir
Landsberg - Gorzow (Poland)
Muskettengabel - a rest for a musket
Pallasch - a sword favoured by Croats and Hussars
Reichsthalers - the coins of the empire: 25–26 grams of fine silver
Secrete - a small helmet hidden beneath a cap or hat
Serpentine - the match holder for the lighted fuse on a matchlock
Stirrup bucket - a way to attach a standard to a saddle
Swetebags - bags containing herbs and concealed beneath clothes to take away the stink of sweat
Tross - the German and Swedish term for the baggage train and camp followers
Quillon - the crosspiece of a sword of the period
Quilitz - Neuhardenberg
Walthame Cross - Waltham Cross
Warkworth Harbour - Amble, Northumberland

Canonical Hours

Matins (nighttime)
Lauds (early morning)
Prime (first hour of daylight)
Terce (third hour)
Sext (noon)
Nones (ninth hour)
Vespers (sunset evening)
Compline (end of the day)

Historical Background

This series is about the war between the Catholics and the Protestants in the early seventeenth century. It was a bloody war that devastated huge tracts of Europe. Between 5 and 9 million soldiers and civilians died in the 30-year conflict. The actual figures were: Military deaths from disease: 700,000–1,350,000. Military deaths from combat: 450,000. Total civilian dead: 3,500,000–6,500,000. Total dead: 4,500,000–8,450,000. The Spanish and Imperial troops were first faced by mercenaries, the Dutch and the Bohemians. Once the Danes and Swedes became involved then the conflict spread. James Bretherton is an amalgam of the mercenary leaders who fought in Europe. Despite being mercenaries, they all believed in their cause. These were not the condottieri who just fought for pay. I have used real battles and events as my structure. I have not glossed over the battles nor made them unduly heroic. They were not. I write about war from the perspective of the soldiers and not the generals.

When Gustavus finished dealing with the Poles then he entered the war and that saw a huge increase in the use of mercenaries from Germany, Scotland and England.

Arminianism: Arminian theology emphasised clerical authority and the individual's ability to reject or accept salvation, which opponents viewed as heretical and a potential vehicle for the reintroduction of Catholicism.

Cavalry at this time fought in a predictable way. They either used the caracole, lines of horsemen riding, firing their weapons and circling while they reloaded, or they halted, fired their weapons and then charged home. There were lancer regiments that did not use gunpowder weapons but there were few of them. The irregulars, the Croats, Hungarians and Finns fought much in the way their ancestors had done. They used weapons at close hand.

Count Tilly was ill served by Graf zu Pappenheim. The massacre at Magdeburg was not Tilly's doing but zu Pappenheim's. When he took his two thousand horsemen to attack the king he lied to Count Tilly about the size of the opposition. He ordered the charge on King Gustavus without asking the count's permission. Like Ney at Waterloo, he cost his leader many horsemen and that would prove fatal. He was a brave and reckless horseman. He is in the mould of Murat, Jeb Stuart, Prince Rupert and George Armstrong Custer. Cavalry leaders like John Gaspard Le Marchant and Lord Uxbridge are rarer.

Heinrich Holk was a real leader. He did switch sides when captured, many men did so on both sides, but he was renowned for his cruelty and the rape and pillaging by his men.

Impropriation, a term from English ecclesiastical law, was the destination of income from tithes of a church benefice to a layman. With the establishment of the parish system in England, it was necessary for all church property and income to have a specific owner. This was taxed by King Charles.

Abatis: a field fortification consisting of an obstacle formed from the branches of trees laid in a row, with the sharpened tops directed outwards, towards the enemy. There is usually a ditch before them.

The words of the king before the battle of Lützen are his and the psalms sung were also reported.

Opinion is divided about whether the prince did or did not kill King Gustavus. What is beyond doubt is that he was shot, first by an enemy and then as his men were killed he was also slain and his body despoiled and stripped. I side with those who have the prince as the killer. As Lieutenant Colonel Bretherton is a figment of my imagination then it follows that the prince's death is also fiction. The battle happened the way I wrote it. It was a bloody battle and like the involvement of the prince there is much debate about the winner. What is true is that Swedish involvement ended a couple of years later. Cardinal Richelieu then took over the war. One theory is that the Cardinal paid assassins to kill the king. Assassination was common. Less than two years later Albrecht von Wallenstein was murdered. It was a brutal war and treachery abounded.

A brigade normally consisted of a pair of regiments or battalions. Sometimes it could be four or five.

The English mercenary will return but not at the head of Bretherton's Horse. That fictitious Regiment died at Lützen.

Griff May 2025

Books used in the research:

The English Civil War - Peter Gaunt
The Thirty Years' War 1618-1648 - Richard Bonney
Imperial Armies of the Thirty Years War Infantry and Artillery - Brnardic and Pavlovic
Imperial Armies of the Thirty Years War Cavalry - Brnardic and Pavlovic
The Army of Gustavus Adolphus 1 Infantry - Brzezinski and Hook
The Army of Gustavus Adolphus 2 Cavalry - Brzezinski and Hook
The English Civil War Armies - Young and Roffe
Lutzen 1632 - Brzezinski and Turner
The English Civil Wars - Blair Worden
The Tower of London - Lapper and Parnell
Dutch armies of the 80 Years War 1568-1648 Cavalry and Artillery - Groot and Embleton
Dutch armies of the 80 Years War 1568-1648 Infantry - Groot and Embleton
Military History May 2017 Issue 80

Other books by Griff Hosker

If you enjoyed reading this book, then why not read another one by the author?

Ancient History

Roman Rebellion
(The Roman Republic 100 BC-60 BC)
Legionary*
Sacrifice

The Sword of Cartimandua Series
(Germania and Britannia 50 A.D. – 128 A.D.)
Ulpius Felix- Roman Warrior (prequel)
The Sword of Cartimandua
The Horse Warriors
Invasion Caledonia
Roman Retreat
Revolt of the Red Witch
Druid's Gold
Trajan's Hunters
The Last Frontier
Hero of Rome
Roman Hawk
Roman Treachery
Roman Wall
Roman Courage

The Wolf Brethren series
(Britain in the late 6th Century)
Saxon Dawn
Saxon Revenge
Saxon England
Saxon Blood
Saxon Slayer
Saxon Slaughter

Lion of the North

Saxon Bane
Saxon Fall: Rise of the Warlord
Saxon Throne
Saxon Sword

Medieval History

The Dragon Heart Series
Viking Slave *
Viking Warrior *
Viking Jarl *
Viking Kingdom *
Viking Wolf *
Viking War*
Viking Sword
Viking Wrath
Viking Raid
Viking Legend
Viking Vengeance
Viking Dragon
Viking Treasure
Viking Enemy
Viking Witch
Viking Blood
Viking Weregeld
Viking Storm
Viking Warband
Viking Shadow
Viking Legacy
Viking Clan
Viking Bravery

Norseman
Norse Warrior*
The Dragon Rock

The Norman Genesis Series
Hrolf the Viking *

Horseman *
The Battle for a Home *
Revenge of the Franks *
The Land of the Northmen
Ragnvald Hrolfsson
Brothers in Blood
Lord of Rouen
Drekar in the Seine
Duke of Normandy
The Duke and the King

Danelaw
(England and Denmark in the 11th Century)
Dragon Sword *
Oathsword *
Bloodsword *
Danish Sword*
The Sword of Cnut*

New World Series
Blood on the Blade *
Across the Seas *
The Savage Wilderness *
The Bear and the Wolf *
Erik The Navigator *
Erik's Clan *
The Last Viking*
The Vengeance Trail *

The Conquest Series
(Normandy and England 1050-1100)
Hastings*
Conquest*
Rebellion*

The Aelfraed Series
(Britain and Byzantium 1050 A.D. - 1085 A.D.)
Housecarl *
Outlaw *

Lion of the North

Varangian *

The Reconquista Chronicles
(Spain in the 11th Century)
Castilian Knight *
El Campeador *
The Lord of Valencia *

The Anarchy Series
(England 1120-1180)
English Knight *
Knight of the Empress *
Northern Knight *
Baron of the North *
Earl *
King Henry's Champion *
The King is Dead *
Warlord of the North*
Enemy at the Gate*
The Fallen Crown*
Warlord's War*
Kingmaker*
Henry II
Crusader
The Welsh Marches
Irish War
Poisonous Plots
The Princes' Revolt
Earl Marshal
The Perfect Knight

Border Knight
(1182-1300)
Sword for Hire *
Return of the Knight *
Baron's War *
Magna Carta *
Welsh Wars *
Henry III *

The Bloody Border *
Baron's Crusade*
Sentinel of the North*
War in the West*
Debt of Honour*
The Blood of the Warlord*
The Fettered King*
de Montfort's Crown
The Ripples of Rebellion

Sir John Hawkwood Series
(France and Italy 1339- 1387)
Crécy: The Age of the Archer *
Man At Arms *
The White Company *
Leader of Men *
Tuscan Warlord *
Condottiere*
Legacy*

Lord Edward's Archer
Lord Edward's Archer *
King in Waiting *
An Archer's Crusade *
Targets of Treachery *
The Great Cause *
Wallace's War *
The Hunt*
The Prince and the Archer*
Warbow

Struggle for a Crown
(1360- 1485)
Blood on the Crown *
To Murder a King *
The Throne *
King Henry IV *
The Road to Agincourt *
St Crispin's Day *

Lion of the North

The Battle for France *
The Last Knight *
Queen's Knight *
The Knight's Tale *

Tales from the Sword I
(*Short stories from the Medieval period*)

Tudor Warrior series
(England and Scotland in the late 15th and early 16th century)
Tudor Warrior *
Tudor Spy *
Flodden*

Conquistador
(England and America in the 16th Century)
Conquistador *
The English Adventurer *

English Mercenary
(The 30 Years War and the English Civil War)
Horse and Pistol*
Captain of Horse*
Lion of the North

Modern History

East Indiaman Saga
East Indiaman*
The Tiger and the Thief

The Napoleonic Horseman Series
Chasseur à Cheval
Napoleon's Guard
British Light Dragoon
Soldier Spy
1808: The Road to Coruña
Talavera

Lion of the North

The Lines of Torres Vedras
Bloody Badajoz
The Road to France
Waterloo

The Lucky Jack American Civil War series
Rebel Raiders
Confederate Rangers
The Road to Gettysburg

Soldier of the Queen series
Soldier of the Queen*
Redcoat's Rifle*
Omdurman*
Desert War*
An Officer and a Gentleman

The British Ace Series
(World War 1)
1914
1915 Fokker Scourge
1916 Angels over the Somme
1917 Eagles Fall
1918 We will remember them
From Arctic Snow to Desert Sand
Wings over Persia

Combined Operations series
(1940-1951)
Commando *
Raider *
Behind Enemy Lines*
Dieppe
Toehold in Europe
Sword Beach
Breakout
The Battle for Antwerp
King Tiger
Beyond the Rhine

Lion of the North

Korea
Korean Winter

Rifleman Series
(WW2 1940-45)
Conscript's Call*

Tales from the Sword II
(Short stories from the Modern period)

Books marked thus *, are also available in the audio format.
For more information on all of the books then please visit the author's website at www.griffhosker.com where there is a link to contact him or visit his Facebook page: GriffHosker at Sword Books or follow him on Twitter: @HoskerGriff or Sword (@swordbooksltd)
If you wish to be on the mailing list then contact the author through his website.

Printed in Dunstable, United Kingdom